A Bus of My Own

JIM LEHRER

A Bus of My Own

G. P. PUTNAM'S SONS
New York

G. P. Putnam's Sons
Publishers Since 1838
200 Madison Avenue
New York, NY 10016

The author acknowledges permission to quote lyrics from "Don't Give a Dose to the
One You Love Most," words and music by Shel Silverstein. TRO © Copyright 1972
Evil Eye Music, Inc., Daytona Beach, Florida. Used by permission.

All photographs are from the author's personal collection.

Library of Congress Cataloging-in-Publication Data

Lehrer, James.
A bus of my own / Jim Lehrer.
p.   cm.
ISBN 0-399-13765-3 (acid-free paper)
1. Lehrer, James.   2. Editors—United States—Biography.
3. Periodical editors—United States—Biography.   I. Title.
PN4874.L365A3   1992   92-7526 CIP
070.4'1'092—dc20
[B]

Printed in the United States of America
1   2   3   4   5   6   7   8   9   10

This book is printed on acid-free paper.
∞

To Kate, Jamie, Lucy and Amanda

■ ■ ■

Introduction

This began as a standard "How I Had a Heart Attack and Bought a Bus" kind of book. There were nearly six years from one to the other, from having the heart attack that caused me to think I was going to die to buying a beautiful 1946 Flxible Clipper bus that caused me to know I definitely hadn't. I thought I might have some things to tell and to say about those years of recovery and survival that could be of interest to anyone confronting a similar experience. But it turned out not to be that simple. There needed to be context and background. So I started putting some in here and there, and then some more here and there, and soon it was something else. It was now a collection of stories and thoughts about my life, of which the heart attack and my bus were only two of the parts. There were also parts about being a newspaperman, a Marine, a fiction writer and a television-news type, among other things.

It remains most selective. I left out pieces and happenings that I decided were irrelevant, boring or too personal to be anybody else's business. The only other big decision was where to begin. And that was easy.

It had to be with buses.

1

May I Have
Your Attention, Please?

There stands an ordinary person with me on a street corner waiting for the light to change. Along comes a bus, let's say a blue and white bus with a running dog and the word GREYHOUND on the side. The ordinary person either sees nothing or sees only a bus with a running dog and the word GREYHOUND on the side. I see my father, my mother, my brother and me freezing, laughing and crying in Kansas in 1947. I see cap badges, bus depot signs, cast-iron toy buses and ticket punches in leather holsters. I smell gasoline and mohair seats, rubber-stamp ink and transmission grease. I remember drivers in starched and pressed gray uniforms driving through snowstorms, ticket agents quoting from memory schedules and fares to cities and towns all over America, mechanics throwing up bus engine hatches and declaring, "Her number-three piston's cracked."

And I remember specific events.

Like the one that happened on a Saturday morning in November 1946, in McPherson, Kansas.

I had gone to the McPherson bus station with my father. He was going to have a cup of coffee with a bus driver, an old friend who would be driving the Salina-to-Wichita bus that morning. Dad said he would give me a nickel to play the pinball machine while he had his coffee. The bus depot was in the lobby of the

Warren Hotel. I knew the place well and had in fact played the pinball machine there many times before. I considered myself a whiz at pinball, in fact. And in fact, I was. But I had never, ever beaten this machine, meaning I had never, ever won a free game off it.

So as Dad went to the coffee shop, I went to the machine and put in my nickel. The second I did, I wished I hadn't. It was cold outside, and when I hit the warm lobby I was struck with a sudden need to go to the bathroom, to do what in polite Kansas company was then called a Number One. But as the machine lit up and I pushed the lever for the first ball, I thought, Oh well, no problem. I'm not going to win any games, anyhow. It'll take just a few minutes to play the five balls. And I'll be on my way.

The first ball went through slowly, beautifully. It popped into the highest-score holes and lit up the best lights and triggered the most glorious sounds on its way down through the machine.

So did ball number two. And three and four. Finally, after ball five I had won three free games. Three free games! The whiz had at last triumphed over that machine! Hip-hip, hooray!

I quickly shoved the lever for another game.

The same thing happened. Each ball, as if on orders from above, went right where it should have, no matter how I shot the ball up the chute or how much gentle pushing and other English I gave to the machine.

I had ten games won. Then twelve. Fourteen!

But my need to go to the bathroom rose with each new game, each new glory. I tilted three games off. I wasted them. But then I played another. This time with no hands on the machine. No gentle persuasion or English. Again, those little silver balls popped into the highest holes.

I kept going. Now I had eighteen games. Then twenty-one. Then twenty-five! More than I had ever won on any pinball machine in the twelve years of my life. It was a Kansas, if not a world's, record, I was sure.

I was now in misery. I crossed my legs. I thought of other

things, such as hamburgers all the way and cherry Cokes, Esther Williams and Hedy Lamarr. I imagined the ceremony where I was crowned Pinball King of the World.

The men's room was on the other side of the lobby. It would take a lot of time to dash over there, do what needed to be done and run back. And some guy would probably come and take over the machine and start playing off my games. He would never believe that they were my games. He would not stand aside and let me continue. All would be lost.

So I decided to go to the bathroom in place. Just a little bit. Just enough to relieve the misery. My skivvy shorts and heavy corduroy pants would absorb the wet, I was sure.

It went to thirty-one games.

And I let go a little bit.

But I could not control it. I felt warm moisture pouring down the inside of my left leg. I could not stop it, and nothing was being absorbed. I had unleashed a rushing river of warmth.

I did not look down. I continued to play the machine like nothing was happening. It went to thirty-two games, thirty-three games, thirty-four.

Then I glanced down. A circle of moisture had formed around my shoes. It was two feet or so in diameter—and still growing.

I heard some blowing into the bus depot public address system. Then came the ticket agent's hard male voice saying: "May I have your attention, please? This is your first call for Santa Fe Trailways Air-Conditioned Trailmaster to Wichita and points south. Now leaving for Moundridge, Hesston, Newton, Wichita, Wellington, Blackwell, Tonkawa, Perry, Guthrie, Edmond, Oklahoma City, Ardmore and Dallas. Don't forget your baggage, please."

The real announcement for me was that Dad would be out of that coffee shop in a second.

I panicked. I splashed and slid through the puddle and ran to the men's room. I went into a stall and locked the door.

Several very long minutes of hell went by before I heard the rest room door open. I knew who it was.

"Son, that's you in there, isn't it?" said my dad.

I said nothing. I was barely breathing.

"That's your mess out there on the floor by the pinball machine, isn't it?"

I said nothing.

"Well, come on out now and apologize. The porter's mopping it up."

I broke my silence. "Dad, please! I can't talk to anybody. I can't come out."

"Okay," he said, "you're going to spend the rest of your life in a men's crapper, is that it? Fine, son. Now how do I explain that to your mother?"

I unlocked the door, opened it and walked out. I did not look at Dad. I ran past him through the lobby and outside to the street as fast as I could. I doubt if I have ever run that fast.

I ran for three blocks, to where we had parked Betsy, our 1938 Flxible Clipper.

She was just down the street from the taxi stand that was our bus depot in McPherson, a town of 8,000 in central Kansas. Santa Fe Trailways would not let us come into the main depot at the Warren because we were considered a competitor. That was a not very funny laugh. Santa Fe, Dad's former employer and a principal in the National Trailways System, ran hundreds of big red-and-cream-painted buses on routes from Chicago to Los Angeles, with feeder lines off in all directions through the Midwest and Southwest. We, the mighty Kansas Central Lines, operated Betsy and two other very mechanically exhausted buses, Susie and Lena, on 125 miles of mostly gravel roads north from Wichita through towns such as Valley Center, Sedgwick, Newton, Goessel, Lehigh, Hillsboro and Marion. The route was an almost perfect T shape, with McPherson on the western tip, Emporia on the eastern.

We didn't know it then, but on that November day in McPherson, Kansas Central had already lived almost half of its life. It opened for business in June 1946, with one full-time and two part-time driver employees. It closed down in July 1947, with no employees. My dad was driving one of the two schedules, my mother the other.

And much of it was Betsy, Susie and Lena's fault. They just weren't up to it. Susie was a bus made by an outfit in Kalamazoo, Michigan, called Pony Cruiser. She had a Ford engine and carried nineteen passengers. Lena was a stretched-out Chevrolet car that carried eleven passengers. Like all buses, they and Betsy had been worn down and out during the war and were mostly junk by the time they got to us. But they came cheap, so that was why Dad bought them. They let in hot dust in the summertime, cold draft in the wintertime. Seldom did two back-to-back days go by that one of the three was not broken down along the side of a road or having some vital part repaired or replaced at high cost in some shop. Dad had financed the purchase of each bus with a separate loan from Wichita banks. Had he been able to buy new buses, a 1946 Flxible Clipper, say, instead of a 1938 model, it might have all turned out differently.

But he had to go into bankruptcy court to seek protection from his creditors thirteen months after our first bus pulled its first run. It was an act of humiliation for him. He was thirty-five years old, the son of German immigrants, with an eighth-grade education and a deep belief that all you needed to make it in this country was a good idea and a willingness to work. He had had both when he quit his clerical job at Santa Fe to start Kansas Central; and he failed anyhow. So the failure must have been somewhere in him, not in Betsy, Susie and Lena. That was how he saw it. And he never got over it. It stuck in his craw and soul for the rest of his life.

The one year of Kansas Central Lines also left its marks on me. Some are from experiences that were wrenchingly sad, having to do with watching my mother and father endure terrific pain. The pain of not being able to buy Christmas gifts for their two sons, of having literally to beg mechanics, gasoline station and restaurant people and others for credit, for more time, for sympathy and understanding. They suffered when they had to lay off our last employee and tell him that not only was he out of work, but there was no way to pay him what he was already owed. They suffered when they had to sell at auction every piece of furniture and other things of value they owned, and when they had to plead with passengers for patience or a second chance when the bus didn't come, because Betsy, Susie or Lena would not start or had broken down on Highway 15 just south of Lehigh.

It left me with an automatic kinship, implanted way deep inside, with anyone who owns and operates a small business. When I enter a restaurant at high noon, say, and there are no customers, I see my father in the guy behind the counter who isn't making it, who may soon have to put up a "Closed" sign, who may have to confess to his sons that he could not make it in business, that he had failed.

It probably had also contributed to my recurring "fired" nightmare. I have been fired from my job—whatever job I might have at the time—and been forced to return to a prior one in a demeaning and humiliating way. The worst scene involves taking a call from a funeral home on the obit desk at *The Dallas Morning News*, with kid reporters one-third my age standing around watching me.

Look at him, one of them says. He can still do it.

Right, says another. Wonder why MacNeil fired him.

Yeah. Well, let this be a lesson to us.

What's the lesson?

That you can't ever relax.

But for the most part, the life and death of Kansas Central Lines was more of an adventure for me than a tragedy. Here I was, by all appearances a mere twelve-year-old boy, but actually a vital player in a most serious grown-up struggle for survival that would surely succeed and lead to Kansas Central Lines' becoming a major force in the intercity bus industry of our nation. That's how I saw it, at least. I saw it that way particularly when I helped load baggage and express, when I jumped out and poured water into a hot radiator, when I quoted schedules and fares to grateful customers, when I assured Mom and Dad that everything was going to get better any day now.

There were also some real adventures.

Like the Saturday night in late August when I came into Wichita on Betsy with our driver Harris Cameron behind the wheel. We had a full load of seventeen passengers, so as "assistant driver" I got to ride where I always preferred to. Right up there on the motor hatch next to Cameron. Betsy was the last of the front-motor buses. From 1939–1940 on, most intercity buses were pushers. The motor was in the back.

As Cameron turned to head up the paved county road for the six miles out to U.S. 81, an unfortunate thing happened. He ran the stop sign.

He glanced back to me to see if I had noticed. Naturally, I had. I noticed everything. Cameron cut his eyes skyward and then back to the narrow road, illuminated by Betsy's headlights.

I looked back at our people. None of them had seen it. Good. But I couldn't figure out what had happened. Cameron seemed like a good driver, even if he had driven only city buses before. Why had he run that stop sign? Now he was probably worried that I might report him to Dad.

I was considering whether or not I would, as the moving headlights from the heavy traffic on the 81 superhighway came into view ahead.

Cameron began slowing down, way down. Slower and slower. Much sooner than he needed to. He was using the gears, going down from third to second and finally to low. But we were still rolling when we reached the flashing red light at the highway.

It was then that I realized Betsy had no brakes.

Cameron couldn't stop her completely, so we crawled right on out into traffic. Cameron was honking his horn and so were several cars, and I heard a screech of brakes and waited for the crash.

It didn't come. We had made it.

Cameron's forehead was wet. So was mine. But as best I could tell, none of our passengers realized yet what was going on. The passenger seats were a bit lower than where Cameron and I were sitting, so our riders really couldn't see very much out the front.

I said nothing to Cameron. I sat there, my bottom frozen to the motor hatch, my mind racing. Should I keep looking straight ahead to see how it was going, or should I keep my head down or my eyes closed? What about Cameron? Before going with us, all he had ever driven was a Wichita city bus. To those of us in the intercity bus business, it was just a notch higher than driving a school bus.

He seemed to know what he was doing. And so far so good now. But he had eleven treacherous, dangerous miles to go. There would be all of those traffic lights after U.S. 81 turned into Broadway, Wichita's main north-south street. There were four or five major intersections—with lights—from the stock-yards on into Douglas and the Eaton Hotel, our bus depot, some twenty blocks south. How in the world could he maneuver Betsy through them? Why didn't he pull over and call Dad, who was waiting with my mother and my brother, Fred, at the Eaton? Or just pull into a service station or something and try to get the brakes fixed?

But I knew the answers. The run-of-the-mill service station guys just threw up their hands when asked to work on air brakes. You had to go to a truck place. There weren't many around. This we had already found out, the hard way. Now was the third or fourth time Betsy had lost the air in her brakes. Because of the war, the essential part required to fix the air tank per-manently was unobtainable, so every repair had been temporary. There was also no point in calling the Eaton. What could they do? Nothing, really. If I could figure all of that out, I was sure Cameron had already done so, too. Also, because the mechanics' bills were mounting, Cameron was under orders from Dad to try to keep the buses moving no matter what. That obviously included driving with no brakes, if necessary.

The first light was at the stockyards at Broadway and Twenty-first. Cameron handled it beautifully. He geared down again, and we arrived as the signal turned green; we cruised on through. No problems.

The next four or five blocks were the same. He moved Betsy

along carefully. The next major light was still a few blocks away, at Central. This would be the toughest one of all before hitting Douglas. Central was a big street. A lot of trucks, crossing town on the north side, used it. I thought about getting broadsided by a big semi, maybe one of the Kenworths. Wichita's biggest funeral home was at the corner of Broadway and Central. How convenient. When I was in the sixth grade—the year before—I had gone to a funeral there for a classmate who had been killed accidentally by his younger brother with their father's shotgun.

Cameron had Betsy at a chugging creep, but I could see a block away that there was no way we were going to make Central before the light changed. No way! The signal was green, yet it seemed it had been green for a long time. Too long a time. I had no idea what Cameron was going to do. From the motor hatch, I could see only the right side of his face. But his eyes were not closed and he didn't appear to be praying. That was a good sign, because he was Catholic. And according to the war movies, Catholics always prayed and crossed themselves before dying.

I felt the motor underneath me barely turning. Cameron obviously did not have his foot on the accelerator at all. And finally he was down to low gear. There was nothing else to do. Cars were parked along the right side of the street. There were no driveways or side streets to provide escape. I wanted to scream or at least yell to the passengers to put their heads down or something.

The light was red now. Cars were moving back and forth in front of us going east and west. There was no way to avoid a collision.

But still Cameron said nothing.

Slowly we arrived at the light. Cameron pressed his right hand firmly down on the horn. There was a weak *beep!* and then silence. Death was here for everything.

Betsy glided right into the middle of the intersection. A car from the west swerved and passed directly in front of us—just inches in front of us, narrowly missing a head-on collision with a westbound car. Others started honking and screeching to a stop. Cameron kept his head erect and his eyes straight ahead. So did I. I wanted to close my eyes, but I didn't.

It seemed as if it took us forever to get across Central. I kept waiting for the crash, the screams, the glass smashing, the jolt to the side of Betsy—either or both sides.

But it was really very peaceful and quiet inside. The motor was barely making a sound now, and the passengers were also silent. Do you remember those scenes from Bible movies where Jesus walked through a crowd, invincible, silent, with the glow over his head and everything seemingly falling away from him? Well, that's what it was like.

As Betsy's rear end cleared the intersection, Cameron stepped on the accelerator pedal ever so slightly. I could feel it underneath me and hear the motor. I realized now that the passengers knew what was going on. But nobody said anything. Not a word.

Cameron, a man in his mid-twenties with a smooth red face and a sphinxlike expression, also said nothing, did nothing, except proceed south on Broadway.

For six blocks, we were in good shape. There were just two more lights to get through before reaching Douglas and turning left for the three blocks to the Eaton Hotel. The worst was over. Assuming Cameron could stop the bus in front of the hotel. Oh my God.

He hit the light at Third Street on the nose. Just as it switched to green. At First Street, the signal was barely yellow when we squeezed through at a good speed, Cameron goosing her to make it.

That left only Douglas, a big street, which ran east and west through the center of downtown Wichita.

Cameron cut Betsy left a block north of Douglas, went over one block east and then turned south for the last block before Douglas.

Everything was perfect. We turned the corner onto Douglas, the light was just changing to green, and we were down to a crawl.

But now the final moment of truth was upon us. We had two blocks to go before stopping at curbside in front of the hotel. It had to be a full stop. No creeping slowdowns would do this time. And I had no idea how Cameron was going to pull it off.

We were in low gear almost immediately after turning the corner. With an occasional but ever so slight touch on the accelerator, Cameron moved Betsy along like a glider plane on the way down or a bicycle after clearing the bottom of a hill.

When we passed the last intersection at the west end of the block where the Eaton was located, we couldn't have been going much more than two or three miles an hour.

Dad, Mom and Freddy were standing on that corner. Dad waved and looked worried. We were nearly an hour late now.

Impulsively, idiotically, I leaned off the hatch, stuck my head out the right-side front window and yelled:

"Our brakes are out! Since Valley Center!"

Dad closed his eyes. Mom put her face in her hands. I didn't notice what Freddy did.

A woman started screaming behind me. "Stop this bus! Let me out of here!"

Then there was a whoop from another woman, and a man was out of his seat, coming up the aisle. "What's going on?"

I had just confirmed at the top of my lungs what they surely already knew, but now it had been said aloud—and loudly—so it was quite permissible to go crazy.

I sat back on the hatch and stared straight ahead. I didn't even look over at Cameron. I knew he was furious with me. He had to be. Mr. Big Mouth, the boss's son.

My family walked briskly on the sidewalk alongside us as Cameron, ignoring the noise of the passengers, calmly rolled Betsy that last little distance.

It was an absolutely incredible performance. We came to a final, perfect stop at the curb exactly in front of the Eaton.

Cameron opened Betsy's door and I got out first. I didn't want to, but I had to. There on the motor hatch, I was blocking Cameron's way. But he and several of the passengers were right behind me as I hit the sidewalk, managing to ignore Mother and Dad and slide along the side of the bus to the rear.

The passengers reacted in one of two extremes. They were either so mad that they were threatening to sue or to never again ride a Kansas Central bus, or scared and thus thankful for Cameron's skill and heroism in bringing them through in one piece.

As Mom and Pop and Cameron talked to them, I stood away from it all, trying to remain out of everybody's sight and consciousness. My brother came over to me. "You scared us half to death," he said.

"What do you think I was?" I replied. "You should have seen us go through Broadway and Central. We were lucky to make it here alive. Cameron . . . Cameron and I did the most fantastic driving job in history."

"Mr. Big Mouth," said my brother. It was a label that fit—and stuck. (Fortunately I chose a line of work for which such a thing is considered an asset.)

I was dreading what would happen when Dad finally got around to talking to me about what I had done. But he never did. There were too many more important things to do. He and Cameron, for instance, had to spend the rest of that Saturday night getting Betsy's brakes fixed so she could be moved and ready for Sunday.

One of the benefits of Kansas Central was that there were always more important things to do than chew out Mr. Big Mouth, the son.

In the long run, the most fun and best benefit of my year of Kansas Central was that it turned me forever into a bus man, into that person on the street corner who sees and smells what others do not.

■ ■ ■

I even had a brief go at being a real bus man. That was seven years later, when I worked as a ticket agent for Continental Trailways. I was also going to Victoria College, a small junior college in Victoria, Texas, a city of 30,000 near the Gulf Coast about halfway between Houston and Corpus Christi. It was a very small school. I was editor of the newspaper the two years I was there because I was the only person who had walked into the faculty advisor's office and asked for the job. My first banner headline in the paper, *The Jolly Roger*, was: VC ENROLLMENT SOARS TO 320.

I loved working in the bus depot. I loved being the guy who breathed into the PA microphone and then cried out to the world: "May I have your attention, please! This is your first call for the Continental Trailways five-fifteen P.M. Air-Conditioned Silversides Thruliner to Houston and Dallas, now leaving from lane one next to the building for: Inez, Edna, Ganado, Louise, El Campo, Pierce, Wharton, Hungerford, Kendleton, Beasley, Rosenberg, Richmond, Sugarland, Stafford, Missouri City and Houston. Connecting in Houston for Huntsville, Buffalo, Corsicana, Dallas, Fort Worth, Wichita Falls, Amarillo, Tucumcari, Albuquerque, Flagstaff, Los Angeles, San Diego, San Francisco, Portland and Seattle. Connecting in Dallas for Tyler, Longview, Shreveport, Minden, Natchez, Jackson, Meridian, Montgomery, Columbus, Fayetteville, Raleigh, Richmond, Washington, New York City and Boston . . . and for Ardmore, Oklahoma City, Wichita, Topeka, Kansas City, Des Moines and Minneapolis . . . Jefferson City, Columbia, St. Louis, Indianapolis, Columbus and Pittsburgh . . . Hannibal, Quincy, Peoria, Chicago, Benton Harbor, Kalamazoo and Detroit. Connecting in Houston also for Baytown, Goose Creek, Dayton, Liberty, Beaumont, Port Arthur, Orange, Lake Charles, Kinder, Opelousas, Lafayette, Baton Rouge, New Orleans, Gulfport, Biloxi, Mobile, Pensacola, Tallahassee, Tampa and Miami . . . All aboard, please! Don't forget your baggage, please!"

It is only good reporting to say my bus-calling became quite famous in and around the Victoria bus station. People didn't exactly come from miles around to hear me call the 5:15, but it was almost that bad—or good. When I first went to work, I read the names from a loose-leaf notebook. But after a while I had them memorized. And I could go through the entire call without looking down. And it was not only the Houston–Dallas route. I also had in my head and on my tongue the call southwest to Inairi, Vidairi, Refugio (pronounced re-*frur*-ee-oh), Woodsboro, Sinton, Odem, Calallen and Corpus Christi. Connecting to Robstown, Alice, Freer and Laredo . . . and to Kingsville, Falfurrias, Raymondville, Edinburg, McAllen, Harlingen, Brownsville and points in Old Mexico. There was also one northwest to San Antonio through Nursery, Thomaston, Cuero, Westhoff, Smiley, Nixon, Pandora, Stockdale, Sutherland Springs and Sayers Crossroads, plus one north to Austin through Yoakum, Shiner, Gonzales, Luling and Lockhart, and another straight south through Bloomington and Placedo to Port Lavaca and the waters of the Gulf of Mexico.

Some of the drivers, particularly a delightful man named Paul Guthrie, used to walk up and stare right at me in mock stunned rapture as I called out the towns one after another in my phony, syrupy, pretentious, Texasy nineteen-year-old PA voice. Paul said I should put out a record titled *Famous Bus Calls I Have Made* by Jimmy Charles Lehrer.

I also loved doing tickets. Long trips meant long tickets, with a separate coupon for each Trailways or other company traveled on. We used rubber stamps for the names of the towns. Again, it is not boastful to report that I became a whiz at moving those rubber stamps along the five- or six-coupon ticket, hitting the proper line as I went with the stamp. I also memorized all of the schedules in and out of Victoria, which was not easy, because in each twenty-four-hour period we had more than forty of them. I knew when the buses left and when they arrived at their destination. I could recite the schedules quickly and pleasantly to anyone who called or came in. The same for the fares. What is the round-trip fare to Fayetteville, Arkansas? Boise, Idaho? Roswell, New Mexico? The chances always were that I knew them without looking them up in the tariff binder.

The man who taught me how to do it all was also my greatest fan. He was Willie Church Porter, who, just like his name suggests, was one of the porters at the bus depot. He was a man of gold teeth and great laughs, and also the smartest man there, but because he was black he was a porter. He would have made a terrific ticket agent or driver, but in 1952 those jobs were only for white people, as were a separate set of drinking fountains, rest rooms, waiting rooms and cafés in the bus depot.

I made one of those local-boy-makes-good returns to Victoria in 1981. Willie was retired by then, but I made sure he was invited to a reception at the college, and I spoke of him and introduced him when I gave my speech the next morning. Fortunately, a young reporter from *The Victoria Advocate* covering it all was wise enough to see what the story was. He interviewed Willie as well as me, and wrote a good piece that appeared on the front page the next day, with a three-column picture of the two of us shaking hands and grinning at each other.

Probably the most important thing I learned from knowing Willie was simply that he existed. Later, as a journalist covering the civil rights movement, it meant that I knew it was more than an idea whose time had come. I knew and was permanently angered by the fact that it was coming too late to help Willie Church Porter become even a ticket agent. Willie died in 1987. I was unable to attend the funeral in Victoria, but his daughter called me to ask if I would mind being made an honorary pall-bearer. "Willie thought you were the best ticket agent he ever saw," she said. I knew he did, because he told me so himself. He also told me that I should not stop there and be a bus man. Go ahead, he said, and finish all of college. Go ahead with being a reporter and that Hemingway man I had told him all about.

Being a reporter was already in me by then. It had begun to seep in in Beaumont, Texas, where we had ended up after the death of Kansas Central. Dad had gone to work first for a small bus line in southeastern Kansas called Kansas Trails, and then for an old Santa Fe friend who ran another bus company called Beaumont–Port Arthur Trailways. He hired Dad to run his company and to manage the Trailways bus depot in Beaumont. In my sophomore English class at French High School, the teacher, Mrs. Mary DeYoung, singled me out for praise. I had written a paper about Charles Dickens's *A Tale of Two Cities*. Mrs. De-

Young told me that I was a good writer. At the same time, I was accepting what had been obvious for years, which was that I was too small, too slow, too soft and too many other things to be the athlete I longed to be. So I became the manager of the French High basketball team and then of the baseball team. And in the course of that I met and talked to a few of the reporters from the two Beaumont newspapers who came to cover our games. It set off gongs that gong to this day. Why not go to football, baseball and basketball games and write stories about them? Why not get paid for having a good time? Why not be a reporter? What could be more fun than that?

Between Beaumont and Victoria there was San Antonio. Dad took a job as the city solicitor for Continental Trailways in San Antonio. We moved ourselves and our few possessions on a Flxible Clipper, the regular overnight run from Beaumont to San Antonio. Greyhound dominated that route, so there were only a handful of passengers on the bus besides my mother, brother and me. At Jefferson High School in San Antonio, I became one of three editors and covered and wrote all of the main sports stories. I also began to learn about and read people like Ernest Hemingway, who not only were newspapermen but also wrote stories and novels and traveled the world in search of women, song, stories and adventure.

But it was later, at the Victoria bus station, that all doubt about what I was going to do with my life was permanently removed. I was exposed there to what I believed to be Real Life, the kind of stuff Hemingway and the rest of us thought good fiction was made of.

One day, a young woman in the uniform of a WAF major came in. WAF stood for "Women in the Air Force." She looked too young and frail to be a major, and she was nervous. I sold her a one-way ticket to Houston. The bus had not been gone five minutes when two well-dressed men were there, identifying themselves as special agents of the FBI. Had I seen a young woman in a WAF major's uniform? Yes, I had. I told them what I had seen and done, and away they went after the bus. The driver told me later that they stopped his bus in Edna, took the young woman off and arrested her. They said she was an enlisted WAF who had "committed a federal offense" and was attempting to escape by impersonating an officer, which was an even bigger federal offense. Wow.

Through the portals of that bus station also came real service men and women of all ranks; drunks, bums, mean truck drivers, salesmen, evangelists, lecturers, oilfield roughnecks, merchant seamen, teachers, farmers, farm hands, blind people with dogs, sick people who threw up in handkerchiefs, elderly people who were not sure where they were going, illegal aliens trying to avoid the immigration police, students of all descriptions, telephone operators and other beautiful women of all ages, including one a driver identified to me as a well-known nymphomaniac, the first of her kind I had ever seen.

The drivers themselves were nothing but stories. There was one named Catfish, who drove the Port Lavaca turn-around. Company checkers caught him keeping cash fares and he was fired. The checkers also caught an old-timer who, every day, pulled into El Campo for a rest stop that was more than rest. A woman, his girlfriend, picked him up in her car, and away they went to her place. The rest stop was supposed to be for only ten minutes, but it often went to twenty or twenty-five. They fired him, too. One driver's wife was so sure her husband could not be trusted that she rode with him on every schedule from Houston to Corpus Christi and return. Every schedule. He never drove alone. Never. There was a driver called the Colonel, because he was the exact replica of a movie version of a white-haired colonel in the Confederate Army. Another was called Preacher because he was terribly religious, did not look at or speak of women and did not use profanity. His schedules were also always late, which the other drivers could not understand. There was a driver who had won a Silver Star in World War II and had returned to drive a bus. He talked mostly about the army and the war and how awful it was to be back among civilians.

Another driver had to leave his job after a tragic accident. Several people flagged him down one night on the highway near Louise, but he saw them too late to stop right where they were. They had a lot of baggage, so to keep them from having to carry it he put the bus in reverse and started backing up along the shoulder of the road. He lost sight of the people in his rearview mirror, panicked, turned the wheel suddenly, and hit and killed three. They were all part of a large Mexican-American family on their way to Houston.

All of us took great pride in a former Houston–Corpus Christi driver who had bid on a new run from Dallas to Amarillo. Once, with a bus full of passengers, he got caught in a sudden snowstorm, and his bus slid off the highway into a huge snowbank. He walked twelve miles through the snow for help. *Reader's Digest* did a story about him and what he did.

It was there in that bus station at night that I wrote short stories on an old upright typewriter, and imagined that I was not only Hemingway but also Robert Ruark, whose syndicated column appeared three times a week in *The Victoria Advocate*. Ruark patterned his life after Hemingway's. He, too, went to Africa and wrote novels about it. He, too, went everywhere, did everything.

It was also at the bus station that I wrote letters to the admissions offices of thirty-seven state colleges and universities, seeking catalogues and other information about transferring for my last two years of college. The final choice came down to Maine, Montana or Missouri. Maine, because I had never been there and it sounded exciting; Montana, because of the reputation of its creative writing and English departments and because I had also never been there; and Missouri, because of its journalism school. I chose Missouri, even though I had been to Kansas City many times. But I had never been to Columbia, and Missouri's journalism school was supposed to be the very best. Hemingway said being a newspaperman was the best route to fiction writing. It forced you to deal with the English language every day, it made it possible to go places and meet people who would later be characters in novels and short stories, and it kept food on the table.

The problem was, Missouri would not take me. Not as a full junior in the School of Journalism. Some admissions person wrote a snotty letter about not being able to accept most of my credits from Victoria College, a school with which Missouri was not familiar. Fortunately, it made John Stormont mad. Stormont was the dean of Victoria College. He asked me how badly I really wanted to go to Missouri. I told him it was a life-or-death matter, which it had suddenly become.

"All right," he said, "let's take 'em on."

Stormont, who was gray-headed and in his late forties, was also a tall, muscular man of fullback dimensions and bearing. Just his saying that gave me confidence. He asked me if I was willing to roll the dice to prove I knew what my credits and grades at Victoria College said I knew. Sure, I said. What did I have to lose?

So Dean Stormont wrote one of the greatest letters of my life. He ripped the admissions man and Missouri for their elitism and shortsightedness, and essentially challenged them to a duel. Send us examinations for every subject you have doubts about, he said. We will administer them to this kid, and you can see for yourselves the kind of person he is and what kind of education we provide here at this little college you have never heard of. Missouri, to both of our surprise, said okay. And a few weeks later, one of the Victoria College faculty members, a delightful man named C. J. Howell, who resembled the actor Clifton Webb in appearance and temperament, was designated to give me the exams. I went to an empty classroom and took one exam an afternoon for four straight afternoons. The exams were in English grammar, basic math, Spanish and typing, one of the Missouri J School's special requirements. I did well enough not only to be admitted as a full-fledged junior but to have my entire English grammar and foreign language requirements waived. It was the single greatest triumph of my life up to that point, and a sure sign that I was destined to be another Hemingway. Or a Spanish-speaking Ruark, if nothing else.

I went to Missouri on the bus. Of course. Continental to Dallas and Tulsa, Southern Kansas Greyhound from Tulsa to Kansas City, and then Southwestern Greyhound on to Columbia, to the University of Missouri. I remember the bus ride, because on the overnight San Antonio–Dallas part I sat next to a guy my age who was in the army. He had a bottle of bourbon, and he drank from it and cried while telling me how he was afraid he was going to die in Korea and never see his girlfriend again. He described her in great detail, saying finally in a whisper that the previous night—hours before he left—she had let him put his hands on her bottom. Both hands, both cheeks. He moved his hands up and down and across them a few times and then she took him to the bus station in her daddy's car. I'd give anything to know what happened to that kid. Several of the guys I knew on the French High football, basketball and baseball teams enlisted in the Marine Corps and went to Korea as a group. I know what happened to them. Two were killed. Another killed himself after getting back home. Others were wounded. One of the casualties was Charlie Whatley, who had been our first-string quarterback. English was not his best subject, and even though he was a senior he'd been in Mrs. DeYoung's sophomore English class with me. We'd sat next to each other. He was killed by a grenade that went off in his hand.

Six years later, fresh out of college, I was in the Marine Corps. The Korean War was over and I had never been at risk. I also seldom went a day without thinking about Charlie and the other guys from French.

■ ■ ■

I had never set foot in Columbia, Missouri, before, and I knew no one there. But it didn't matter. Hemingway, Ruark, Dean Stormont and Willie Porter had prepared the way.

So had Sticks Strahala.

Sticks was a reporter/photographer for *The Victoria Advocate*. He was a real newspaperman, the first I had ever known, not counting the Beaumont sportswriters. I saw Sticks at the *Advocate* when I took our college paper in to be printed, but I saw him and got to know him mostly at the bus station. Many Friday evenings he came in to buy a ticket for the 6:40 to Yoakum, where his mother lived. He always had on a dark suit, a large knotted tie and a felt hat. He was probably the only man in Victoria who wore a felt hat every day, summer and fall, winter and spring.

One evening I told Sticks I wanted to be a reporter and writer like him and Ruark. He told me it was the greatest work there was, the only way he had ever heard of to make a living that made sense, the only life he ever wanted to lead. He was probably in his forties, but at that time in my life everybody older than I seemed probably in his forties. Sticks said he had worked in San Antonio for the *Express-News* and for some other papers in Texas before coming to Victoria. He told me about covering murders and head-ons and crooked politicians and gambling raids. He remembered hard-nosed editors who could kill with a stare, hard drinkers who, drunk out of their minds, could write better prose than ordinary mortals could sober in their minds.

He was there the night of the most awful real-world experience I had while I was a ticket agent.

The 9:30 P.M. bus on its way from Corpus to Houston was in the depot for its ten-minute rest stop. The driver came out of the coffee shop and said to me, "Give me a first." I went to the PA mike and gave him a first call. The full treatment—to both Coasts, and to Minneapolis to the north, Miami to the south.

In a few minutes the whites' waiting room, which was about forty by forty feet square, was empty and quiet. And in a few minutes the driver, who was the guy who had won the Silver Star as an infantryman on Saipan, returned with a handful of tickets. He separated them into little stacks there on the ticket counter in front of me so he could count them. This many here going to Houston, those going to Wharton, these to El Campo.

There was a scream. A woman's scream. An awful sound. It

came from the women's rest room, the white women's rest room. The driver ran toward it. I raced from around the counter and followed him.

The rest room door was wide open. An elderly woman was standing there with her hands over her eyes. "My God! My God! She's dead! She's dead!"

The driver stepped past her to a body lying on the floor in front of a stall. It was the body of a young blonde woman. She was dressed in a tacky, dirty blue dress. Her hair was stringy and needed combing. Her shoes were white sandals. The strap on one of them was missing. Blood was pouring from both of her wrists. Her skin was the color of gray enamel. I could not tell if she had ever been pretty.

It was the first time I had ever seen blood flowing from a body like that. I stepped back. I was about to be sick.

The place was soon full of police officers in uniform and plainclothes, and ambulance attendants in white coats. Then in came Sticks Strahala, dressed in his usual way.

I moved away and back behind the ticket counter. It wasn't long before the driver was there with me, wiping the blood off his hands with a paper towel. "She's a goner," he said. "I knew guys who would have given anything to stay alive, and they died. She was alive, and what does she do? She dies. Add it up if you can." He grabbed up the tickets and said, "All of this has made me late. Give me a last." He looked up at the clock on the wall above me. It gave the time and the Continental slogan, "Always Going Your Way."

I brought the PA mike to my mouth and gave him a last call to Houston, Dallas and all points east, north and west.

And after a while, Sticks came over to the counter. "She's just a kid," Sticks said. "Why did she do it? She had no ID. The driver said she wasn't on his bus. So she was from around here probably. Did you ever see her before?"

I said I didn't remember seeing her.

"There's a story here somewhere," he said. "Somewhere there's a story." He started to walk away. "I guess doing stories about dead little babes in bus depot crappers doesn't seem like a fancy reporter thing to do, does it?"

He was so right.

"Well, that's what we do," said Sticks. "You'll get used to it or you'll quit."

• • •

Making bus calls went on to become my party thing to do. Other people sit down at the piano or pick up a guitar or break into "Danny Boy." I put an empty water—or wine—glass to my mouth and do a bus call. There are few people in any of my walks of life who have not at one time or another heard me say: "May I have your attention, please! This is your first call for the Continental Trailways five-fifteen P.M. Air-Conditioned Silversides Thruliner to Houston and Dallas . . ." and so on to "Don't forget your baggage, please!" I did it first at a party of J School students at Missouri. I did it as a newspaperman in Dallas at a company Christmas party while standing on a table at the Dallas Press Club. I did it in a speech in the ballroom of the swanky Inn on the Park Hotel in Houston, at a luncheon at the even swankier Waldorf-Astoria, and later from the stage of the Alley Theater in Houston. I have done it in commencement addresses, at book-and-author luncheons in Washington and Boston and on Long Island, at a quiet Christmas Day open house in the Georgetown section of Washington, and even on national radio and television. I have done it for my children and other people's children, for mature adults, for sophisticates, for rednecks, for journalists, for people who hate journalists, for bus drivers and bus company owners. Few have escaped. It is the only thing I do that few if any others do. There is something to be said for that. And I just said it.

It is one of several things that have kept buses alive in my life. Another is also the result of something that few if any others do. It is The Collection. My collection of intercity bus memorabilia, one of the finest of its kind anywhere, because it is also one of the fewest of its kind anywhere. I have more than three hundred bus depot signs. No one anywhere has more. I have more than three hundred bus driver cap badges. Only one or two fellow Americans have more. I have running dogs and silver and golden eagles off the sides of real Greyhound and Trailways buses, toy and model buses, ticket punches, tickets, baggage checks, express waybills, posters, depot clocks, timetables, playing cards, matchbook covers, ashtrays, destination signs, ticket validators, card ticket dispensers, drivers' and agents' uniforms, belt buckles, tie clasps, cuff links, photographs and drawings and paintings of buses, bus company magazines, coin changers, fare boxes and most everything else having to do with buses it is possible to collect. Much of it is on walls and shelves in my house or my office in Washington. Instead of window shades, my office at home has destination sign rolls that can be pulled down to expose in white letters on black the names of towns in Texas like Clarksville, Paris, Commerce, Honey Grove and Bonham. Oklahoma towns such as Ardmore, Durant, Ada, Idabel, Waurika, Broken Bow and Lawton. I found the rolls in abandoned 1940s Flxibles in a junkyard outside Ada, Oklahoma.

Some of the depot signs are of tin and wood, but most of them, the best ones, the prized ones, are porcelain-enameled. The process involves applying a colored design, in the form of molten glass, to a piece of heavy metal at furnace temperatures ranging from 2,300 to 2,400 degrees Fahrenheit. The end result is a sign that is close to indestructible, resistant to rust, dirt, weather and most everything else, short of a .22 rifle and other bullet shots. Some signs in my collection shine today with the same newness they had when they were made more than sixty years ago. Many have depictions of old buses. I have one from Santa Fe Trail System, the forerunner of Santa Fe Trailways, where Dad began his bus career. The sign has a 1928 Mack, with the driver and his passengers clearly drawn in the windows. Another sign, a Santa Fe Trailways, has a 1938 ACF, again with the driver and passengers riding proudly. I have all breeds of Trailways and Greyhound and a variety of independent companies that go back to the very major beginnings of national bus travel in the 1920s.

My cap badges do the same. They have company names like Yelloway, Colonial, Great Eastern, All American, Tamiami, Alaga (for Alabama and Georgia), Arkomo (for Arkansas, Oklahoma and Missouri), MKO Coaches (for Missouri, Kansas and Oklahoma), Pickwick, Blue Ridge, Great Falls, Bowen, Indiana Motor Bus, Quaker City, Queen City, Safeway, Safety Transit, Mt. Hood, North Star, Northland, Overland, Interstate, Trans State, Carolina Scenic, Harmony Short Line, Gulf Transport, Brooks, Sunnyland, Sunset, Sunshine, Dixie, Lake Shore, Arrow and Zephyr.

There is very little, short of murder, armed robbery and/or burglary, that I have not done to add to my collection. I extort from public television stations and others who want me to do things for them. Would you do a question-and-answer session at our annual dinner, please, Mr. Lehrer? Yes, sir, if you can come up with an old sign from such and such a bus company. I went to Wilkes-Barre, Pennsylvania, for a Martz Trailways sign; Springfield, Missouri, for a Missouri Transit Lines; Spokane, Washington, for a Boise-Winnemuca Stages and a Northwestern Stages; Minneapolis for a Zephyr Lines; Green Bay, Wisconsin, for a Wisconsin-Michigan Coaches; Roanoke, Virginia, for an Intercity Bus Lines. I appeared at a dinner in Lincoln for Nebraska public television so I could spend the afternoon rummaging through some priceless old files of Burlington Trailways and American Buslines, two companies that had been headquartered in Lincoln before they merged, went broke and disappeared into the Continental Trailways system.

The biggest extortion haul was from a speech I gave to the annual meeting of the American Bus Association in Portland, Oregon, in 1977. My "fee" was bus memorabilia. Badges and signs galore poured in to me. A wooden depot sign from Vermont Transit and several items from Public Service in New Jersey were probably the tops from that appearance. But other items, from Jefferson Lines, KG Lines, TNM&O Coaches, New Mexico Transportation Company and Gulf Transport Company, also came in.

I began collecting after my father died in 1970. He had been the Continental Trailways bus depot manager in San Antonio at the time. In going through things afterward, my mother came across a box of cast-iron and other toy buses that Dad had given my brother and me when we were kids. I looked at them and loved them all over again. Before I knew it, I was picking up other toy buses to go with them. Then I found a Pickwick Greyhound sign, bent and rusted, in an antique store in Dallas. I bought it. My wife and daughters gave me a six-foot-long Greyhound dog off a Greyhound bus. It, too, came from an antique store in Dallas. Then, after we moved to Washington in 1972, I went to an antique-advertising show in Gaithersburg, Maryland. Somebody was selling a Queen City Trailways cap badge. I bought it. And I was off.

I wrote letters to bus companies, I went to flea markets and antique shows, I began driving up and down the back roads whenever I could, looking for lost and forgotten bus depot signs swinging from poles. One of my best signs I found that way. I was driving with the family through upstate New York on one leg of a big Northeast college visiting tour for our oldest daughter, Jamie. On the way from Colgate in Hamilton to Vassar in Poughkeepsie, we went through a small town called Davenport Center. My practiced eye, able to spot bus depot signs from hundreds of yards at all speeds, saw something on the side of a general store. The sign said "No Parking." But underneath that, barely visible, it looked like there might be a picture of a bus or the word "Depot." I spun the car to a stop as my wife and daughters said it was nothing more than a "No Parking" sign, and if it was more, whoever it belonged to would never part with it, so why couldn't we just go on? I ignored them, of course, and inspected the sign at close range. Sure enough, it was a painted-over bus depot sign for Adirondack Trailways. A 1940s vintage GM bus was depicted in the center. I went inside the store and asked a young woman there if I could buy her sign. I offered her fifteen dollars; she frowned, so I immediately said twenty-five. Okay, she said. She then loaned me a ladder to take it down. No wife, no daughter, got out of the car to help me. But I did get it down and I did take it to the Holiday Inn in Poughkeepsie that night, and with fingernail polish remover I did remove the white-and-black "No Parking" to reveal a mint-condition red-and-cream-and-black Adirondack Trailways sign.

I have a Crown Coaches sign that John David, a friend in Joplin, Missouri, heard about from a traveling salesman, who said it was still hanging in Perryville, Arkansas. Another friend, Bob Sells, with whom I had gone to Missouri, drove to Perryville from Little Rock and took it down for me. I made him. He wanted me to come make a speech before the Little Rock chapter of the Society of Professional Journalists. I said I would if he got that Crown sign. As I said, there is little I will not do.

Not all my tries have happy endings. The worst experience involved an Indiana Motor Bus Company sign I found hanging at a small store in Schoolcraft, Michigan. I found it on a weekend, and there was nobody around to ask about it. Attempts to raise somebody later by phone did not work, either. A few months later, *Smithsonian* magazine asked me to write a piece about my bus collecting. So I quite cleverly used this sign in my opening anecdote. The grabber. "There is a 12-by-24-inch metal sign hanging outside an appliance store in a small town in Michigan," I wrote. "It is green, orange and white with the word BUS in the center of an oval and 'Indiana Motor Bus Company' in small letters surrounding it. I want that sign. I want it so badly it hurts." Well, that did it. With the *Smithsonian* name and the article behind me, I finally found the woman who was responsible for the sign. She said she had forgotten it was out there and, sure, she would sell it to me. We finally agreed on a price of sixty dollars. She said she would get somebody to take it down and send it to me. She did in fact send it, but it never in fact arrived. Somebody called a "consumer advocate" for the U.S. Postal Service did a full investigation after I complained of its disappearance. What his investigation revealed was that the woman at the appliance store had taken the sign to her local postmistress in Schoolcraft and had been told the sign did not have to be wrapped. It could be sent as is, with a label on it. The sign had definitely been put aboard a mail truck in School-craft, because the man who had taken it remembered. But some-where in Detroit or elsewhere, it disappeared. The consumer advocate told me he did not believe it had been stolen.

"What does one do with a hot bus depot sign, anyway?" he said, trying to be friendly and funny.

I did not laugh. He went on to make matters worse by giving me his investigative theory of the case. I do not paraphrase.

"One of our people probably assumed it was trash," he said. "You'd be surprised the kind of stuff people toss into mailboxes. We've found dead cats and other things I will not mention. Sorry."

It never turned up. But I have since acquired two Indiana Motor Bus signs, so all is not completely lost. These signs are very different in style and vintage from that oval one, though.

There are probably serious sides to my collecting. A friend recently told my wife that it was my way, conscious or other-wise, of showing a reverence for my father. By collecting the remnants of what he did for a living, of his career, of his life, I am saying that what he did mattered as much as what I did and do. The friend may be right. I hope she is. All I know is that I love everything about it—the hunt, the find, the possession, the touching, the oohing and ahhing.

It is also an absolute delight to be obsessed with something other than what I do for a living.

2

Jim and Charlie

My full name is James Charles Lehrer. James for my mother's father, James Chapman, a master preacher. Charles for my dad's father, Charles Lehrer, a master plumber. They would have been an odd couple if they had ever met—which they never did—as were their daughter and son, who not only met but married.

The Chapmans, my mother's family, were a royal family of the Church of the Nazarene, a holiness denomination that believed jewelry, makeup, movies and cooking on Sunday, among a terribly long list of other things, were sinful. Mother was no longer a practicing Nazarene when she met my dad in Washington, D.C., in 1930. He was a U.S. Marine corporal; she was a secretary at the War Department.

She had gone to Washington on her own after teaching school in Oklahoma and Idaho. She had a degree from Oklahoma City University and had done some graduate work in English at the University of Kansas.

Dad had an eighth-grade education and had worked as a messenger for the Corn Exchange Bank in New York City before he joined the Marines. He was seventeen years old when he saw a recruiting poster in a store window. "Join the Marines and Learn to Fly," it said. Dad decided he would love to learn to fly. He enlisted for four years, spent all of his time in the infantry at Quantico, Virginia, and in Haiti putting down rebellions, and never laid anything but eyes on an airplane.

Dad and Mom went to Kansas after they married, because he could not find work on the East Coast. He had gone from the Marines right into the middle of the Depression, and the best he could do was sell men's socks door to door in Boston. They went west for him to take a job with Southern Kansas Stage Lines, a bus company in Wichita. Mom's sister Grace and her husband, Al Ramquist, had told them about Kansas and the job there.

Dad seldom talked about his family back in New Jersey. We made only two trips there, and they were after Grandfather Lehrer died in 1943. All Dad ever told us was that his father, our grandfather, was a master plumber, such a good one, in fact, that he had done plumbing for Thomas Edison, who lived nearby in Menlo Park. That was about it. The only other things he told us about growing up were that his family had four or five types of cheese on the table at every meal, and as a result he hated cheese of all kinds; and that although both of his parents had come from Germany, they never allowed anyone to speak German in the house because of World War I, and because they wanted everyone to be American now.

It was only in the mid-1980s, long after both Dad and Mom were dead, that I found out more about the blood that flows through me from the Lehrer side. It is extremely more interesting blood than I would have ever thought—or dreamed.

A New Jersey cousin of mine, Dorothy Lindblad, and her husband, Harry, came to our house in Washington one evening for dinner. In the course of that night, Dorothy told us the following story:

Grandfather Lehrer and Grandmother Amelia came to the United States from Germany in the late 1800s with their respective families. Both were teenagers. Both their families were free-love socialists who had left Germany to escape jail and other persecutions from people who did not like free-love socialists.

Free-love socialists, Dorothy?

That's right, Jimmy.

Both families settled in a commune in the Yorkville section of Manhattan. Charles and Amelia fell in love—real love—and decided to get married. But they stayed in the commune and apparently in the swing of things.

That changed when Amelia got pregnant a short while later with their first child.

We must leave here and this life and have a normal life, said Grandmother to Grandfather.

Fine, he said. We will go west.

One Saturday morning soon after the baby was born, they packed up their belongings and went over to the Hudson River docks and boarded the ferry for Hoboken, New Jersey.

They got off the ferry, declared New Jersey to be the west, and settled in for the rest of their lives.

They were lives lived mostly in a storm. Grandmother was a devout Catholic, Grandfather a stubborn Lutheran. In accordance with historic precedent, they could not resolve their differences. So they decided to divide up the children. Every other one would be raised Catholic. They had four children in all. Dad's number happened to come up Lutheran.

Grandfather apparently never got over his free-love upbringing. He had a second passionate love, for alcohol. He drank lots of it every day. It made for a terrible marriage.

This was not helped by a third passion of his: politics. He decided to run for the city council of West Orange, the New Jersey town where they lived—and he was elected, thus becoming the first socialist city council member in the history of West Orange. Maybe in the history of New Jersey, for all I know.

Dorothy said he would probably have gone on to be mayor of West Orange if he hadn't been such a drunk. He died just before Christmas 1943, of a burst appendix. Dad's younger brother, Walt—my uncle Walt—was with him. Uncle Walt said his body temperature rose to 107 degrees before he died.

Uncle Walt himself told me some terrible stories of how, as a kid, he went around on plumbing jobs with his father, and how at the end of the day, and often much earlier than that, he would be left outside barroom doors to wait while his father got smashed, and then had to help him home.

The only physical image I have of this man Charlie Lehrer, for whom I am named in part, comes from an old photograph. He jumps out as a large, big-nosed man of noise and charm.

Obviously, that was all his son Fred, my father, wanted me to know.

I knew exactly what my grandfather Chapman looked like. He was completely bald, a little on the pudgy side, wore rimless glasses and had a chocolate-bar deep voice.

I also knew everything about the Chapmans, his and my mother's family. They were in Wichita and Oklahoma and Kansas City and elsewhere around where we were. Grandfather Chapman came to see us regularly. Mother was in contact with him and her four sisters and brothers regularly.

Jim Chapman, like Charlie Lehrer, was a charmer. From the time he was sixteen until he died, he spent most of his time traveling, spreading his version of the word of the Lord.

He was some preacher. I heard him preach several times, and even though I was a kid and thought what he had to say was boring and irrelevant and too religious, I do remember that everyone else always listened carefully to him. And shouted along with him.

Amen, Dr. Chapman! Amen, brother. Preach the word, Brother Chapman! Say it, say it!

My favorite eyewitness story about his preaching is what happened one night at a revival meeting outside Oklahoma City. Some kind of regional or district meeting of the Nazarenes was the reason for the gathering. Mom had taken Freddy and me there to see the family rather than to participate as Nazarenes.

But on the night Grandfather preached—he was already the senior general superintendent of the church, the biggest of the big deals—it was a command performance even for nonbeliever grandchildren.

Grandfather had been talking for less than ten minutes when

a *crack* rang out, and there was a crashing sound of glass right behind him and above his head.

Somebody had fired a shot through the window!

A deep breath of panic came from all of us in the tabernacle, and then the beginning of some rustling and some screams.

And then I noticed that Grandfather was up there, still talking. He had not even glanced around! He just kept preaching.

In a few seconds, the panic and the noise were gone and the place was absolutely quiet again; people went on listening to Dr. Chapman as if nothing had happened.

The shots turned out to be only rocks thrown by some pranksters. The coolness in Dr. Chapman, said everyone, was the work of the Lord.

Whatever, it only locked in even more the hero worship I had for Grandfather Chapman. He was the leader of the Nazarene Church and yet here he had a daughter, Lois, and her husband, Fred, and their two sons who were not Nazarene. Her husband even smoked cigarettes. Cigarettes! Her sons went to movies. Movies! Grandfather never seemed to hold any of that against any of us, and more important, he never tried to preach to us. Just the opposite. He played with us—Freddy and me, plus our cousins Tom and Gloria Ramquist. They were Aunt Grace and Uncle Al's kids.

See this? he'd say, holding out a twenty-five-cent piece.

Yes, sir, we'd say.

See this? He held out a bar of soap.

Yes, sir.

Whoever bites this bar of soap in two gets this quarter.

Tommy would reach out and bite the soap in two before anybody else could say or do a thing.

Good job, Tommy.

Then he'd give a half-dollar to Freddy—or to me or Gloria—for not being stupid enough to bite into a bar of soap for money.

The next time, he would offer the two bits to anyone who would run up a flight of stairs backward. None of us would do it. Too bad, he'd say, and put the quarter back in his pocket and resume reading the newspaper.

I was never sure whether there was a life's message in any of his games other than, Stay loose, boys and girls, but it did not matter. He was an important man and he paid attention to us nobody, no-Nazarene Lehrer kids.

He was also the strongest man I had ever known. He could put a Coke or Pepsi bottle lid between the thumb and forefinger of his right hand and bend it in half. I never saw him do it, but it was gospel that as a young man he never used a jack handle to raise the car to fix a flat. He picked up the car himself and somebody slid the jack underneath.

And there was the watermelon story. When he was a kid, he entered a watermelon-eating contest at some fair. Whoever ate the most watermelon got a quarter. Jim Chapman won, hands down, by throwing up between watermelons. He ate a watermelon and then went behind a shed, stuck a finger down his throat and vomited it up, returned, ate another. He kept doing that until all of the other competitors had given up.

Grandfather, like my father, had no formal education beyond the eighth grade. He had discovered Jesus on his own one day in the small town in Oklahoma where he lived, and he took to the life of the Bible from that day forward. He just declared himself a preacher at the age of sixteen and hit the road with other preachers.

A schoolteacher named Maude Frederick, of Palestine, Texas, came to one of his meetings in nearby Troup. She saw something in this young man and she took him away to another world. The world of language and knowledge. After they married, she sat in the front row every time he spoke and then critiqued him afterward. She corrected his pronunciation, expanded his vocabulary and taught him how to write grammatically and well.

He went on to be editor of *Herald of the Holiness*, the denomination's main magazine, and president of a couple or so Nazarene colleges before being elected senior general superintendent of the church. At the time of his death in 1947, he had written

sixteen books. They were mostly religious writings, and in looking through them recently I found them to be mostly religious
gibberish. But they were not that, and are not that, to people
who are Nazarenes. His name is magic in the church to this day.

I was there when he died, on July 30, 1947. It was at his
house on Indian Lake, outside Vicksburg, Michigan. There was
a Nazarene encampment by the lake, and Grandfather had a
summer home and several outbuildings there. Freddy and I, and
later Mom, went up there after the death of Kansas Central,
while Dad remained in Kansas to close down the bus line and
find a job.

On this particular evening, I had made a date with Grandfather. I had spent the day fishing out on the lake in a rowboat,
the same one Freddy and I used when Dad came to row him
out on the water and out of sight so he could smoke. On this
day alone I had not worn a shirt. So my back was badly sun-
burned.

I'll put some lotion on it before you go to bed, Grandfather
said at dinner.

But when it came time to go to bed, I was told Grandfather
would have to pass. He had had a tiring day and was feeling a
bit down. That message came from Louise Robinson Chapman,
Grandfather's second wife. We grandchildren called her Miss
Louise. She had been a missionary for twenty years among the
Zulus of South Africa. She and Grandfather had married a couple of years after Grandmother died in 1940. I loved her stories
about Africa.

Freddy and I, who were sleeping in the room directly above
Grandfather and Miss Louise's, woke up to the sounds of shout-
ing and crying.

It was still dark outside.

We went to the door. It was two o'clock in the morning.

Mom came up the stairs to our room and told us what had
happened.

"Grandfather is dead," she said. "He died in his sleep."

The next day was a terrible day. There were people I had

never seen before around everywhere. Everyone was crying. Or trying to remember the last thing the Great Man had said to them or others.

Somebody had told somebody else that I had been the last person to see Dr. Chapman alive.

No, I said. He was going to put suntan lotion on me, but he didn't.

I got tired of saying that to people, who were then disappointed that they were not talking to the twelve-year-old grandson who had been the last one to see Dr. Chapman alive and who had heard him say . . .

The worst thing about what happened the next day involved the sheets. The sheets on which Grandfather died. I came across Miss Louise frantically hanging them up on the clothesline behind the house.

I said nothing to her. I didn't have to. "Nobody should see these," she said. "Nobody should see these."

There were huge brown and yellow stains in the center of the sheets. She had tried to wash them out by hand, obviously, but it had not worked. It made me sick and it scared me.

Grandfather was sixty-three years old. He had had a series of heart attacks, and it was another, in his sleep, that had killed him.

I knew nothing about heart attacks, except that they could kill people. It was to be thirty-six years before it occurred to me that there was a connection between what had happened to my grandfather and what happened to me.

3

Always Faithful

There were buses and there was the Marines.

There was never a time I did not want to be a U.S. Marine. It came with being a son of Fred Lehrer, who had entered the Marine Corps in the twenties and never quite gotten over it. Nobody who does ever does.

I went into the Marines in the fifties without so much as a moment's thought or hesitation. So did my brother, Freddy. We had made the decision to be Marines years before, when we had seen brown-tinted photos of Dad in his uniform in Haiti and when we had played Marines in the backyard in Kansas during World War II and watched Randolph Scott, John Payne and Robert Taylor be Marines in movies. By the time we were five years old, we knew that the Marine motto, *Semper Fidelis*, meant "Always Faithful," and we knew all of the words to all three verses of the Marine Corps hymn and that you had to stand at attention whenever it was played or sung.

Dad was barely five feet, seven inches tall and he was thin-boned, but he seemed larger because of his bearing and style. He always carried himself in a military manner and groomed himself with care, spit and polish. The joke was that he wore ties to picnics and to carry out the trash. It was barely a joke.

Maybe he would have been that way even if he had not been a Marine, but I doubt it.

Dad and the movies and my imagination had prepared me for the best of what it meant to be a Marine, but unfortunately not for the worst.

Freddy went first, in 1953. He came back from a summer of officers' training at Quantico, a shaken and battered young man. While at the University of Texas, he had joined a Marine officers' training program called PLC, for Platoon Leaders Class, which required him to go to Quantico for a form of boot camp between his junior and senior years. He told me of mental harassment and physical brutality and screamed profanity and other kinds of awfulness that were completely unimaginable to me.

I could not believe the U.S. Marine Corps actually treated good people like us like that.

They did.

At the train station in Quantico two summers later, between my junior and senior college years at Missouri, my turn began.

Some fifty of us new PLCs had come on the same train from Washington, D.C. I had flown there from San Antonio, the first airliner ride of my life. The plane, a Constellation operated by Eastern Airlines, had broken down in Atlanta (some things never change), so I arrived late in Washington and late at Quantico. We were met at the train by a drill instructor—a DI. He was a tall, thin sergeant in heavily starched khakis with perfect creases. He was terribly annoyed with all of us, not just for being late but for merely existing.

He called us "candidates" in a way that made it sound like the name of a dreaded insect, and he had us line up in formation in front of him on the train station platform. He told us to stand at attention and keep our eyes staring straight ahead.

He began calling out names.

He got to mine. "Leer!" he barked.

"Leh-ra," I yelled back. It was a reflex.

There was silence. A silence of danger. Of doom. I dared not move my eyes. But I heard two feet moving toward me.

"Where is the little baby shithead candidate who just opened his pussy little candidate mouth?" said the voice of the sergeant.

I could feel him coming. Good-bye, Marine Corps. Good-bye, life. Freddy had warned me. Never say anything about anything. Never. Shut up and stay shut up. But Mr. Big Mouth could not do it.

Sorry, Pop, but there was this guy calling out our names. He mispronounced our last name. *Your* last name. So naturally I had to correct it. After all, it's important to pronounce our name the right way. Right, Pop? You always said it was. I have always corrected people when they mispronounce it. They don't mind. They want to get it right. Everybody wants to get everybody's name right. . . .

"Here, sir," I said, straight ahead of me as quietly as humanly possible to still be heard. Freddy had told me to say "sir" all of the time. When in doubt about anything, say "sir." Sir, sir, sir. Always say "sir."

"I can't hear you, candidate!" screamed the sergeant, his voice closer.

"Here, sir," I said at full volume.

And there he was. The man who was going to end my Marine dream and maybe my whole life right here at this train station. His face came right into mine, the rim of his campaign hat up against my forehead, his nose not more than an inch from mine.

"You listen up, little college-baby pissant, and you listen up good!" The force of his breath, which smelled of beer and potato chips, almost knocked me over. "If I say your name is This Little Piggy Shit Went to Market, your name is This Little Piggy Shit Went to Market. If I say your name is Cunt Who Jumped Over the Moon, your name is Cunt Who Jumped Over the Moon. Do you hear me?"

I heard him.

That pretty much set the tone of my twelve weeks as a PLC that summer of 1955. It occasionally got slightly better than that, but only around the margins.

I went back to Quantico after I graduated from college the following summer. Now I was a commissioned officer, a real second lieutenant, which was a terrifically big deal to Dad, who had been a corporal, and to me and a few others back in Texas and elsewhere, but at Quantico it was nothing. It was less than nothing. Everybody who walked the Quantico earth seemed superior in every way to second lieutenants.

I spent nine months there, the first six in officers' basic school, and came out with the best occupational specialty there was—0302, infantry officer. I learned how to fire an M-1 rifle, a .45-caliber pistol, an M-1 carbine, a Browning automatic rifle, .30- and .50-caliber machine guns, rocket launchers, 60- and 81-millimeter mortars, and a flamethrower. I learned how to throw a hand grenade, dig a foxhole, mold and detonate yellow plastic explosives, lay land mines, inspect a rifle bore for rust, and count cadence for close-order drill. I studied map reading, infantry tactics, hand-to-hand combat, amphibious warfare, the uniform code of military justice, and battlefield first aid. I was told Marines never leave their dead and wounded behind, officers always eat last, the U.S. Army is chickenshit in combat, the Navy is worse, and the Air Force is barely even on our side.

I got used to hearing the word "fuck" used—with or without a suitable prefix or suffix—as a noun, verb, adverb, adjective, gerund, participle or anything else in the English language, and at any place in a sentence and at any time or place or occasion in daily life. I was—and remain—amazed at the number of such things an average U.S. Marine could cram into any sentence about any subject.

Hey, Lieutenant, my fucking sister sent me some fucking peanut butter fucking cookies. Can you fucking believe it? Fucking peanut fucking butter fucking cookies. I hate fucking peanut fucking butter fucking cookies. How about you, sir? Would you like one of these fuckers?

I stayed at Quantico as a platoon leader at officers' candidate school for three months before going to the Third Marine Division on Okinawa. I spent fourteen months there in One-Nine—First Battalion, Ninth Regiment, Third Division—as commander of an antitank assault platoon (rocket launchers, mortars, flame-throwers and demolitions), then as an infantry company executive officer, and finally as an S-1, adjutant and personnel officer with additional responsibility for classified documents and morale. I was supposed to keep the classified documents locked up and morale high. No problem with the documents. Not much with morale, either.

How's morale out there in the battalion, Lieutenant?

Not good, Colonel.

What can we do about it?

Have a free-beer party, sir.

Great idea, Lieutenant. Get it done.

Aye, aye, sir.

■ ■ ■

I spent my last six months of active duty at the Parris Island Recruit Depot in South Carolina. I arrived hot and ready to pass on to new young recruits the wisdom I had acquired in a so-called Ready Battalion overseas. But I got waylaid by the colonel who was in charge of assignments. He saw from my personnel file that I had a journalism degree.

"How would you like to be officer-in-charge of *The Boot*, our little weekly newspaper here?" he said.

Thinking it to be a question, I replied: "No, thank you, sir. I'm an infantry officer."

"You're needed at *The Boot*, Lieutenant."

So. I never exchanged one word of wisdom or anything else with the recruits, and I saw them only from a distance as I went each day between the Bachelor Officers' Quarters—the BOQ—and the Quonset-hut offices of *The Boot*.

And on a day in June 1959, I departed Parris Island and the Marine Corps to take up where I had left off three years before in becoming another Hemingway.

■ ■ ■

I came away from the Marine Corps with much more than I had gone in with. I fired no rounds in anger at any enemies of the United States and/or of life, liberty and the pursuit of happiness. And none was fired at me. I jumped on no hand grenades, pulled no wounded out of harm's way, danced through no mine fields, cleared out no sniper nests, destroyed no tanks. I had no close calls, no rendezvous with danger, no skirted destinies with death.

What I had was a chance to discover and test myself, physically and emotionally and spiritually, in important, lasting ways.

I discovered that I, a small-muscled male of barely average size—five-nine, 155 pounds—with no athletic skills or special coordination or stamina, could accomplish stunning physical feats, just because somebody ordered me to and I had no choice but to do them.

Such as hiking around the island of Okinawa, a distance of more than a hundred miles, in five days. Doing 100 push-ups, 75 sit-ups, 30 chins. Double-timing around a parade field singing obscene songs for nearly an hour. Shinning up and over a wooden barrier the height of a telephone pole. Leaping across a small gully on a rope like Tarzan. Deflecting and then tossing to the ground and disarming somebody coming at me with a knife.

There were many moments of truth, times when I was sure I had finally come to the end of the road. Here now was something that I simply could not do.

The moment I remember best was in Basic School, the morning we had to cross a river. It was more than fifty yards wide, deep and running. A steel cable was strung across it. One at a time, in full battle dress—helmets, packs and M-1 rifles—we lieutenants-in-training were to grab the cable with our hands, wrap our legs up and over it and then pull ourselves across the river backward. And upside down. A couple of boats with enlisted Marines were down below to pull those of us who did not make it out of the water.

I was certain I would be one of those. One of those candy-asses who belonged in the Air Force or the Boy Scouts. I was now going to be found out. There was simply no way I could do this. My arms and hands did not have the strength to pull me across. I would fall into the water, drown or be saved. I saw both results as about equal.

And suddenly it was my turn. I made sure the strap holding my helmet on was secure. I checked my rifle. The sling held it tightly over my back and pack.

"Come on! Come on! Come on!" yelled somebody. He gave me a gentle shove toward the cable. "Move, move, move."

I reached down and grabbed the cable and slid out from the bank, turning backward as I threw my legs up over the cable. I had done it right! I was in position. I moved my left hand down the cable and pulled my body after it. I moved! All of me! I repeated with my right. Look at me!

I could hear the water below, but my eyes were on my hands, the cable and the sky. After what seemed like hours, I figured I was only halfway across. But I hadn't fallen. I hadn't fallen! I started moving my hands faster and thus me faster. I felt like a million dollars. I felt like Superman.

I felt like a Marine.

I thought of all the girls I had ever panted for unsuccessfully. If only they could see me now!

Seconds later, I was on the other side. I did not fall, I did not drown, and I did not humiliate myself.

"Good work, Lair," said the captain who was our platoon commander. He patted me on the helmet and I double-timed over to a clump of trees where we were to reassemble.

I know it sounds stupidly melodramatic now, but thirty-odd years ago I ran over there with my head and body and soul screaming with the glory and the pride and the sure knowledge that I could do anything. Anything at all.

It was the first time in my life I had ever felt that way.

And by the way, that "Lair" back there was not a typo. That was what the captain called me from the first day. I had elected not to correct him.

Quick-Study Leh-ra, they called me.

▪ ▪ ▪

I learned about all kinds of responsibility. In the Marine Corps, a nineteen-year-old corporal way down in the ranks can screw up, and smelly things can hit the fan for forty-year-old colonels and a lot of lieutenants, captains and majors, among others, in between.

One particular case I remember: It was 1958. The Red Chinese were bombarding two offshore islands called Quemoy and Matsu, which were still under the control of Taiwan and Chiang Kai-shek.

A joint U.S.–Taiwanese marine landing exercise was planned on a beach in southern Taiwan. Twelve hundred U.S. Marines would be involved. The idea, apparently, was to scare the Chinese into stopping their shelling.

Good idea, don't you think, Major? We'll show those commie bastards. . . .

But General, there are 900 million of them and only 1,200 of us.

That's about even odds for the U.S. Marine Corps, I'd say.

Yes, sir.

One-Nine, fortunately, was not involved, so I had no command responsibility. I was there on temporary duty as an umpire, my job being to move about the battlefield observing firefights and then deciding winners and losers between the invading Marines and the enemy, also marines, dressed up in weird, communist-like uniforms.

The whole thing was probably stupid to begin with. But it was made much, much more so by some staff sergeant who had failed to get the proper clearances signed by farmers and others who owned the land on which this show-of-force make-believe war would be fought.

So. Our landing force came ashore, the farmers would not let them go into their rice paddies, the "Red enemy" mowed down the good guys, who were forced to walk down the roads, and the other umpires and I had no choice but to declare the Reds the winners. Some U.S. news correspondents who were in the area covering the real war over Quemoy and Matsu got the story. And heads started to roll. In fact, as I heard it, just about everybody in the higher reaches of the Marine Corps with a head lost it. I don't even want to think about what happened to the staff sergeant and to the poor lieutenant, captain, major or whatever who was his commanding officer.

They teach this kind of responsibility early. And with a whack. My first PLC platoon once had to double-time around the parade field ten more times one muggy Quantico afternoon because one man in the platoon—only one—had failed to pass a physical fitness test of some sort. The DI put it to us ever so delicately: "When they're shooting at you, one candy-ass can get everybody killed."

The rest of us made damned sure that one guy passed the physical fitness test the next time.

I learned another kind of responsibility the day I showed up at a tent camp on Okinawa where One-Nine was temporarily housed. It was nighttime, and it was raining and muddy. I ended up in the headquarters tent, where the duty officer, a first lieutenant, told me where my BOQ tent was and gave me my assignment to Weapons Company and the antitank assault platoon.

"Here, sign this," he said.

"What is it?" I said.

"It makes you responsible for all of the eighty-one mortars, flamethrowers, rocket launchers and other equipment in your platoon."

"Where are they?"

"Somebody'll show it all to you tomorrow morning."

"Why sign this tonight, before I even see it?"

"Because I have been told to have you sign it. Welcome to One-Nine."

I signed it. I was now responsible for more than two million dollars' worth of equipment on which I had never laid an eye.

It was a dramatic introduction for me into the world of being a platoon commander. Responsibility for the forty or so members of that platoon had no limits. I comforted NCOs older than I who had received Dear John letters from home. I helped a young PFC write his own letter to a girlfriend he no longer wanted. Out in the field, where we spent fifty percent of our time, I had to make sure everyone in the platoon was fed, bedded down, clean, clean-shaven, sober, orderly, trained in all of our weapons and tactics, and reasonably happy.

I was twenty-three. Where else but in the military could a punk fresh out of white bucks and yellow corduroy pants get that kind of a real-world responsibility?

■ ■ ■

I learned about melting the American pot. I learned it most loudly and clearly when I was a platoon leader, before going to Okinawa, back at officers' boot camp at Quantico.

It was the first night after the arrival of a new PLC platoon. There was a knock on the door of the small office the platoon sergeant and I shared in the headquarters Quonset hut.

"Who is that knocking on my door?" I shouted, in accordance with the accepted style.

"Sir, candidate Jones, sir." Jones is not his real name. I do not remember it.

"Get in here!" I ordered.

Jones marched in and to the front of my desk. He was a burly, handsome kid from a southern state. I had been told by the company commander that he had made second team All-American as a running back. He looked the part. He would have no trouble with any of the physical training in the next few weeks.

"What is it, Jones?"

"Sir. A nigger is sleeping on the rack above me, sir. I'm not sleeping with a nigger, sir."

The Marine Corps does everything in alphabetical order. If there was no such thing as an alphabet, some commandant would order some gunnery sergeant to make one up. There was a black in the platoon, among the very few the Marine Corps had or was bringing into its officer corps in those days. The alphabet had dictated that he have the bunk—"rack" in Marine talk—right over Jones in the sleeping area—"squad bay" in Marine talk.

It took me a count of only two or three to decide what to do.

I stood up, leaned across the small desk and said in my toughest voice:

"Candidate, hear me well. You have exactly ten seconds to decide between racking where you are told or getting your ass thrown out of the United States Marine Corps. I am counting. One . . . two . . . three . . ."

"Sir, I want to be a Marine, sir."

"Four . . . five . . . six . . ."

"Sir, you mean I sleep with a nigger or I'm out, sir?"

"Seven . . . eight . . . nine . . . ."

The kid was still at rigid attention. His eyes, probably used to watching people run from him or be run over by him, flickered.

"Sir, all right, sir."

I leaned across the desk again into his face. "Candidate," I said, "nobody knows about this unless you tell them. You tell anybody and cause any problems for this platoon about it, you can count on more hell in your life than you ever thought existed. Do you hear me?"

"Sir, yes, sir."

"Now get out of my sight."

He took two steps backward, as we had already taught him, did an about-face and got out of my sight.

Jones made no problems about the young man sleeping above him. When the summer ended, he and the black candidate were terrific friends, probably the first friend of the other's race each had ever had.

Both had experienced the mostly mythical American melting pot—by force.

In the course of my time in the Marine Corps, I served with the son of Wayne King, the "Waltz King," and the son of John Charles Daly, the famous TV man and host of *What's My Line?* A scion of the famous Bingham family of Kentucky was in the next platoon in Basic School. I bunked with the son of the chief executive officer of one of the largest paper-manufacturing companies in the country. But just across the squad bay was another like me, a kid from a small state school in Illinois who had never been farther east than Indianapolis before he had gone into the Marine Corps. On farther down were the son of a New Jersey carpenter and the son of a San Jose, California, cop. They were all there, the rich, the poor, Catholics and Jews, Baptists and atheists, slicks, slows, cools, hots. One of my best friends on Okinawa had gotten a Great Books degree at Duke. There was a guy from California who wanted nothing more in life than to sing with the Kingston Trio when he got out. Some wanted to spend their lives being Marines. Others were planning graduate school or law school. A guy in One-Nine was going to go to theology school to be a Presbyterian minister. There were some with drinking problems, others who never drank, some who never spoke of sex or women, others who spoke (and, as best I could tell, thought) of nothing else.

It was amazing, the numbers and kinds of young men I came across in the Marine Corps. It is amazing, the times since then I have had occasion to remember.

Old Smitty there across the office is a left-handed, horny, teetotaling Chicano with a degree in Oriental philosophy who grew up on a farm in northern Minnesota and worked his way through Yale selling condoms door to door.

Right. I knew a guy like that in the Marine Corps.

Knowing somebody helps avoid a lot of knee-jerk clichés about people later in life. Like those two in my PLC platoon. My guess—and it's just a hopeful guess, because I have no idea what happened—is that if that former football star got involved in a conversation with one of his fellow rednecks and heard somebody say something sweepingly negative about black people, he would think—and, I hope, say—Wait a minute. I knew a black guy in the Marine Corps who was terrific.

I hope and believe the young black candidate would now say the same, no matter what, about white people.

I honestly and sincerely believe those two men are better persons and citizens because of their military experience. I know

I am. The things I learned and experienced came at me in a way and at a time that left lasting impressions.

I firmly believe everybody should have that experience. Not have the opportunity to have it, but *have* it. And that, of course, means some kind of mandatory national service. The Marine Corps and the military are not for everybody, but God knows there are plenty of needs in this country and abroad that could be met with various kinds of alternative government service.

Freddy and I joined the Marines because there was a draft. If we had not signed up for the Marine PLCs or some similar program, eventually we would have been drafted into the army. The same was true for Jones and his black friend, and the Bingham and Daly and King boys. And the kid from Illinois and the one from New Jersey, the New York slicks and the Montana slows.

I know there are many other aspects to the argument for national service. I know it would be expensive. But at this particular time in our country, when we are dividing along class and racial lines, it seems to me it would be cheap at any price to have a national program that puts the young unemployed black from the ghetto street corner into the same world with the sons and daughters of the white, rich and famous, and forces them to serve and suffer and laugh together. And get to know each other.

And depend on each other.

We of *MacNeil/Lehrer* have a professional obsession against taking public positions on current events and issues that we cover on the program. I realize I have just violated that. But I do know what being forced to perform a national service did for me, and I hate it that there is not such a program for the young people of today, men and women.

The same kind of transformation happened to me about guns. I learned to fear and loathe them. Having been expertly trained to use handguns against human beings—particularly all of the body-splitting automatic and semiautomatic weapons—I find it impossible to see them as anything but tools of death and injury.

They are not sports equipment. They are not croquet wickets or autographed Louisville Sluggers, basketball kneepads or tennis racquets. They are made to cut people in half, to blow holes in their chests, to splash their heads on the pavement.

In my opinion, only the untrained and the ignorant play word games about the magic manliness of holding a gun, hunting deer with an AK-47, protecting one's VCR from a drug-crazed burglar with an Uzi, or holding back the Marxist hordes at Harlingen, Texas, with a Saturday-night special.

I am grateful to the Marine Corps for having taught me that in a way that stuck forever.

■ ■ ■

Before I leave the subject of the Marines, let me say (à la *MacNeil/Lehrer*) that I am aware there is another side to it. I have emphasized the positive elements of my three-plus years in the Corps because I believe it was the pluses that took in me, rather than the negatives.

There *are* negatives.

I came across some really lousy people in the Marines. Sadists, masochists, fascists, racists, nasty drunks, monsters, idiots, liars. Majors who would run over not only their own mothers but everybody else's as well to make lieutenant colonel. Captains who shaved their heads like billiard balls and took their companies on forced marches in the middle of rainstorms at midnight just to prove how strange and tough they were. Officers of all ranks who were scared to make any decisions because they were afraid they might be wrong and thus damage their careers. NCOs who stayed in the Marine Corps only so they could humiliate fellow human beings. It was their favorite pastime and they got addicted.

There is a Jesus factor, as it is called, in the Marine Corps, and it is funny only in hindsight. A regimental inspection is called for 0900. The uptight battalion commander calls one in advance at 0800. The company commander does his at 0700, the platoon leader his at 0600, the squad leaders at 0500, the fire team leaders at 0400. By the time 0900 comes, the troops are half asleep, exhausted.

It must also always be remembered that the Marine Corps is an organization created and designed to be in combat: intense, close-up, forward-position combat. There is nothing more frustrating to a well-trained outfit than not having an opportunity to demonstrate their fitness and their abilities. This breeds a kind of warmongering sickness among some. They talk like little boys of getting out there and blowing up things and killing people. They crave medals and battlefield promotions and casualties and running for cover and storming machine-gun emplacements. They were very much in the minority where and when I served, but they were there. And they gave me the creeps.

And while the real gung-ho types would probably strongly disagree, the truth is, the best thing about being a Marine is being a *former* Marine. There is a spectacular grin of recognition that comes onto the faces of two men when they discover both have been Marines—no matter the rank or station, no matter the time or place. It is a grin of shared experience, probably not unlike that exchanged between members of some mysterious, exclusive society.

It is also the grin of a shared secret. The non-Marine public, for the most part, thinks highly of the Marine Corps and those who have served in it. They bestow attributes of great skill and courage on them, among other things. The secret shared by the Marine grinners is that most of the praise is not deserved. But so what? If people want to think I'm great and special because I was a Marine—well, why not let them?

Maybe, in the most final personal analysis, the best thing being a Marine did for me was make it unnecessary for me ever to have to prove my masculinity to myself or to anyone else. It was as if I had gone through a ritual to manhood, such as Indian tribes and others once practiced.

I know I can pull myself across a raging river on a steel cable.

Whatever, being a Marine was also in full step with the Hemingway doctrine of having experiences, of living life out there, of doing things that would help me be a better newspaperman and writer of fiction.

Being a newspaperman was what I did next.

4

Thank You, Felix

It was Saturday night, just after midnight. I answered the ringing phone on the city desk.

A hysterical female voice cried out: "This is *Time* magazine in New York! I need help!"

Time magazine in New York! Hello, Big Time.

"I need to know John Connally's middle name," said the voice. "I'll be killed if I can't find it. We're on deadline. Please. Please!"

I held the phone away from me and yelled over to the copy desk, some twenty yards across the newsroom. "Anybody over there know John Connally's middle name?"

Hardly even looking up, one of the copy editors said: "Bowden. Spelled B-O-W-D-E-N."

I repeated that into the phone.

"Are you certain?" said the woman.

"Are you certain?" I yelled back at the copy editor.

"As if it were mine," he replied.

"I am certain," I said into the phone.

"Oh, thank you. Thank you. What is your name? What is your Social Security number?"

I gave her both.

Five days later I received a Time Inc. check in the mail for fifty dollars.

Hello, Big Time.

It was July 1959. I was a few weeks into my first newspaper job as a night rewrite man at *The Dallas Morning News*. While winding up my time at Parris Island, I had written four I-want-to-be-a-reporter letters. United Press International never answered. The Associated Press responded with a polite "We have no openings." The *Fort Worth Star-Telegram* came with a less polite "Sorry, we're not interested." It was the *News*, after my letter number four, that brought the only answer I wanted. You look good on paper, they said; come see us after your discharge.

I came two months later, they saw, and I was hired at $82.50 a week.

Sticks was right about what a newspaperman was all about. Particularly the part about death.

In ten years as a reporter in Dallas, I covered many stories about people dying. They died in plane crashes, head-on auto wrecks, tornadoes, flash floods, house fires, love triangles, hold-ups, cop-and-robber shoot-outs, loaded-gun accidents, knife fights, wife and child beatings, and assorted other violence. Some of them even died of natural causes. I saw and smelled some of their bodies and interviewed some of the people who loved them.

I learned about heroes.

I stood outside a burning two-story slum house while two firemen went through a window filled with smoke and flame, and came out carrying two tiny, silent children. I watched with the children's screaming mother and neighbors in gagging awe as these two men put their mouths on those kids' and tried and tried and tried to breathe them back to life. They pounded the little ones' chests with their fists and pleaded and finally gave up in exhaustion and tears.

I learned that even murderers, con men, sex deviates, burglars, embezzlers and bank robbers have faces and family. So do their victims. So do the police officers, deputy sheriffs, FBI agents, prosecutors, defense lawyers and judges who work the cases. So do the people who run for office, who work in district and county clerk offices, who collect taxes, who pave roads, who type letters, who teach school, who run corporations, who sue corporations, who picket, who protest, who preach, who pray.

I interviewed Elvis Presley (before he died). He came through Dallas on a sleeper train on his way from Memphis to California after being released from the army. He appeared on the rear of the train platform like he was Harry Truman or somebody running for president.

"Ah just woke up," he said to us thirty waiting reporters and female fans.

One of the reporters—not I, I swear—shouted out a question about Elvis's father's recent decision to marry a young divorcée back in Memphis.

Elvis said he didn't mind.

"Is he with you on this trip?" somebody—I, to be embarrassingly exact—hollered.

"Wahll, no. While I was in the army, the house in Memphis got kind of run-down. . . . The grass grew up tall and the patio furniture got messed up. So he's staying there to get it all fixed up."

Great moments in journalism, and I was there.

I was also there when Steve Lawrence, another singer-soldier, came through Dallas. I interviewed him between planes at Love Field. Elvis had been a truck driver in the army. Not Lawrence, Eydie Gorme's husband.

"I don't think the army gets the full benefit of a singer's abilities if they put him behind the wheel of a truck," said Lawrence in his exclusive interview with me. "The singer doesn't benefit, either."

Great moments in journalism II.

As a general-assignments reporter, I spent a lot of journalistic moments at Love Field interviewing people of prominence and purpose who arrived or passed through. At one time I was referred to as the only foreign correspondent in American journalism who never left the city limits of Dallas. If anybody with an accent came into town, I was there.

I developed a standard repertoire of questions for all visitors from all countries. How do you like America? How do you like Texas so far? (Yes, some replied that they had just arrived and it was a little early to say.) How does it differ here from your country? How close are the communists to taking over in your country? What do you want the United States to do to help you?

My favorite Love Field story involves a reporter for KLIF radio in Dallas. He and two other reporters and I were there to cover the arrival of a Cardinal from St. Louis. When first given the assignment, I thought it was Stan Musial or Enos Slaughter, but I was quickly told this Cardinal was the Catholic cardinal of St. Louis. He was coming to Dallas to make some kind of speech.

I was not Catholic and I had no idea what to ask him. How close are the communists to taking over your country? was not quite appropriate.

So I was delighted that there were other reporters there to ask questions. But in the few minutes before the cardinal's plane actually arrived, we compared notes. Nobody had an idea—a prayer, you might say—as to what to ask.

And then suddenly there he was. A big black-haired man in a black suit. An aide-de-camp priest introduced us all around, and we followed them into a small interview room.

"Well, now," said the cardinal. "Who wants to go first?"

Silence.

"Don't be bashful," said the cardinal. "We must move on to our appointments in a few moments."

More silence. I could not think of a thing. I was embarrassed and mortified and all of those things. But my mind was frozen. How do you like Texas, Your Majesty? How do you address cardinals, anyhow?

The cardinal started to move toward the door.

"Your Grace," said the KLIF reporter. "I have a question."

The cardinal, obviously pleased, sat back down. "Yes, my son?" he said.

The KLIF reporter said: "How do you like being a cardinal?"

The cardinal looked stunned. But after a beat or two he smiled and said: "It is a glorious job, thank you." And he went on and on for several minutes about how he enjoyed ministering to the needs of the Catholics of St. Louis, running the parochial schools, the hospitals and all the rest. I do not remember every detail, but I do remember that I got enough out of it to write a four-hundred-word story under the headline CARDINAL LIKES JOB.

And I immediately added, How do you like being a Yugoslav businessman (or whatever)? to my repertoire of Love Field interview questions.

My first front-page byline story was about a kid who put a pigeon egg on top of a television set. The warmth from the TV caused the egg to hatch. My memorable lead: "A 17-inch television set gave birth to a baby pigeon Saturday morning in Oak Cliff." My first "copyrighted" front-page story was based on a telephone interview with the Texas pianist Van Cliburn in New York, about his being invited to a reception in honor of the visiting leader of the Soviet Union, Nikita Khrushchev. Among my stupidest leads was the one I put on an account of a press conference held by the Duke of Edinburgh, who was in Dallas pushing British-made airliners to Braniff: "Prince Philip, husband of the Queen of England, was asked in Dallas Saturday if he wears polka-dot underwear. 'Let's leave that under wraps, shall we?' replied the prince."

My first big investigative series was about the Communist Party in Texas, followed by one on the John Birch Society and another on the civil defense operation in Dallas. The civil defense stories were the reason I went from the *Morning News* to the *Times Herald*.

It is my only Hero Lehrer story.

I worked for several weeks running down and confirming a basic fact about the civil defense operation in Dallas. It was handing out right-wing, Reds-behind-every-bush propaganda while ignoring its real job of preparing the city of Dallas and its people for nuclear attack and other inevitable calamities of that year, 1961. It had, for instance, published an evacuation plan that called for citizens to evacuate to safe places in rural counties surrounding the city. I went through the plan in detail and called the authorities in each of the counties that had been designated to receive people from Dallas. Few of them knew anything about it, and they were most upset when I told them. None of the citizens who were to do the fleeing when sirens sounded knew about the plan, either. The whole thing was ridiculous, and my series of five stories laid it out.

But the publisher of the *Morning News* was called by some friend on the civil defense board of directors, and my series was killed. So I quit. Literally, within an hour of having been told my stories would not be published, I had cleaned out my desk and left the building.

"That's crazy," said Johnny King, the city editor. "Where are you going?"

"I don't know," I said.

And I didn't. Fortunately, I was able to get a job with the afternoon competition, the *Times Herald*.

I had made only one phone call before telling Johnny King I was quitting. That was to Kate, who had just been forced to leave her job as a junior high English teacher because she was pregnant with Jamie, our first of three daughters, and was beginning to "show" too much.

"I don't want to work here anymore," is what I said to her.

"Then don't," she said, without even a second's hesitation. "Get out of there."

So I got out of there. Kate did not say a word about where I was going to find a job. She also did not remind me that we were without savings or assets, and that with a baby coming maybe this was not the best time for the family's remaining breadwinner to become unemployed.

Kate was the Hero Lehrer I was referring to.

She was also with me when I came within a hair of throwing in the whole journalism towel and got saved only by the God-playing arrogance of my boss.

I was making $115 a week at the *Times Herald*. We now had Jamie and Lucy, daughter number two, and were living in a two-bedroom duplex in northwest Dallas. Once our rent and other essentials were paid, not only was there nothing left, we were always in the hole. Always. It became a case of writing checks to cover bills and then rushing to the bank with money to cover the checks. If something had ever happened to us on the way to the bank, we would have probably gone to jail for writing hot checks. Because technically that's what several of them were—every month—when we wrote them. And frankly, if it had not been for Kate's mother, a traveling credit supervisor with the Sears catalogue stores division, Jamie and Lucy would never have had any new clothes and we, as a family, would never have been able to go to a restaurant.

Sticks Strahala, a bachelor, had not warned me about this. I had begun to think that maybe I was not going to be the Big Time success I had dreamed of being. I was almost thirty years old. I was down and disagreeable and depressed most of the time about where I was headed, and that I was taking Kate and our girls with me.

And along came a man from Texas Power and Light, an electric utility that did business throughout the state. The company was looking for a young newspaperman to join its public relations staff. The top PR man was already contemplating retirement, and in a year or two and if it worked out, the new young newspaperman could move into the top slot. That was the way it was presented to me. I was then the *Times Herald*'s federal reporter and backup political man.

Kate and I were taken to dinner at a country club. A country club! This was after first having drinks at the top man's house. It was a real house, with a yard and everything. The man had real liquor—scotch, even!—that he offered us. And he had a car. A company car! He was able to travel to Austin and other places. Travel! And his wife could go, too, all expenses paid. Hot damn!

The pay was almost double what I was making at the *Times Herald*. I told the man I was interested.

"Well, let me go see Felix," he said. Felix was Felix Mc-Knight, the executive editor of the *Times Herald*, the man who had hired me after I had walked out of the *Morning News*. He was a former Associated Press man who many years before had himself come over from the *News* to the *Herald*.

"I don't get it," said I. "Once we make a deal, I will go see Felix and turn in my notice."

"No, no," said the electric utility man. "First I have to get permission to talk to you. We cannot afford to alienate a big newspaper like the *Times Herald*."

Two days later, I was summoned to Felix's office. I came in, we shook hands, and I had barely sat down when he said: "No way."

"No way? How can you say 'No way'?"

"It would be a mistake for you," said Felix. "You are not a PR man. You would hate it. I will not let you do it."

I stood up. "It's not your decision, God damn it!"

"Yes, it is," he said. "Forget it. You're a newspaperman."

"You can't do this!"

"Get back to work. Good story on the Pleasant Grove bank robbery, by the way."

"How about a raise, then?"

"Nope. Not right now. Things are tight."

"Damn you, Felix!"

"Some day you'll thank me."

I walked out of there in a rage. How could this man play God with my life like this? It was unconscionable. Outrageous.

Thank you, Felix.

■ ■ ■

Let no one tell you there is no such thing as the Power of the Press. Particularly, let no one in the press tell you that. Such a person is either an idiot or a liar, for one thing, and is surely an irresponsible and lousy journalist, for another.

We in journalism are essentially in the dynamite-handling business. We hold in our hands the power to blow reputations and ideas and all kinds of other things to smithereens, or the other way, to the heavens. Billions of dollars and hours are invested by corporations, politicians, authors, movie stars, millionaires and public and private interests from the left, the right and all other directions in attempts to influence what is said, reported and commented upon in the printed and electronic press. A bad review of a play can close the play and end a playwright's or actor's immediate future. A story based on a leak from an FBI investigation can end or seriously impair the future of a governor, congressman or county commissioner. A positive story about a senator can launch a presidential "possibilities" campaign. A negative story about a new product can throw a corporation into bankruptcy. And so on.

It could be that the play was terrible and the leak was correct and the product was bad and the end result was not only desirable but in the public and national interest. The point is that it was helped along, if not precipitated by, stories in the press. If that is not power, then the word simply has no meaning.

I learned the lesson early.

In the fall of 1959, less than six months into my life as a reporter, I covered a hearing before a federal magistrate in Dallas, the U.S. commissioner. A fifty-seven-year-old man had been arrested by postal inspectors on an indictment returned in Atlanta. He was one of twenty-four people charged with participating in a nationwide loan racket that got businesses to pay fees in advance for loans that never seemed to come through.

The arrested man, well dressed in a coat and tie, came over to me while we waited in the U.S. marshal's office for the commissioner to arrive.

"You're a reporter for *The Dallas Morning News?*" he said.

"That's right," I said in all my importance.

"You're not going to do a story about me, are you?"

"Yes, sir, I am."

He said: "No, please. I only worked for that company in Atlanta for six months. I didn't know anything wrong was going on. I used to drive a car in car shows. Daredevil stuff. They called me Flash."

"I'm only a reporter," I said.

"Hey, listen to me, young man," he said. "My lawyer tells me that they're going to dismiss all charges against me in another week or so. Please don't do a story."

I shrugged, looked away and wondered where in the hell the commissioner was.

"If you do a story, it'll ruin me," said the man. "I just resettled here in Dallas with my son. There he is, over there."

I looked at his son. He was a blond kid standing against a wall trying hard to be invisible.

"He's had problems in school, but now he's clicking. I've got a job as salesman for an outfit that makes car-wash gear. They'll fire me. It'll throw me and my son for another loop. Please don't do a story."

I told him it was not my decision to make. I was only a reporter.

The commissioner finally arrived. There was a brief hearing to establish only that Flash was in fact the man named in the indictment. Bail was set at $10,000, and the man and his son left.

My story the next morning was two columns on the main local news page. DALLAS SALESMAN INVOLVED IN RACKET read the headline. My lead paragraph:

"A one-time 'daredevil' car driver, now a Dallas salesman, was involved Wednesday in a nationwide loan service racket that bilked 13,000 businessmen of $10,000,000."

The fifteen-paragraph story had details of the indictment, plus the accused man's denials.

Two weeks later, I received a phone call from the man called Flash.

"I told you those charges were going to be dropped," he said. "Well, I just wanted you to know they were today."

"I'll do a follow-up. . . ."

"Too late for that," he said. "I was fired, just like I said I would be. And I can't get my son to go to school. He hasn't been since your story. We're packing up again. Going to Houston to try again. I just wanted you to know what your story did to me."

I'm only a reporter.

No, I did not say that again to him. He had hung up. But I did say it to myself, and I have said it many times since: I'm only a reporter. But with the power to do to others what I did to that man named Flash. I still do not believe I did something wrong in going ahead with the story. Reporting the arrest of a person on a serious charge like that was certainly fair and justified game. I had neither the authority nor the responsibility to grant a form of press clemency to the man for two weeks or so to see if the charges were dismissed.

But. But my story contained the power to damage a person's life. And it did. It was the first time I had seen it happen like that and been a party to it. It scared me, and it still does.

The power to do good is also there, of course. I learned that other side a short time later, in January 1960, with a story about Brother Bill's annual shoe party in west Dallas. Brother Bill was a Baptist minister in his late fifties who for years had collected shoes and then given them away to poor kids in a west Dallas housing project at a shoe party. On this particular Saturday, it turned bitter cold. Joe Laird, the photographer on the assignment with me, took a magnificent photo of three little tow-headed brothers standing in line in the cold. My story related the unfortunate fact that by the time the sponsors got to them, all the shoes in their sizes were gone. Both picture and story ran in the center top of the front page the next morning.

The phones rang all day at the *News*. People volunteered shoes, clothes, money and everything else imaginable for those three little boys. The Associated Press sent Joe's picture plus a small piece of my story all over the country. Calls and telegrams and letters and checks then began pouring in from outside Dallas and outside Texas. People said they had never seen anything like it.

And later, as a courthouse reporter, I did a story about a Mexican-American man whose wife came to the courthouse press room claiming the police had wrongly arrested him for armed robbery. As a result of my story, the DA's office looked at the charges closer and quicker, and sure enough, he was the wrong man. The charges were dismissed and he was freed.

A terrific reporter-editor named Lewis Harris and I did a series of stories about the connections between a state senator in
West Texas and some gambling and liquor interests. Conse-
quently, the man was defeated for reelection.

The wonderful power of the press in action. My stories are
not special or heroic. Anybody who has reported more than a
handful of local stories has experienced the positive power of
cause-and-effect journalism. And, one hopes, been humbled and
instructed—and scared—by it, as well as by the negative power.

There were other lessons to learn about journalism in those
beginning days. Such as the fact that people lie. I learned it hard
from a well-known black disc jockey who had been arrested and
charged with raping a young white Freedom Rider from Britain.
I interviewed him in the Dallas County Jail after his arrest. With
a straight and impassioned face and voice, he swore to me that
he had touched and felt the woman, but had not had sexual
relations with her. He claimed he was being persecuted because
he was black. Please help me, he said. I believed him, and I
helped him with a major interview that I persuaded the city
editor to display prominently on the front page.

A few months later, I was sitting at the press table in the
courtroom when he went to trial for rape. The alleged victim
testified in great detail about how the man had taken advantage
of her pro–civil rights attitudes to force himself on her.

Then, with an occasional eye flashed toward me, the defendant told the judge and the jury a story that in no way resembled
what he had told me. Yes, he had had intercourse with the
woman. He described it in full detail. But, he said, it had been
done with her full cooperation and acquiescence. The jury
bought his story and he was acquitted. Black-on-white may have
been important to a jury in Texas in 1960, but the fact that the
woman had put herself in what was seen as a "welcoming" position was more important.

"You lied to me," I said to him in the hallway, during the first
break after he testified.

"I had to," he said. "I had to get some good early publicity
right then. My lawyer told me to do it."

My lawyer told me to do it. That was another line I was to
hear often in my five years as a courtroom reporter. It was the
most exciting and revealing and instructive five years I have had
in journalism. Every day in courtrooms there were people facing
the loss of their liberty against people trying to get justice
for the loss of a loved one or a car or a twenty-dollar bill or
whatever. In between them stood the words, shouts and decisions of lawyers, judges and cops. There is nothing more exciting, more gripping, in my opinion, than watching two evenly
matched top trial lawyers go at it in a courtroom presided over
by a judge who cares about what's going on. The most revealing
and instructive thing for somebody in journalism is witnessing
the phenomenon called perspective. That thing that turns issues
and events from black-and-white to gray.

Time and time again, I would listen in a courtroom while a
prosecutor laid out his case with his witnesses. I would conclude
without question not only that the accused was guilty as charged,
but that he or she should be taken immediately to prison and
locked up there forever. Then I would listen while the defense
laid out an entirely different way to look at that same set of
facts, and I would conclude that the defendant was clearly the
wrong person or, if the right one, definitely did not deserve to
go to prison. Or whatever. And then I would look over at the
twelve men and women chosen to make a decision and feel
grateful that it was they, not I, who had to decide.

The lessons for somebody in journalism, of course, were simply that there is always more than one way to look at things,
and that when two or more people look at the same thing they
will always see it differently. Always. Good criminal lawyers
know that the least reliable witness is an eyewitness. Good reporters learn it, too.

■ ■ ■

A courtroom, for all the gray and glory, is also a good place
to learn about lying. I listened to lawyers and defendants and
witnesses, including some law enforcement officers, hold up
their hands and swear to what I was certain were lies. It pro-

vided training for sorting through the comments of others—
thousands of others—I have since interviewed for print and
television.

Thirty years of such sorting has led me to conclude that truth
as purely defined by some philosophers and preachers does not
flourish in the world of public discourse.

Mr. Lieutenant Governor, did you take a $5,000 bribe from
the magnolia tree interests?

No, sir.

I have a notarized receipt signed by you and a videotape of
your actually accepting the money.

I thought the money was for me to deliver to the Salvation
Army to feed the poor.

Great answer, Mr. Lieutenant Governor. Moving on now to
the crisis in education . . .

We, the interviewers and journalists, are continually saying,
"Great answer, Mr. Lieutenant Governor," and moving on. The
public figure is judged not on whether or not he or she answered
the question, but on how. How the question was handled is the
test, which is a lot different from how it was answered. Much
of the blame for this lies with us, the journalists and interviewers. We have set a standard of style rather than substance. Just
look at the wreckage of politicians who did try to answer difficult
questions honestly. George Romney was laughed out of the 1968
presidential race when he admitted the generals brainwashed
him in Vietnam. Same thing happened to Edmund Muskie when
he had the honesty to show anger and passion over an editorial
attack on his wife. Barry Goldwater told the truth about Social
Security and paid through the political nose. The list of wrecks
is a long one.

It was this system that allowed John F. Kennedy, Gary Hart
and others to live personal lies, and Richard Nixon, Ronald Reagan and many others to tell political and official ones. Even the
current post-Watergate tell-all atmosphere hasn't changed much
except in matters of the flesh and the buck. Truth in sexual,
financial and other so-called personal ethics areas is now re-

quired, but that's about it. The style-over-substance system still encourages lying about opinions and issues.

Senator, you are from a cranberry-growing state. Is that the reason you are in favor of continuing the cranberry subsidy program?

Certainly not. I vote only in the national interest.

Great answer, Senator. Moving on now to arms control . . .

Everyone in earshot of that kind of exchange—and such exchanges go on every day by the thousands at courthouses, White Houses and other kinds of houses all over America—knows that it is a dialogue of lies. But everyone winks. It's a small business-as-necessary lie. Obviously, the senator protects his political base. Obviously, that is why he votes the way he does on cranberry matters. But he is neither encouraged nor, in my opinion, permitted to lay it out. He must tell a lie or wake up to a headline like: SENATOR ADMITS TO NOT VOTING IN THE NATIONAL INTEREST!

It's a stupidly dishonest way to do business. It will not change until we journalists figure out a better way to encourage and nurture truth-in-answering, or until a few politicians are successful at trying it on their own in a dramatically new way.

Meanwhile, the scandal of tolerating statements such as the president's that Clarence Thomas was nominated for the Supreme Court because he was the best qualified, and race had not one thing to do about it, will go on. You do not have to be anti-Thomas to shout, Lie! Mr. President, that is a lie! You just stood there on your front lawn at Kennebunkport and told a lie! A lie, sir! Stop it! Don't do that anymore, sir! No more lies! None! Stop it!

But nobody said that. The people of America, not even the journalists of America, rose up to shout, Lie! We all just kind of smiled and said, Oh, my. That certainly isn't right, but please, pass another beer—or martini or glass of milk or Diet Pepsi. Our president lies, life goes on. What if it didn't go on when a lie was told? What if there was a National Truth Squad made up of rotating Americans who knew lies when they heard them, who called the hands of liars? Maybe the squad could be made up of old journalists like Fred Friendly, Scotty Reston and Walter Cronkite, and old politicians like Howard Baker and Tip O'Neill, and some old Supreme Court justices like Lewis Powell and William Brennan, and some old preachers and teachers and screamers and others. And every time somebody like a president or a presidential candidate or senator or House member or governor or whatever, of any party, or newspaper columnist or television commentator told a whopper, the squad would go on *The MacNeil/Lehrer NewsHour* and every other news program and outlet in the nation and shout, Lie! Lie! Lie! Maybe we could stop this craziness of judging public people not on what they say but on the way they say it.

▪ ▪ ▪

And speaking of telling lies: I learned another early lesson about that. I learned that reporters do it, too. Even to each other.

I was involved in an effort to unionize the newsroom of the *Times Herald* for the American Newspaper Guild. At the time we launched it, we had no holidays off and no overtime pay and lacked most of the other basic amenities of the workplace. Texas and Dallas were not places that welcomed any kind of pro-union activity, so it was a tough go in most every respect from the beginning. But labor and management, for the most part, conducted their respective sides of the campaign cleanly and without too much open hostility and fireworks.

With a few days to go before the representation election, all of our face-to-face polling showed that we were going to win. The overwhelming majority of the newsroom employees were going to vote for the union. Then, for personal reasons completely unrelated to the union election, an assistant city editor cut his wrists. He survived, but the nerves of everyone involved in the weeks of campaigning did not. Management came to the five of us on the publicly declared organizing committee through an intermediary and offered us a deal. Call off the election and we will give you everything you want without it. The unspoken sweetener was that all would be forgiven, the five of us as well. No hard feelings, and all the rest. Let's get on with the glory of newspapering and the *Dallas Times Herald*, rah, rah, rah, and all the rest.

We five met in a downtown hotel room with Jim Ceznik, the Guild's professional organizer from Washington, D.C., who was a straight and honest man. These were the most wrenching, difficult couple of hours I had ever spent. The issue, at its most unvarnished, was simply that it was in the selfish interest of us organizers to make a deal. We could claim we had accomplished what we wanted and walk away from it as heroes to most everyone concerned, and with few scars.

We smoked a thousand cigarettes and drank a thousand beers and screamed a thousand cusses of anguish and disagreement. And finally we decided to do the right thing. We concluded that we really had no right to make the decision. The troops had gone this far with us. We could not walk away from them.

Over the next twenty-four hours, every one of the eighty-five *Times Herald* employees eligible to vote in the election was contacted by one of us in person. Eye to eye, we laid out the offer from management, and then asked only one question: What do you want us to do—take the deal or remain on course for a union?

The tally was clean and overwhelming. More than sixty wanted us to stay the course.

We passed on the no to management, and two days later we lost the secret-ballot vote by thirteen votes. Some twenty-five of our fellow/sister workers lied to us eye to eye and left us out to dry. And to perish. Why? Not because they were evil people, but probably because they simply did not have the courage it took to tell us the truth: that they were not with us and never had been. They had lied.

A victory party had been scheduled at our house that night in northeast Dallas. Kate and I had drink and food for sixty people and their spouses and/or companions. Only eleven people and their spouses and/or companions showed up.

Of the five of us who had openly identified ourselves with the union effort, three were gone from the staff and Dallas within a few months. The two of us who remained went nearly two years before getting a raise or much of anything else.

And life has gone on for me. Now I am a member of a management at *MacNeil/Lehrer* that opposed an attempt by the Writers Guild of America to organize our employees in 1986. I found myself telling our employees things similar to what Felix McKnight and others in *Times Herald* management had told me and my colleagues twenty years before. I am certain that the union organizers on our staff went through many of the same wrenches and strains I had gone through back then.

Life and perspective go on.

▪ ▪ ▪

The most important news event in my newspaper life in Dallas, of course, was the assassination of President John F. Kennedy. I have little of consequence to add to the thousands of remembrances and observations that have already found their way into print and other things. As a reporter for the *Times Herald*, I covered the President and Mrs. Kennedy's arrival at Love Field and stayed more or less on the assassination story for the next two years. I covered the Dallas parts of the Warren Commission investigation and was on a team that covered Jack Ruby's trial, and as the federal reporter I generally stayed on top of other events and developments in the story. I have loosely followed what has come in the years since, but I do not claim to be a maven of assassination lore.

Do I believe Lee Harvey Oswald was the lone assassin? Not really. Do I believe there was a conspiracy? Not really. What I do believe is that the lone-assassin thesis is full of unexplained holes and hard-to-swallow leaps of fact and faith. The only things more difficult to believe are the conspiracy theories. Or to put it another way: I have seen no conspiracy case that is any more factually convincing than the original Warren Commission finding that Oswald did it by himself. That includes most assuredly the claims of former New Orleans district attorney Jim Garrison, all of whose books and other writings I have read.

I found it astonishing that, of the numerous conspiracy theories, Oliver Stone chose Garrison's to chronicle in his 1991 movie *JFK*, because Garrison's were the only ones that had been tested in court and been found not just wanting but mostly laughable. Stone clearly shares Garrison's inability to distinguish between incompetence and conspiracy. And I must say I felt the reaction to Stone's movie was excessive. It was tedious as a movie, poorly written and acted, and was both too long and too preachy. Its pre-release praise/hype by movie critics, major magazines and TV programs was a mystery to me. As far as its political and editorial slant, an equal mystery was why it unglued so many attacking columnists and commentators. The movie, in my opinion, ended up making Garrison and Stone and their ideas look idiotic. So why the storm? I went to the movie expecting to leave captured emotionally and enraged editorially. I was neither.

It was only the elitist libeling of a whole class of Americans, my own class, by the Stone fiction that brought real heat and red to my face and soul. The movie, directly or indirectly, alleges that hundreds, thousands, of working CIA, FBI and other federal agents; police officers, deputy sheriffs, Warren Commission staffers and congressional investigators; and reporters from news organizations of all sizes, persuasions and resources were not interested in finding out who killed Kennedy, or worse, were either involved in the assassination and/or the cover-up or manipulated by evil higher-ups who were. It is an absurdity beyond all honest imagination to claim people of such independent minds and spirits could be so involved or so used in killing a president of the United States. Any person with any experience in or knowledge of this real world knows better. Spies, cops, reporters and writers are the worst kinds of conspirators. They are suspicious, they are antiestablishment and antiauthority, they are patriotic, they are ambitious, they trust no one, they talk. Only in a never-never land of the ignorant and the careless would such an idiotic conspiracy idea be taken seriously. It is a blood libel to repeat it in public, particularly in a large-screen $40 million movie. And it says more about the people who make, finance and appear in movies these days than it does about who killed John F. Kennedy. And what it says is mostly what we already knew: There is nothing they will not do to make a buck, including showing Kennedy's head being blown to bits in slow motion.

But to repeat: I would not be surprised if someday the AP news computer on my desk bulletined a story about the deathbed confession of a guy who was the "driver" or "lookout" or "paymaster" or whatever for some group who had plotted and committed the assassination of John F. Kennedy—with or without Lee Harvey Oswald. My guess is that if it ever does happen, it will be more along the lines of the real fiction conspiracy in Charles McCarry's novel *Tears of Autumn*. Oliver Stone could not have made a movie of that book, of course, because McCarry is a former CIA agent and thus undoubtedly one of the thousands, millions, who were part of the Garrison/Stone version of the conspiracy.

I am tied to the Kennedy assassination in another way, which has nothing to do with my reporting. I wrote some words that are now etched forever into the marble at the Philip Johnson "open tomb" memorial two blocks from the assassination site in Dallas. John Schoellkopf, an old and good personal and *Times Herald* friend (we covered the courthouse together) who went on to become a civic leader, was chairman of the citizens' committee in charge of raising money for the monument. When it came time to dedicate it in 1970, he asked if I would write something that could go with the memorial. A statement on behalf of the people of Dallas. We agreed that it should be done anonymously, so as not to confuse things. I was then running an experimental news program on the public television station in Dallas, which had filed suit against the presiding judge of the Dallas County Commissioners' Court for violating the Texas open-meetings law. The county judge had responded by calling me, the program and the station Communist, among other evil things.

Schoellkopf was asked many times back then who had written

the inscription, but he never said. I've decided after twenty years it no longer matters.

What I wrote was this:

The joy and excitement of
John Fitzgerald Kennedy's life belonged to all men.
So did the pain and sorrow of his death.
When he died on November 22, 1963, shock and agony touched
human conscience throughout the world.
In Dallas, Texas, there was a special sorrow.
The young President died in Dallas. The death bullets were
fired 200 yards west of this site.
This memorial, designed by Philip Johnson, was erected by
the people of Dallas. Thousands of citizens contributed
support, money and effort.
It is not a memorial to the pain and sorrow
of death, but stands as a permanent tribute to the joy
and excitement of one man's life.
John Fitzgerald Kennedy's life.

No, it's hardly Nobel Prize material. And if written now, it would surely say "to all men and *women*." But it is there on marble at the entrances of the memorial.

"This will last longer than anything else you will ever write, Lehrer," Schoellkopf said to me.

Right, John.

And I do have one assassination-reporting story. It is not one of conspiracy or intrigue. It is one of the many personal what-ifs that ricocheted through hearts and minds after the assassination.

Mine is about a Secret Service agent.

My assignment on that November 22 was to cover the president's arrival at the airport, stay there until he came back, and then report on his departure. The visit was happening right in the middle of our major deadlines, so virtually everyone on the city staff was involved in the coverage.

I had a telephone against a fence right in front of where the president's plane would taxi up. It was an open line to our rewrite desk downtown.

Just before the plane was scheduled to leave Fort Worth for the short flight to Dallas, the rewrite man, Stan Weinberg, asked me if the bubble top was going to be on the presidential limousine. It would help to know now, he said, before he wrote the story later under pressure. It had been raining early that morning, and there was some uncertainty about it.

I told Stan I would find it. I put the phone down and walked over to a small ramp where the motorcade limousines were being held in waiting. I spotted Forrest Sorrels, the agent in charge of the Dallas Secret Service office. I knew Mr. Sorrels fairly well, because I was then the regular federal beat reporter. After he had found out that I had been a Marine, he had even tried to recruit me as a Secret Service agent. That had gone nowhere because I wasn't interested, particularly when he'd said all agents being hired right then had to take special training to become expert swimmers, sailors and horsemen. That was because of the Kennedys.

I looked down the ramp. The bubble top was on the president's car.

Rewrite wants to know if the bubble top's going to stay on, I said to Mr. Sorrels, a man of fifty or so who wore dignified glasses and resembled a preacher or bank president.

He looked at the sky and then hollered over at one of his agents holding a two-way radio in his hand. What about the weather downtown? he asked the agent.

The agent talked into his radio for a few seconds, then listened. Clear, he hollered back.

Mr. Sorrels yelled back at the agents standing by the car: "Take off the bubble top!"

Just over twelve hours later, I was part of the bedlam at the Dallas police station along with hundreds of other reporters. I went into the police chief's outer office to await the breakup of a meeting in Chief Jesse Curry's main office. I had no idea who was in there.

The door opened and out walked several men. One of them was Forrest Sorrels. He looked tired and sad. And bewildered. He saw me and I moved toward him. His eyes were wet. He paused briefly, shook his head slightly and whispered: "Take off the bubble top."

He was gone before I had a chance to say, It was all right, Mr. Sorrels. It wasn't your fault, Mr. Sorrels.

It wasn't *our* fault, Mr. Sorrels.

■ ■ ■

My newspaper, the *Dallas Times Herald*, died just before Christmas in 1991. The competition, my first newspaper, *The Dallas Morning News*, bought it and closed it down. After I had left the *Times Herald* in 1969, it went from local ownership to the Times Mirror chain and finally to two consecutive young newspaper entrepreneur-owners. I read several stories about what caused the *Times Herald* to fail, and all of them said it was the combination of the recession and the built-in disadvantage for afternoon newspapers.

Old newspapermen tend to get sappy about the death of newspapers they once worked for. They talk about them and mourn them like they were people, exotic people, magic people, important people. I did that about the *Times Herald*. But I did it in the context of memories that were beautifully mixed, beautifully newspaperlike.

City editor was my last job at the *Times Herald*, my last newspaper job. It was awful. Truly awful.

I was offered the job by the managing editor over lunch, the first one I had ever been taken to by a *Times Herald* editor or executive. He said management had all but forgotten—and maybe even forgiven—my Guild activities, I had done well as the political writer-columnist, and frankly, there was no one else left who knew downtown Dallas from Oak Cliff. How about it?

How much does it pay? I asked.

Ten thousand a year, he said.

I will do it for eleven. Not a penny less.

That would make you the highest-paid newspaperman in town.

So?

They met my price—or they at least came close. And there I was. The only good thing about the job was saying I had it.

What do you do, Jim?

I'm the city editor of the *Times Herald*.

Wow.

The day my new position was announced, Dad took Mom to the most expensive restaurant in San Antonio to celebrate. It was a French place called La Louisiane. I heard about it from a Dallas friend who just happened to be in San Antonio that night and just happened to have gone to La Louisiane for dinner. He heard a commotion from the other side of the restaurant.

What's going on over there? my friend asked his waiter.

There's a couple celebrating their son's being made editor of something, said the waiter. Something in Dallas. The man's buying drinks for everyone.

The friend went over and introduced himself. Dad made him join them for a drink. Dad, as the Continental Trailways bus depot manager in San Antonio, was making less than I would be in my new job.

The problem for me was the job itself. I went to work at five-thirty every morning and was seldom home before six or seven in the evening. What I did most of the day was fight with the managing editor and the assistant managing editor and juggle too many assignments among too few reporters. The courthouse man was sick, so the federal reporter would have to cover for him. A general-assignments reporter would go by the U.S. district clerk's office on his way to Love Field to interview some accented west Hungarian businessman about how he liked being a west Hungarian businessman. And so on.

It was as city editor that I finally and irrevocably learned the basic truth of journalism. It ain't history, friends. It ain't science, either. And it sure as hell ain't art. In the course of my twelve-hour days, I would make 150 or so decisions. Some of them very small, like throwing a particular story inside the paper or deciding to run a picture two columns wide instead of three. Others involved sending a photographer or not sending a photographer, or covering story A instead of story B, just because something in my gut told me A was better.

Over the first few hellacious weeks, I discovered that no matter how hard I worked, no matter how much intellectual energy I put into it, I still made mistakes. Cropped the picture wrong. Misplayed an important story. Covered the wrong story. Photographed the wrong event. Killed the wrong story. I came up with a rough count that I was right about seventy-five percent of the time. That meant, of course, that I was wrong twenty-five percent of the time. That, I have since discovered, is about the way it is in daily journalism. Making fast decisions on deadline on the basis of a fragment of a sentence or thought from a young reporter or even an old source is the name of the game. It's an exciting game, but it is also a dangerously selective game. Let no one tell you otherwise.

The pressures of the job can be used as an inexcusable excuse for carelessness with simple facts and quotations. What all newsrooms need are a few firings. Firing a few people for not caring enough to get a few simple facts absolutely correct would do wonders. Being the subject of stories, as Robert MacNeil and I have been, can open your eyes forever to just how casual so many reporters and editors are about getting things right. It is too bad all practitioners of journalism cannot be the subject of a few stories as part of their training, to see how it feels to be misquoted, misborn, misaged, misaddressed, miseducated.

I once asked Ben Bradlee, when he was executive editor of *The Washington Post,* "Have you ever had a story done about you by anybody in any medium that was completely accurate?"

No, he replied.

There are few in or out of journalism who would reply any differently. That is, to borrow Jimmy Carter's favorite word, an outrage.

■ ■ ■

Upon his retirement in the summer of 1991, Ben Bradlee said something in a *NewsHour* interview that was also relevant to my time as city editor of the *Times Herald.* He said the first thing it takes to be a successful newspaper editor is a good owner.

Unfortunately nobody named Graham owned the *Dallas Times Herald* in 1968. The people who did were mostly good, solid, honest people. But their view of running a newspaper was sometimes not in sync with the view of those of us who worked for them. Things got out of hand in their use of the paper's news columns to further their own purposes. Some of those purposes were, in my opinion at that particular young, hotheaded time of my life, idiotic and irresponsible.

For instance: In 1964, one of the top executives of the paper was a close friend of John Connally. With or without Connally's encouragement, he decided it was only right that Connally place Lyndon Johnson's name in nomination at the 1964 Democratic National Convention. Johnson, who had other national political fish to fry, had said no. But nobody knew this. Nobody but the *Times Herald* executive. He went to the paper's political editor and said he had a story for him. And the story was simply that Johnson had chosen Connally to nominate him at the convention. Who is the source? asked the reporter. I am, said the executive. I'll have to check it with Johnson's people, said the reporter. Don't do that, said the executive. Just write it. I have made arrangements for it to go on page one. And we'll get it to the wires. And hopefully on the nightly news programs tonight.

The political reporter smelled a rat. But he did not own the paper. So he wrote the story and asked that his byline not be on it. The rest, as they say, is tainted history. The story did go on the front page, and on the Associated Press wire and Huntley/Brinkley that night. Johnson was then forced to select Connally to share the nominating with another person. To have done otherwise would have embarrassed Connally.

Another instance in which I was involved: the Reverend Martin Luther King, Jr., fresh from having won the Nobel Prize for Peace, came to Dallas for a speech at Southern Methodist University. The student government association had invited him. There had been only a small story way inside the paper about his coming. Our archcompetitor, *The Dallas Morning News,* had run a similar small inside story.

I was assigned to cover King's day in Dallas. That morning

at the city desk, the city editor told me that a publisher-to-publisher deal had been worked out. SMU was in the middle of its annual fund-raising campaign, and it was decided that King's coming there might hurt fund-raising efforts among "the people who were considered the major contributors." So the story was going to be lowballed. I was not to ask any questions at King's news conference. I was to write a story only 350 words long. It would run inside the paper. The *Morning News* was going to do exactly the same thing. The city editor, a man of integrity named Al Hester, spat out the words to me. He was embarrassed and angry that he had to say to me what he was saying. But he, too, did not own the paper.

I did not do exactly as I was told. I asked several questions at the news conference. So did the guy from *Morning News*. I also wrote a story that was nearly three thousand words long. It was cut down and run at the desired length. But at least I didn't do it.

When I became city editor myself a few years later, I was prepared for the worst of this kind of thing. And I was not disappointed. Once the publisher himself came into the newsroom and asked the managing editor to see a story our federal reporter had just done about a lawsuit against the leading wholesale liquor dealer in Dallas. The publisher, using his own pencil, removed everything that referred to the defendant and his company by name. The end result for the reader of the *Times Herald* was a story that made no sense.

Why are you doing this? I asked the publisher.

Julius—the liquor dealer—was good for and to Dallas, answered the publisher.

A worse incident happened one Saturday afternoon. The publisher had, through the managing editor and assistant managing editor, ordered the coverage of the arrival of Gloria Vanderbilt, the New York socialite-designer, and her writer husband at Love Field. They were flying in in the late afternoon, when there was only one "swing" general-assignments reporter on duty. But that was no problem. Nothing else was scheduled to happen in Dallas right then.

But. Just as the reporter and photographer were about to leave the newsroom, the police reporter called the city desk. Bulletin! A Navy fighter plane had crashed at the Grand Prairie Naval Air Station, between Dallas and Fort Worth. There was at least one fatality. Maybe more on the ground.

Without so much as a second's hesitation, I scrubbed the socialite-arrival assignment and sent the reporter-photographer team to Grand Prairie. They got the story, we put it in on page one, and I thought I had gone home with a job well done.

I was wrong. On Monday morning, after we got past our first-edition deadline, the assistant managing editor put on one of his funeral faces and asked me to join him in his office.

What happened Saturday? he asked.

Nothing but the plane crash, I replied. And we got it.

Gloria Vanderbilt at Love Field, said the assistant managing editor. She was not covered.

That's right, I said, still not picking up on what was going on.

The assistant managing editor cleared up my confusion. Gloria Vanderbilt and her husband were houseguests of the publisher. He had even had a party for them Saturday night. He had assured them they would be met at the airport and interviewed for a story that would appear in the Sunday paper. But this did not happen. And not only was the publisher embarrassed, he was furious.

You mean I should have skipped the plane crash for that?

Yes, said the assistant managing editor. A must story from the publisher takes precedence over all other stories. Always and completely, now and forevermore. Amen. I thought he might cross himself the way Catholics do before eating. He, I reminded myself, did not own this paper, either.

I do not mean to suggest that the downside of being city editor was entirely the fault of editors and executives from above. Those below also supplied their share of grief.

Newspaper reporters—the good ones, at least—tend to live close to the edge in most everything they do.

One story:

For Veterans Day one year, I assigned our best general-assignments man to write profiles of three Dallas area service-men—one who had gone to Vietnam and come back, one who had gone and not come back, one who was about to go. I gave the assignment to the reporter on Monday. The profiles were due Friday for the Sunday morning paper.

Friday afternoon he turned them in. They were short, but they were terrific. He had found the perfect three servicemen. There would not be a dry eye in any *Times Herald* home on Sunday morning. The stories were so good I took them imme-diately to the managing editor to sell them for page one. He bought. Across the top of the page is where they belong, he said. Get me a one-column picture for each, he said.

Aye, aye, I said. I went to the reporter, praised his stories, reported on their selection for page one and instructed him to get photos.

Aye, aye, he said. But a few minutes later he was at my desk pleading with me to join him for a cup of coffee in the coffee shop. It was urgent, he said. *Really* urgent.

I made up those three soldiers, he said over coffee. They do not exist.

You're fired, I said. Clean out your desk and get the hell out of my sight, my life.

Wait a minute, he said. What if I can find real ones before deadline Saturday? Stories and pictures. On your desk ready to go. Please. Let me try. I'm having trouble at home. They're foreclosing on my house, car and furniture. A cat burglar stole my baby's toys. My mother-in-law has just moved in. My first wife is suing me for back child support. My mother has a ter-minal disease. My father is already dead. There are holes in all of my shoes and I haven't eaten in two weeks. Or something like that.

So I said okay, not believing for one minute that he could pull it off.

He did. I do not know how he did it, but he found three real people who were just as good as the phonies. He got their sto-ries and pictures, and there they were, on my desk at noon the next day.

The managing editor, who knew nothing about what was going on (of course), had some problem swallowing the idea of three new soldiers. My lie was simply that the other three would not agree to being photographed. So we had to find three others. And here they are. Their stories are just as good, and isn't it all simply wonderful. Happy Veterans Day, sir.

Then there was the time the managing editor put out a memo lamenting the lack of names in the *Times Herald*. He reminded us that names make news, names *are* news. Put them in your stories, he ordered. No story should be without them. Lots of them. One of the reporters (Bill Sloan was *his* name) followed the memo in a matter of minutes with a story prominently and anonymously tacked on the newsroom bulletin board.

The story said something like:

"More than 75,000 people came to the Cotton Bowl in Dallas Saturday to watch Southern Methodist University play Texas Christian University.

"They were:

"Josef Caldwell, Louise P. Caldwell, Robert Compton, Lee Cullum, Billy Bob Dunn, Bob Finley, Sarah Finley, Larry Grove, Martin Haag, Stanley Marcus, David McManaway, Robert Miller, Shirley Miller, Patsy Nasher, Raymond Nasher, Jerry Richmond, Peggy Schoellkopf, Debbie Shelton, Keith Shelton, Fred Smith, Jerri Smith, Libba Weeks, John Weeks, Frances Williams . . ."

No more newspaper stories. It is time to move on: to *Viva Max!*, the book and the movie, and to KERA, the job—and another way of life.

5

Here Comes the Sun

Hemingway said newspapering was a good place for a fiction writer, but only if he or she didn't stay in it too long.

How long is too long, Papa? somebody allegedly asked.

Oh, about two years, Papa Hemingway allegedly replied.

At ten years, I was already way over the Hemingway rule. I had written fiction, ever since being at Victoria, but I had always felt slightly embarrassed to tell people that. I wasn't even comfortable saying I wanted to be a writer of fiction. There was something presumptuous and egotistical about it. Why in the world did I think I would ever be good enough to walk down the same road as Ruark, Hemingway and all of the rest? There were people in that sophomore English class in Beaumont, on the high school paper with me in San Antonio, in journalism school and in every newsroom where I worked who were better writers than I was. I knew it. And I knew everybody else knew it, too. So why me? The answer was simply that that is what I wanted to do with myself. Nobody chose me. I chose it.

Another reason to remain silent about my writing was that I did not do very well at it. None of the fiction I had written had been published. Not one word.

At the University of Missouri, I took short story–writing and playwriting courses. Dr. William Peden, the distinguished liter-

ary critic who taught the fiction course, said my main strength
was titles. The playwriting teacher identified my strength as typing. "Having a good clean script is important, though," he said.

I did not let this kind of ill-informed comment stop me. What
did they know? Anyhow, not everyone blooms early. I also had
a sniff of some truth about writing. Ninety percent of it is keeping your bottom on the chair. Certainly, you have to have some
semblance of ability and you have to have something to say, but
all of that is for naught without the drive and discipline it takes
to keep the pen in hand, the fingers on the keyboard. Bars,
newsrooms and university faculty clubs are full of great writers
who never wrote much more than their names on a few checks.

I said things like that over and over to myself.

And I hung in there. While in the Marine Corps I wrote short
stories on a very small portable typewriter I bought at the Air
Force PX on Okinawa. I sent them off to magazines. None was
published.

Kate and I courted over conversations about writing and literature. She was impressed that I had read James Joyce's *Ulysses*
while in college. We argued about the poetry of Gerard Manley
Hopkins. I thought his poetry was awful, she loved it. She
burned as much as I did to be a writer. The coming of babies
made it hard for her to do much about it, but she kept the air
and the space clear for me to write in the evening on the dining
room table. Right after we were married, I wrote story after
story and sent them to magazines. None was published.

Then, when I came to the *Times Herald*, I met A. C. Greene.
He was on the rewrite desk during the day and was the paper's
book editor in the evening and on weekends. He and I became
real and fast friends. So did Kate and his wife, Betty, and our
respective kids. Books, writing and all matters literary were what
drew us together.

A.C. put it to me straight: Forget short stories. Nobody's
publishing them anymore. Write a novel. That is the only way
to make a start as a writer. Okay, I replied. And I set out to
write a novel. But about what? Then I remembered an idea I

had been kicking around in the courthouse press room. In those days, everyone in press rooms was also either writing fiction or talking about it. That was the journalism of the Hemingway generation. It went with the territory.

My idea was: What if the Mexican army tried to retake the Alamo in San Antonio? Right now. In contemporary, 1960s, times. Look at all of the commotion and controversy and wonderful events it would trigger!

My press room friends, also newspaper, radio or TV reporters, thought that was a great idea to play with.

I began playing with it on the dining room table. And also during the day on typewriters hidden away in small offices at the courthouse and later in the law library of the U.S. attorney's office when I moved to the federal beat. John Schoellkopf was my *Times Herald* sidekick at the courthouse. He covered the civil side, I covered the criminal side. When I was writing, he covered for me. (For the record, I did the same for Schoellkopf, then a bachelor and man-about-town, when he was recovering from one of his many hangovers. Ah, newspapering.) The book became a driving force in my life. Kate and I talked endlessly about how it would be published, then made into a movie, and how everything we had hoped for and thought we could get at Texas Power and Light would come from this Alamo novel.

Eventually, I had enough to give to A.C. to read. He liked it and made some suggestions, which I quickly accepted and acted upon.

He also helped on the title. I called it "Remember Max!" as a takeoff on the line "Remember the Alamo!" Max was the nickname of my main character, Maximilian Rodriguez de Santos, the Mexican general who mounted the new Alamo invasion with a hundred of his troops from the Nuevo Laredo garrison of the army of Mexico.

No, no, said Greene. "Remember Max!" sounds like it's about a Polish butcher from the Lower East Side of New York. Get something Latin in there. How about *"Viva* Max!"?

Viva Max! it became. A.C. sent it off to an editor friend of his at Doubleday. She said she liked it, but not enough to publish it. But would I mind if she sent it over to an agent she knew?

Did I mind?

It was under "serious consideration" at another big-time publishing house when President Kennedy was assassinated. One of my characters was a young president of the United States from New England. The book was withdrawn. And I assumed that withdrawn and in a drawer was where it would remain forever.

But A. C. Greene would not be denied. Two years later, when he was the editor of the *Times Herald* editorial page, he had lunch with an editor from Duell, Sloan & Pearce, a subsidiary of Meredith Press. Did A.C. know of anybody in Texas who knew how to write? Anybody who might have a book that might be publishable?

He mentioned me and my dead Alamo book. The guy said for me to send it to him. So I got it out, removed all references to a young president and did some other rewriting, and sent it off. He bought it for $5,000. And in the spring of 1966, it was published.

Look at me now, Sticks. Papa and Robert. And you Missouri professors. I didn't even write the title, Dr. Peden!

Viva Max! caused no sensation. It was reviewed in about a dozen newspapers, and mostly favorably. But none of that mattered. I was a published novelist. Me. What I wanted to be I had become. I was a newspaperman who wrote novels. Me. Just what I set out to be.

Before long a man named Mark Carliner became the most important person in our lives. He was a young—early-twenties young—junior executive at CBS television in New York, but he wanted to produce movies. One of the things he did was read the weekly summaries of plots of just published novels that were circulated among people in the movie business. He had been in the Air Force in San Antonio. The idea of a book about a modern-day retaking of the Alamo intrigued him. He sent a secretary out to bookstores in New York to find *Viva Max!*

None of the stores had the book. Of course. He called Duell, Sloan & Pearce. And before long he offered us a deal. He had no money, but if we would give him a six-month option on the book and he was able to put a deal together, he would give us a percentage of the budget of the movie. Up to $50,000.

We had nothing to lose. The deal was made, and Kate and I went off into fantasy conversations about how we would spend the money and who should play Max in the movie. Bogart? No, too thin. Cooper? Too tall. Jimmy Stewart? Too Jimmy Stewart.

We knew enough to know that the chances of Carliner's pulling off such a deal were about a million to one. But at least there were odds. It was a possibility. Why not dream about it?

He did it. And as I said, it changed everything, just the way it was supposed to. We got $45,000, which was the full $50,000 minus ten percent, which went to our agent. Kate and I had been waiting for this day since the first day of our life together. It was the full-time literary life we wanted, and I hated being city editor of the *Times Herald,* so it was a remarkably easy decision. Even with our kids—now three—and one mortgage, we figured we could live four, maybe five, years on $45,000.

"Let's do it," Kate said.

"Let's do it," I said.

The managing editor took my resignation calmly. So did Felix McKnight. It was one thing to quit newspapering to be a PR man, quite another to quit to become a novelist. None of us knew at the time that it would also lead to my going to KERA and public television.

■ ■ ■

There were other good things that happened because of that movie.

Carliner put together a cast that included Peter Ustinov as Max, plus Jonathan Winters, Pamela Tiffin, Harry Morgan and John Astin. They all came to San Antonio in the spring of 1969 to shoot the exteriors. The Daughters of the Republic of Texas, proprietors and keepers of the Alamo, would not let them shoot inside the hallowed grounds and building. So a replica of the Alamo was built in Rome for that purpose.

We had some great family moments during the filming in San Antonio. Right after it started, there was a huge party for the stars of the movie and of San Antonio. Kate and I drove down in a very excited state, trying our best, of course, to act like this was nothing to us. After all, I had written a book, not a movie. We were people of literature, not of show business. But it would be good for my mother and dad, who lived in San Antonio, to have a piece of the enjoyment. Our involvement would facilitate theirs. Noble, noble, noble. There was also the Peter Ustinov factor. He was more than a movie star. He wrote books and plays. It would be terrific and worth it to go to the party to meet him, if nothing else. He was of our high quality and caliber.

The drive from Dallas to San Antonio took five hours down I-35. By the time we got to the party, we had convinced ourselves the only reason we were going was to meet the great Peter Ustinov. A man soon to be our friend because he would certainly want to be friends with the distinguished man of letters who had written the novel *Viva Max!* and his wife, a distinguished lady of letters. Certainly.

Well. The party was in a restaurant on the grounds of HemisFair, the 1968 World's Fair. When we arrived, Ustinov was not there yet. But he was expected. Any moment. There were two hundred or so other happy people there, all listening to a Dixieland band, none paying any attention to the fact that the author and his lady had just arrived. None.

We got drinks and stood back against a wall with my parents, as people we had never laid eyes on laughed and played at a party honoring the cast of a movie based on our novel. *Our* novel. None of you would be here if it weren't for us!

After a while, there was a rustle in the crowd, as they say. Then a buzz. Ustinov's car had just driven up. He was on his way in. Dad disappeared.

And in a few minutes a little knot of people moved our way. In the middle of the knot, I saw our great friend Peter Ustinov. There he was, coming right to us. I knew it!

I chose to ignore the fact that my dad was pulling the knot our way.

"Right this way, Mr. Ustinov," he said. I heard him say it several times.

And finally there he was. Dad and the knot parted.

"This is the author of *Viva Max!*" my dad said, as if he were announcing the arrival of the pope (or the Cardinal of St. Louis).

The great Peter Ustinov stuck out his right hand toward me. I grabbed it like it was gold.

"How nice," said the great Peter Ustinov. And he walked on away with his knot, never to return.

"How did you like him, son?" Dad asked.

"He was great, Dad. Thanks."

Kate stood there holding my other hand through it all. We looked at each other and laughed at each other for the fools that we were.

But it got better the next morning. Carliner arranged for us to visit a set where a scene with Ustinov and Pamela Tiffin would be shot. An interior of the Alamo's gardener's shack had been reconstructed in a building on the old HemisFair grounds. It was the eighth birthday of our daughter Jamie, and I told Carliner it would be a terrific thing for her to be able to see some of the shooting.

Ustinov talked to us briefly during a break, like we were real people, which I appreciated and dined on for years afterward.

But the big event was Jonathan Winters. He showed up to watch the shooting. One of the movie PR people had told him it was Jamie's birthday. He put on a private little show for her, telling stories and impersonating people and making faces and weird sounds.

A reporter for the *San Antonio Express-News* saw it all. He did an absolutely wonderful story, which appeared under an absolutely wonderful headline: JAMIE LEHRER HAS 8TH BIRTHDAY WITH STARS.

I had asked Carliner for another favor. There was a part in the movie for a bus. Could it be a Continental Trailways bus? I asked. Why not? Carliner replied. Could he make my dad, the Continental bus depot manager in San Antonio, the main contact man? Sure, said Carliner.

He had his production manager work it out with Dad, who then worked it out with Continental headquarters in Dallas. In exchange for the use of a bus and a driver during location shooting down around Laredo, the movie people would have a Continental Silver Eagle in the movie itself. Carliner and his people would talk only to Dad. It was a glorious thing for the Dallas executives to be told they *had* to go through Fred Lehrer to deal with the movie people about the bus.

Later, when exterior shooting began on the streets outside the Alamo, Dad went down there. He took pictures of Ustinov and Winters and everybody else, and had pictures of himself taken with them.

The best thing happened right before the movie company closed up shop in San Antonio and headed for Rome. Carliner and Jerry Paris, the director, were grateful for the cooperation the city of San Antonio officially and unofficially had given in the making of the movie. So they had a party to view a rough-cut version of some rushes at the St. Anthony Hotel, then the nicest and fanciest in San Antonio. All of the biggest of the city's big shots were there. So were my mom and dad. Kate and I drove down from Dallas.

Dad was in his element. The element he wished he were in all of the time. This was where he belonged, by God. He may have been only a bus depot manager, but this was his rightful place. I had never seen him more happy, more exhilarated, more full of an occasion.

At one moment late in the evening, with some scotch and emotion brimming over, he came over to me and said: "Son, I can't believe this. But I just told some guy *I* wrote *Viva Max!*"

That was fine with me, Pop. Pop was what my brother and I called him most of the time.

The movie premiered in San Antonio in early December 1969. There were parties and ceremonies all over the city that we all went to. My brother, Fred, and his family—Joan and the kids, Fred III, Paul and Cathy—came from Gainesville, Georgia, where Fred was working as a Southern Baptist minister. He had returned from the Marines to go to law school at the University of Texas. But Jesus intervened and Fred went off to the Southwestern Baptist Theological Seminary in Fort Worth to become an ordained minister instead. He pastored at several small churches in Texas before moving east.

The premier turned out to be a special occasion for all of us in a way we were not really aware of at the time. We knew Dad was not feeling well. He was losing weight for no particular reason. He was already a thin man, so it showed. The doctor had told him it could be something wrong with his colon. But none of us had any idea it was very serious.

On New Year's Day, just four weeks later, he went into Nix hospital in San Antonio for what was billed as an "exploratory" operation. The doctor had warned him that it might be cancer. It was. He survived the operation, but the cancer had spread to the lymph nodes. It could be several months or even a couple of years, but he was a goner, said the doctor. Dad was eventually sent to a regular hospital room for a few days before being discharged. Mom, Fred, Kate, Joan and I discussed how Mom and Dad might do some traveling and some other things in whatever time Dad might have left.

Then one morning, before Mom got there to spend the day with him, Dad's heart suddenly stopped. By the time a passing attendant noticed, it was too late. He hung on for a while, in a more or less vegetative state, before he died.

This experience spooked me forever about hospitals. Dad had walked in there under his own power and at full stride. I was with him. I know. Six weeks later, he was dead.

I know the medical reasons for what happened. And I am not alleging any wrongdoing or incompetence on the part of anybody. But the inescapable fact is that if he had stayed away from that hospital, he might have lived for several more months, possibly even a few more years.

And that bothers me.

My opinions about hospitals weren't helped by an incident that happened an hour before Dad actually died. My brother and I were standing in the hospital room when a lab technician came in. He nodded and smiled, and we did the same. He went to Dad's thin, limp, already black-and-blue right arm and extracted some blood for testing. It didn't make sense. Dad was already in a coma and the doctor had told us he had only a few hours left. Why would they be doing a blood test on this dying man?

But Fred and I said nothing to the technician, and went on talking. Probably about something stupid. Like buses. Fred and I, to the annoyance of our wives and children, talked about buses a lot. We did so primarily because neither of us had anyone else in our normal everyday lives to do it with.

The lab technician finished his work, put everything back in his portable carrier and headed for the door.

"Are you related to Mr. Schwartz?" he said at the door, in an obvious attempt to be friendly.

"Schwartz?" Fred said.

"Yes, sir. The patient." The man motioned toward Dad.

"Lehrer," said Fred. "His name is Lehrer. Fred Lehrer."

"Oh my goodness," said the technician. He looked at some papers. "Isn't this room six-oh-seven?"

"It's six-oh-nine," I said.

"Sorry," he said. He left, and Fred began wondering about poor Mr. Schwartz. What if he was in the hospital to have a toenail fixed or some such thing, and lo and behold, the blood test comes back and shows that he's dying of colon cancer, a failed heart and many, many other things?

We started laughing. It was so strange to be laughing at that particular moment, but we could not help it.

And it did beat the alternative.

■ ■ ■

I had just left the *Times Herald* when Dad had his operation. I had just gone to KERA, the public television station in Dallas, when he died.

Ralph Rogers, the KERA board chairman, and Bob Wilson, the general manager, were already at work changing my life forever. I had appeared three or four times as a guest interviewer or some such on KERA and other local stations, but that was it as far as television was concerned. And I had the normal news-paperman's attitude toward television. It was there mostly to make people giggle and to show the Dallas Cowboys winning NFL championships. With some exceptions, the on-air report-ers were deep-voiced, hair-enthralled former disc jockeys who had turned to news because they couldn't keep up with the changes in rock and roll. Rogers and Wilson kept telling me public television was different, and I was sure it was. Although I seldom watched enough to know for myself.

They made me a terrific offer to be director of news and public affairs. They said that since their station did very little local programming, and had very few funds at the moment to do more, I would have to work only two or three days a week. That would still give me plenty of time to do my writing. It was an ideal situation.

But Wilson had another idea. KQED, the public station in San Francisco, was doing a nightly local news and public affairs program that had grown out of a newspaper strike there. The Ford Foundation was now underwriting the program, called *Newsroom*, and was interested in putting money into similar *Newsroom*s in other cities.

Let's you do one here, Wilson said.

I wouldn't know how or even where to begin, I replied.

Begin with a proposal, he said. Write a proposal.

So I wrote a proposal. And I met a good man named David Davis with the Ford Foundation. He encouraged and helped us, and eventually brought us to New York to meet Fred Friendly, the Foundation's main television man and the one who would make the decision. Fred Friendly, somebody I knew of only in Superman terms. Edward R. Murrow's partner, who had quit his job as president of CBS News because the network would not preempt *I Love Lucy* reruns for Senate hearings on Vietnam.

In a matter of seconds after I walked into his office with Davis and my two Dallas friends, I was mesmerized by Friendly. He talked and gestured and breathed in huge gulps and swings, in a way that consumed and dominated all that he chose to survey. On this particular afternoon in the Ford Foundation's glass building on East Forty-third Street, it was Ralph Rogers who got the Friendly treatment.

"Why have you hired Lehrer here to run the program you want to do?" Friendly asked, after the small talk was out of the way.

Rogers, a man of force equal to Friendly, said some nice things about me as an editor and reporter.

"Are you prepared to let him do his job?" Friendly boomed.

"Yes!" Rogers boomed back.

"Well, let's see if you are," said Friendly.

What followed was a short course/oral exam on journalism management.

Friendly got Rogers to concede that as a successful businessman—he had founded Texas Industries, a giant concrete firm—and leading civic leader—he had been chairman of the Dallas Symphony, the United Fund and many other projects before taking on KERA—he was a hands-on manager.

Nobody makes major decisions without consulting you? Friendly asked.

That's right, Rogers said.

Well, Lehrer will never consult you, and you should fire him if he does.

Rogers swallowed. And then he listened as Friendly explained that journalism must be left to journalists. Fire Lehrer after the fact if he screws up, but stay out of his hair before.

Rogers said sure.

Then came some specific hypotheticals. After determining that Rogers was a major Republican, albeit a rare-for-Texas moderate Republican, Friendly asked:

"Do you know Senator John Tower?"

"I do," replied Rogers.

"Well?"

"Very well."

"Let's say he calls you about a story Lehrer's people are doing.

Let's say he says it's an unfair, untruthful story that will damage him, the Republican Party and the United States of America. What do you do?"

When Rogers did not answer immediately, Friendly said:

"Do you tell the senator, 'I'm sorry, but I have nothing to do with the news operation. Call Lehrer'? Or do you say, 'I'll call Lehrer and see what's going on'? And then, when you hang up, do you call Lehrer and ask him about the Tower story?"

After a few seconds of silence, Rogers said, "I take it from your leading question that I should not call Lehrer?"

"Absolutely not."

"Well, if you say so."

"Can you do that? Can you tell someone like John Tower or someone who is a powerful business- or civic-leader friend that you do not have the power to decide what runs on your own channel's news program? Can you do that, Mr. Rogers?"

"Yes, I can. Call me Ralph."

"There aren't many people who can admit they have no power," said Friendly. "I'm Fred. Are you sure?"

"I'm sure."

"Even if you personally believe Lehrer and his people are wrong?"

"Try me, sir," said Mr. Rogers.

We all shook hands and Friendly tried him. We got a $500,000 grant to do a *Newsroom* in Dallas.

Less than two weeks after we went on the air, Rogers was tried. Our courthouse reporter discovered some unusual buying-up of downtown land by Trammell Crow, Dallas's leading developer. The word was, it would be the site for a very tall skyscraper. Maybe the tallest skyscraper in Dallas, if not in all of Texas. Big story, in other words. The reporter, John Tackett, put together as much as he could and then called Crow. It was only a matter of minutes before many and much hit the fan. Crow called Mr. Rogers. Mr. Rogers called me to say only that Crow had called.

"I told him it was not my decision," Mr. Rogers said. "He said all of the details of the deal were not in place. He said he wanted to announce it properly and when the time was right. He could not understand why it could not wait. I told him it was not my decision."

I did not say a thing. Mr. Rogers said one more time it was not his decision, and we said our good-byes.

A few minutes later, I lost a friend. He was a guy who worked for Crow and whom I had gotten to know socially through Bob Wilson because of his volunteer work for KERA. He and his brother were terrific good old West Texas boys who had gone to Harvard, then to the Marines at the same time I had, and finally to Dallas to make their marks and fortunes.

"I told Trammell I would call and take care of the problem," he said to me. "I assured him you were a reasonable, responsible person."

I agreed with him about my reasonableness and responsibleness, and then told him what he did not want or expect to hear. The story was going to run on *Newsroom* that night.

"That is ridiculous!" he said. "What possible purpose does that serve? We will tell you when the story can run. And you can run it first."

I tried to do for him what Fred Friendly had done for Mr. Rogers, but it was no use. He did not understand why I could not allow him or anyone else to kill a story like that. There was an issue of independence at stake that went beyond friendship and all the rest.

He got truly angry. He said he would no longer support public television. He would no longer support me. He would no longer do much of anything that I liked or approved of, and he let me know pretty much that I was history in his life. It was sad that he had probably told Crow and/or his people that he and I were friends, and he was sure he could do what Ralph Rogers had been unable to do. Now he was going to have to go back to the boss and admit impotence, something he dearly did not want to do. I sympathized with him on a personal basis, but as I told him repeatedly, this was not a personal matter. It was professional.

The man kept his word. He did not speak to me again.

Neither did another young Dallas businessman who called me a few minutes later. He, too, wanted the story killed, He, too, had been active in KERA fund-raising. He, too, thought I was an irresponsible idiot for what he said was "jeopardizing the financial future of KERA." He, too, "dropped" me from his social world and looked away whenever our eyes met anywhere, anyhow, for the next two and a half years before I left Dallas for Washington.

The skyscraper story did run that evening, and Mr. Rogers not only remained true to his word and the Friendly doctrine, but actually seemed to enjoy exercising his power to protect *Newsroom* rather than rule it.

Newsroom survived that opening storm, but others were always on the horizon. The program had a look and a feel to it that simply annoyed some people. It was 1970, please remember. Our opening theme music was "Here Comes the Sun" by the Beatles, and we went out over the sounds of the Edwin Hawkins Singers belting "Oh Happy Day." I am proud to say that on *Newsroom*, Dallas got its first serious media, consumer and environmental reporting, as well as its first clean journalistic looks at the gigantically powerful First Baptist Church of Dallas, the glittery local world of debutantes, the then depressingly secret world of homosexuality. Two of our ten on-air reporters were black and one was Hispanic, at a time when there were neither on the major Dallas newspapers. One of the four women reporters wore her hair in hippie stringy style and two of the white men had beards or mustaches—or both. Some people went crazy and red in the face just looking at us.

Our format was 1950s amateur. The reporters' desks were arranged in a large circle in the middle of the newsroom. They worked at them during the day, and then at airtime the cameras and I came in. I sat in a swivel chair in the center of the desks and essentially debriefed the reporters one at a time on their stories. After I was through, the other reporters could ask questions. We also took viewers' feedback every night. Volunteers accepted questions and comments, and we read and reacted to them at the end of the program. We had the flexibility to spend the entire thirty minutes—later increased to an hour—on one subject or on several. We even ran a few pictures, most of them black-and-white stills taken by a young photographer named Gary Bishop. At the beginning, his pictures were about the only ones we had that came out focused. Eventually, we developed an ability to take pictures that moved like those on everybody else's television news programs. That was after Ken Harrison came aboard as a filmmaker. Ken went on to become a celebrated movie director, working on *On Valentine's Day*, with the great Horton Foote, and other films.

We did special all-evening editions during elections and during the heated debates about desegregating the schools. We interviewed Buckminster Fuller for forty-five minutes, and afterward we all agreed that we had not understood one word the man spoke. Ella Fitzgerald came on and hummed for us. John Gielgud read for us. Harry Reasoner, then the new anchor at ABC News, talked TV and journalism with us. I. M. Pei explained why he had designed the new Dallas City Hall to look like an upside-down half-pyramid. Roger Kahn talked about the Brooklyn Dodgers of the forties, the Boys of Summer, my boyhood baseball heroes.

Was it good television? No, not really. But the journalism was first-rate. As a newspaperman with no television experience or knowledge, I hired only newspapermen and newspaperwomen as reporters. We filled the airways with a lot of "uhs" and "you knows," sentence fragments and long pauses. But we broke a lot of reporting and personnel taboos that very much needed to be broken in that conservative city, and for this I am unashamedly proud. Our main value was in our influence on the two daily newspapers, my immediate past employers. Reporters and editors at both the *Times Herald* and the *Morning News* were able to use us to get things into their own papers.

We can sit on this and the *Morning News* can sit on it, said the reporter to the city editor, said the city editor to the managing editor, and the managing editor to the publisher. But the freaks over at *Newsroom* will run it anyhow, and there we'll be.

Right, said all of them in their own ways.

On more than one occasion, reporters for one or the other paper actually brought us stories that they could not get in their own papers. We ran them, and then their papers ran them.

We had some terrible television moments. One of the most terrible was on the first Earth Day, in 1970. We had planned our whole program to be devoted to the subject of the environment. Every reporter and filmmaker had a special project. It was to be our first full-court press on a major subject. The pressure to do well was on even more, because two executives from the Corporation for Public Broadcasting in Washington, D.C., were coming to observe us in action. CPB, along with a local foundation run by computer millionaire Sam Wyly, had added some small grant money to our funding from the Ford Foundation. CPB was the outfit that had been set up by Congress to clear federal money before it was sent to public radio and television. It was—is—ruled by a board of presidentially appointed and Senate-approved members.

On that Earth Day evening, the Beatles sang "Here Comes the Sun," and then, as always, I came up on camera to say who I was and that this was *Newsroom*, "a program of local news, analysis and opinion." I said some appropriately heavy words about the Earth and the need to preserve and celebrate it, and then introduced our first film piece. I looked to a TV monitor as the film came up. Then I noticed something was missing. Sound. There was no sound. After a few seconds, I said to the audience that clearly we were having audio problems on that particular piece and they would soon be fixed.

I introduced another film piece. A floor manager was desperately trying to tell me something. Something like: Forget it. Talk. Talk. *Talk!* So I turned to the reporters and we talked about what we had planned to talk about *between* the films. Because the films had not run, the talk made no sense. But we had no choice. We talked about rivers and streams, grass and flowers, mountains and valleys. We soon ran out of things to say. We kept talking.

Finally, the floor manager signaled. Introduce the films. All of them at once. There was not enough time left to run them all, but we would get on as many as we could. What followed was an incoherent assortment of reports of varying lengths and Earth subjects.

So. Kate and I and Bob Wilson and his wife, Laura, went to dinner afterward with the two CPB men. They were pleasant and sympathetic, but when I left to go home, I swore off television to Kate. No more of this. Who needs this in his life? Who needs to work in a business where a faulty tape machine can destroy many weeks' work done by many people with many things riding on it? All I wanted to do was stay with my fingers on a typewriter and my mind and nerves making up stories to be read rather than watched and heard.

But by the next morning I was better. And besides, there was another program to do that night. There was always another program to do that night. That dailiness is the joy of daily journalism. It leaves little time to sulk and sweat about what happened in yesterday's newspaper or last night's broadcast. It is always: On to the next story, the next edition, the next broadcast.

The crisis that almost ended it for *Newsroom* was the open-meetings storm with the county judge.

Darwin Payne, an old friend from *Times Herald* days, covered media subjects for *Newsroom* on a part-time basis. His real job was teaching journalism at Southern Methodist University. The Dallas County Commissioners' Court had held a meeting—and others were scheduled—that Darwin believed was in violation of the Texas Open Meetings Law. We checked with a lawyer friend of Wilson's, who agreed. We served notice on the commissioners' court and County Judge Lew Sterrett, who, under the Texas system, presided over the court meetings.

The court and the judge stiffed us. Go away, they said.

Let's sue them, Darwin said.

Okay, I said.

Okay, Wilson said.

So sue we did. And bananas went Judge Sterrett. Real bananas. I knew Judge Sterrett from my courthouse reporting days, but it did not matter. We had challenged him, and he already did not like our variety of skin colors, gender mix and hairstyles. He set out to destroy us. He accused us of being part of a left-wing plot to discredit him and the good, clean, all-American government of Dallas County. He also challenged the propriety of a public-supported organization to file such an outrageous suit. And he openly called for our demise. Others joined him. One in particular who did was the president of the city's third largest bank. He was on the KERA board of directors and a semi-leading fund-raiser for the station.

Ralph Rogers, our protector, was out of the country. Wilson and I talked to him on the telephone. It was not a good connection, but he seemed to understand there was trouble at home. Big trouble. I gave him our reasons for filing the suit. We read him what the judge and others had said in the papers. He said he would be back in a few days. Meanwhile, sit tight, and don't do anything stupid. Yes, sir, we said. I think he meant anything *else* stupid.

The suit stayed filed. The banker organized an effort to get us off the air. A support group sprang up to defend us. Our lawyer, who took the case for no fee, said it was going to be tough. There was a good chance we would eventually win it, but there was no guarantee. The law was new, and no cases had been filed under it yet. Ours was the first.

Mr. Rogers returned. He held a news conference and said things that I wished he had not said—for instance, that he did not agree with the filing of the suit. But the decision to file it was mine, and that was that. He also worried out loud about what this might cost the station in public and financial support.

As he explained to me later, it was one thing to go or not go with a story. It was another to file a lawsuit that jeopardized the survival of the station. He didn't say it directly, but he said loud and clear otherwise that the Friendly rule did not apply here. This case was different. But again and as always, he said to me what he had said in public. He would stand with me and Wilson and the staff. Uncomfortably, but he would stand.

A few days later, I caved. Sterrett and the banker kept the public heat on. I began to feel it simply was not worth all of this. I decided to withdraw the suit; we should go on about our business. I told the staff, and then Wilson and Mr. Rogers. And that night I announced it on the air at the end of our program. I said the suit was being withdrawn because it was our job to report news, not make it, and because there was evidence the already frail financial status of the station was being made even frailer. I could barely get the final words out of my mouth. They were simply that "the decision to file the suit was mine and the decision to withdraw it was mine. Thank you and good night."

I have no regrets about any of it. We did the right thing in filing the suit, and we did the right thing in backing off. I was accused of buckling under to pressure, and that is exactly what I did.

There was a delightful irony in my leaving Dallas for Washington, less than two years later. In the eyes of Judge Sterrett and friends, I was Dallas's worst example of a leftist commie pinko press sympathizer, now moving on to Washington, where my kind belonged. But in Washington things were seen very differently. *The Washington Post*'s very small story about my PBS appointment said I had come from conservative, Republican Dallas in a move clearly designed to win favor and soothe attitudes about public broadcasting within the Nixon White House.

6

PBS Blues

We Lehrers came to Washington in May 1972, shortly before Nixon's boys broke into the Watergate. That is important and relevant, because if it hadn't been for that burglary and all its subsequent trimmings, it is quite probable there would be no public broadcasting anymore.

It is an absolute certainty there would be no anything called *MacNeil/Lehrer*.

So for the record let me say (in italic type for emphasis): *Thank you, Nixon. Thank you, Messrs. Liddy and Hunt, Dean and Colson, Haldeman and Ehrlichman. We could not have done it without you.*

It's a lovely story of how good triumphed over evil. More or less.

I will try my very best to tell it straight.

Nixon, with egging on and encouragement from Pat Buchanan and various later-to-be-unindicted and -indicted aides, hated public TV and radio, as he apparently hated a lot of things in the spring of 1972. He, and they, were not about to allow federal money—"our" money, they called it—to be used to create a fourth network news operation that could spread the anti-Nixon, pro-Kennedy doctrine of the leftist press. Nixon vetoed bills for the funding of public broadcasting and, through his people in the White House telecommunications office, kept up a steady hammering on the national public broadcasting establishment and local station managements and lay board members.

The message was simple and direct: Get rid of the liberals, or we'll get rid of you. The focus of the attack was Sander Vanocur, a former NBC correspondent who had joined public television to coanchor special coverage of the 1972 presidential election campaign. The other anchor was another former NBC man, Robert MacNeil. *The* Robert MacNeil. The Nixon people saw Vanocur as a Kennedy-lackey leftist of the worst order. Memos and tapes released after Watergate show that the idea of Vanocur's covering the campaign, and being paid out of public money to do so, absolutely incensed Nixon et al.

They used the news of Vanocur's and MacNeil's salaries to draw blood. Sandy's was $85,000 a year, Robin's $65,000. Both sums exceeded what anybody else in public broadcasting was being paid, but more important, they also exceeded the salaries of members of Congress and other high federal officials. Some Nixon-friendly congressmen brought the matter up at hearings, as did some Nixon-friendly PTV executives at national meetings.

How can you defend paying a leftist, Kennedy-lackey television news correspondent more than a clean, conservative, pro-Nixon Republican member of Congress?

I can't, sir.

Why do you do it, then?

I don't know, sir.

That, I am sorry to say, is a fairly good characterization of how the dialogue was going. Nobody in or outside public television had anything much to say, other than a scared "I don't know, sir."

It was into this World of the Cowed that I, Mr. Communist/Conservative from Texas, arrived to "coordinate" the Vanocur–MacNeil coverage, as well as all other news and public affairs programming on PBS.

It was a new job; nobody had ever done it before. I was told mostly just to do my coordinating through the enforcement of a new code of standards and practices for such programming that the Nixon assault had frightened public television into adopting. There wasn't anything wrong with the code. I had helped write it, in fact, as the boonie representative on an outside committee of journalists that had been appointed to do the work. The committee had been chaired by Elie Abel, a former TV correspondent who was then dean of the Columbia University School of Journalism. Another member had been David Webster, a distinguished journalist who was then head of the BBC news operation in North America. There was nothing in the final product that any working journalist could or would object to. And none did.

It did not take but a few hours for me to discover what "coordinating" meant to some people. George Wallace was shot at a political rally in Maryland the afternoon of my first day on the job.

There were questions about whether Wallace would survive, among other things, and it made logical sense to keep public television viewers informed through the night. I made arrangements for the Vanocur–MacNeil team to do one-minute news cut-ins that evening during the PBS prime-time feed, most of which was to be a live opera broadcast with simulcast stereo sound on public radio. Gerry Slater, vice-president and general manager of PBS, made the decision to run the news spots. PBS president Hartford Gunn, Jr., was out of town and out of pocket.

MacNeil, whom I still barely knew, did the on-air work, and Slater and I went away late that night satisfied that we had done the right thing for PBS and America.

We were wrong to be satisfied. The next morning, my second day on the job, we were both screamed at by the just returned Hartford Gunn, on behalf of station executives far and wide. One of the cut-ins had gone a few seconds over. It had fouled up the simulcast sound!

Gunn was really upset. "That opera had been in the works for months! You ruined it! And for what? News! We are not in news! We are in public affairs!"

We are not in news? We are in public affairs?

That's right, stupid.

It turned out "We are not in news, we are in public affairs" was one of the key mantras of survival against the Nixon onslaught. I had just been clued in on my second day on the job.

I began to wonder if KERA would consider taking me back.

Within a few days, I was told that WNET, our New York station and principal national program producer, was working on a special about venereal disease that would be broadcast on the PBS system in a few months. It was called *VD Blues*. Dick Cavett was the host. Large promotions and educational tie-ins with schools and community service health groups were planned. It was to be a very big deal. "Coordinate" the program, were my orders. Make sure there isn't anything in it that violates the PBS standards and practices. Or anything else.

Aye, aye.

I had had some unsuccessful experience in the field of venereal disease abatement. For several months, one of my additional duties for Weapons Company One-Nine, First Battalion Ninth Marines, on Okinawa, had been as VD control officer. Then, my orders had been to make damned sure our VD rate, which was usually somewhere between twenty-four and twenty-seven percent of all the young Marines of Weapons Company, never exceeded that of the other three companies in the battalion. I tried to do that by having an NCO armed with a .45-caliber pistol force all Marines returning from liberty to take two penicillin tablets. Even if they said they had been in church, they had to take the pills. Even if they had just gone to the movies with nuns, they had to take the pills. The plan did not work. Our resourceful young Marines, who believed penicillin would make them impotent and sterile for life, figured out ways to hold the penicillin in their mouths without swallowing it, and then spit it out once they left the battalion headquarters tent.

So I instituted a form of public humiliation. Each Marine who came down with clap—the main venereal disease of choice, formally known as gonorrhea—was called by name to come front and center in a company formation. There he ceremoniously turned over to the next painted wooden number on a contraption I had made and nailed on the bulletin board. The idea was shame. The effect was just the opposite. Instead, cheers rose from the ranks for each fallen Marine, who usually responded by flexing his muscles and with other gestures of manhood as he walked to and from the bulletin board.

Now, on life's second major VD assignment, I flew to New York on the Eastern shuttle to see a rough cut of *VD Blues.* Fortunately, the men who ran WNET, Jay Iselin and Bob Kotlowitz, were friends. They took me to a screening room in a spirit of friendship and cooperation.

"It's all right," Bob said.

"It really is," Jay said.

Thanks, guys.

The program opened with a terrible-looking rock group singing a cute little ditty:

> *Don't give a dose to the one you love most.*
> *Give her some marmalade, give her some toast.*
> *You can give her a partridge up in a pear tree,*
> *But the dose that you give her might get back to me.*

A real toe tapper. But what followed was a very funny, beautifully written and acted collection of songs and skits and information that made *VD Blues* a potential milestone in PBS history. I could hear people laughing at their television sets all over America.

And I could hear something else, too: cries of outrage. As the program went on, I realized through tears of laughter and joy that I had one huge problem on my hands. It was something called survival. Sandy's and Robin's salaries were child's play compared with someone's singing "Don't Give a Dose" on banker- and doctor-supported public television stations.

That was what I thought. But what I said to Jay and Bob was

mostly things like: Well, yes. It's certainly provocative. Yes, sir. Well done. You bet.

Thanks, guys.

And I got on a plane for Washington as quickly as I could. On the flight, I realized that there was only one thing worse than broadcasting *VD Blues*. And that was *not* broadcasting it. So by the time I got back to the PBS offices at L'Enfant Plaza in Washington, there was no question what I had to do. I had to figure out a way to get *VD Blues* on the air in a way that did not bring down the house of PBS.

I had no idea how I would accomplish that.

But the two wise men who ran the programming department of PBS, Sam Holt and Bill Oxley, came to my rescue. We worked out a strategy that was a modified emperor-has-no-clothes approach, with a little full disclosure and public service shame thrown in for seasoning.

Said Holt: Establish a process and be rigid in following it. Said Oxley: Get as many people under the tent with you as early as possible.

I certified to everyone at PBS that, in my professional opinion, the program did not violate PBS standards and practices. I coupled that with a flag notifying PBS staff executives that there were some language and taste situations that might present problems for some of the stations in the system. Oh my, yes. I strongly urged all PBS personnel to watch the rough cut to be prepared for any negative reactions that might come.

Then, at Oxley's brilliant suggestion, I got Iselin and Kotlowitz to agree to a national closed-circuit screening of the rough cut for all public TV stations. It was the first time anything like that had ever been done. Oxley, Kotlowitz and Iselin were all smart people.

Process. Inside the tent.

And it worked. After the rough cut was viewed, only the public TV network in Mississippi and a few other stations in the South declined to run the program. There were complaints and screams of anguish and alarm from several others, but no storms.

Because they had had enough advance notice, and because they were now under the tent, they mounted medical panels, call-in segments and other ways of mitigating the problems that the content of the program might have caused.

I was delighted at the way the overwhelming majority of the people in public television handled the whole thing. And frankly, I was somewhat ashamed of my initial sky-is-falling reaction to that original screening in New York. My public broadcasting colleagues were a lot stronger and smarter than I had given them credit for.

The program received good reviews and much response. It was in every way a huge success.

But it wasn't quite over yet.

Just before the special went on the air, a new man had taken over as president of the Corporation for Public Broadcasting. John Macy, a distinguished man with Democratic lineage, had been quietly removed, and replaced by Henry Loomis, a distinguished man with a Republican lineage. Within days of his appointment, Loomis came to PBS headquarters for a get-acquainted courtesy call. It happened to be the day after *VD Blues* had aired.

After Loomis was shown around the place, Hartford Gunn assembled eight or nine of us (*Variety* called people with our jobs "PTV Web Moguls," which we in turn called ourselves) in a conference room to talk with the new CPB man. Everything went fine for a while, until Loomis suddenly asked:

"How did that VD program get on the air last night?"

Gunn pointed to me and said I—that person over there, Lehrer—had put it on and could explain how it happened.

I then explained the rough cut, the process. Loomis, a pleasant man of tight lips and thin ties, age fifty or so, listened attentively and then, as I recall (nothing was recorded), said:

"So there was a process of review?"

"Yes, sir," I replied.

"You decided that program was tasteful and responsible?"

"Yes, sir."

"Using what measurements?"

"These."

I handed him a copy of the PBS standards and practices.

He took them and moved on to another subject. He had been had. And we had won. For now. In order to raise hell, Loomis had to disagree with all TV critics and most of the people who ran and who watched public television. In order to change things, he would have to change everything. Theoretically, CPB and PBS were separate organizations. CPB was ruled by a presidentially appointed board that laundered and then doled out the federal money to public broadcasting. PBS was an organization the stations had created to run a national programming service.

Holt and Oxley knew what they were doing. We did it right.

But frankly, I saw it as only a small battle won. The power to fund is the power to starve, and thus to control. We were clearly in Nixon's sights. We being people like us PTV Web Moguls who used Richard Nixon's money to broadcast programs about people catching clap.

And as the next few weeks and months went by, our political strength in Congress and the system waned. The Nixon people were winning. There was even serious talk of reducing public affairs programming dramatically. Some people in the system were suggesting we eliminate it altogether and stick to things for children and adults who liked classical music and English drama. Nixon's overwhelming reelection made it clear to most of us that it was only a matter of time before he had his way with public broadcasting.

A few of us Web Moguls mounted some guerrilla attacks through leaks and other methods, but it was a losing battle. I thought it was, at least.

My major contribution to the effort was to join with Fred Friendly and others in suggesting and then facilitating the coming of Ralph Rogers to the national fight for survival. As a Republican businessman with energy and clout, he was the perfect person to lead our effort. As the lay chairman of the board of

KERA, a leading public television and radio station, his PTV credentials were also in perfect order. He had become chairman of a national group of lay public television board chairmen. Perfect.

What was not so perfect were his Republican credentials. He had supported Nelson Rockefeller against Nixon for the 1968 nomination, one of probably three Republicans in all of Texas to do so. Oh, well.

Kate and I decided we must take the girls out every weekend to see a different monument, museum, Civil War battlefield or other national landmark. It was clear it would not be long before we would be headed back to Texas.

What happened up there, Jim?

I got Nixoned, Felix.

I told you you were a newspaperman.

Thank you, Felix.

■　■　■

Then along came providence and the Senate Watergate hearings to keep me in television and us Lehrers in Washington. Sandy Vanocur was the providence. He chose to leave public television after the election, and I was offered his job. Well, not really his job, but a job as a correspondent teamed with Mac-Neil. Robin would be the senior man and I would be his junior. It was terrific for me. I hated being a "coordinator" and I very much wanted to get back to reporting, the only thing I did reasonably well and was comfortable doing.

Robin and I were teamed together in a series of weekly documentary programs that were broadcast under the umbrella title *America '73*. It was not a pleasant experience. The organization we worked for, the National Public Affairs Center for Television, or NPACT, was run by ex–network television news people who considered correspondents "raw meat" or "talent," rather than journalists. I was of even lower worth because I had had no commercial television experience of any kind, much less with a network. And to make matters even worse, I had no national working time or name of any kind, even in print. I was pure boonie. Their attitude kept me in a state of anger most of the time. But that muddy water has already flowed under many bridges, and it should be left where it is. With a couple of monumental exceptions, the people involved were terrific professionals and people. The rubs were about approach and philosophy.

Another reason to remain silent is that my side of the argument has some thin-ice problems. While I was sure of myself journalistically—defensively arrogant about it at times, I am afraid—I was terrible on the air. My Dallas *Newsroom* experience had taught me little about how to walk, talk or do much of anything on the air except smile. And I didn't even do that right. MacNeil could open up an encyclopedia to any page and read it to the camera so it sounded like something important. My reading of an encyclopedia would sound like the reading of an encyclopedia—or worse. I spoke in a lazy Texas slur with inflections that went up when they should have gone down, and vice versa, and a tone that got higher and more nasal the longer I talked. My movements and facial expressions also never quite worked. I tended to grin when the news was grim, frown when it was happy. And do things like say, "It goes to the head and the heart of what government is all about," while pointing first to my heart and then to my head.

This is not phony false modesty. I was truly awful. If I had my way, all videotapes of those early NPACT programs on which I appeared would be shredded. And burned.

Thank God for the Watergate hearings.

Gerry Slater, still number two at PBS, got the hearings on the air. He posed a should-we-do-it question to the stations that would have done any professional pollster proud. It was geared to get a yes answer, and it got that from a small but deciding majority. Mr. Rogers, by now the elected chairman of the PBS board, had some doubts about broadcasting the hearings. He was an easy sell, but he told Robin and me, when we went to Dallas to persuade him, that there was a bigger story out there that nobody was paying any attention to.

What story? we dutifully asked, more out of a desire to humor than to learn.

Energy, said Mr. Rogers. There is an energy crisis coming in this country like nothing we have ever seen before.

Sure, we said.

What did he know? we thought. And pressed on to do the Watergate hearings.

Robin and I coanchored the Watergate broadcasts all day for three straight months, and then set them up and analyzed them again with expert guests on tape for prime time. We alternated closing each night's broadcast with what was labeled a "commentary." Looking back in pain now, I realize some of the things I said were truly stupid and irresponsible. The worst was on the night I predicted John Ehrlichman would probably go bananas when he testified the next day. I actually used the word "bananas." Some points I made on other nights were even worse. So much worse that I have put them out of my mind forever and have absolutely no interest in browsing through transcripts to be reminded.

As programming, the Watergate broadcasts were a terrific hit with the audience and the stations, and established once and for all that real public affairs programming had a permanent place on public broadcasting. That was what Robin and I claimed, at least.

As justice, it was pure delicious. We were being bailed out by the sins of a president who was trying to do us in. He and his minions were so distracted with the crumbling of his presidency that the plan to crumble us was abandoned and forgotten. But I remained convinced that if Watergate had not happened, they would have been successful. Public broadcasting would have been eliminated or at least deballed. Probably permanently. We would never have been able to do the programs that built the constituency that now keeps any president or member of Congress of any stripe or party from our door.

I still hope that someday a long-lost Oval Office tape will turn up at the National Archives that will recount The End. Nixon

and Ehrlichman, say, will be talking about Watergate hush
money or some such, when Haldeman comes rushing in.

> HALDEMAN: Mr. President, I have some terrible news!
>   NIXON: [Expletive deleted]!
>   H: Public broadcasting lives!
>   N: [Expletive deleted]!
> EHRLICHMAN: We tried, Mr. President. We lied, we connived, we
>   threatened, we vetoed, we deprived, we spit and we
>   bribed, but nothing worked.
>   N: [Expletive deleted]!
>   H: It's not too late.
>   E: Yes, it is. Dean is talking.
>   N: [Expletive deleted]!

The hearings helped me personally because they got me on
the air a lot. Performing on television is like playing the piano
or robbing banks. It takes practice and repetition to get it right.
Watergate got me on the air sitting next to Robert MacNeil.
By example and by quiet words of advice, he taught me how
to be what I was already being paid to be—a television correspondent. Over those days and weeks in a Washington television studio, he gently told me that if I planned to make a career
and/or a mark in television journalism, then maybe I ought
to take a few days and learn how to do it. So I did that.
I practiced reading a TelePrompTer and all of those other
performing things that I had resisted for juvenile, I-am-a-
serious-reporter reasons.

Robin also suggested rather pointedly that I practice pronouncing each and every syllable in each and every word. And
that I think as "crisply" as I spoke. And that I imagine a head-
shot photo of Kate, my mother, or somebody else real that I
could automatically flash in front of me when I delivered something directly to the camera. It would help me speak more con-
versationally and thus curb my tendency to read copy in a PA
shout, in the apparent belief that if the people in Roanoke,

Nashville and points west and elsewhere were going to hear me, I had to really yell it out to them.

Robin's most important piece of counseling was that I simply relax and be whatever I was. Don't even try to be Robert Mac-Neil, he said.

The most important happening during Watergate for me, of course, was that Robin and I became friends.

Our friendship had grown naturally, out of amazingly similar views of what we wanted to do in journalism and with our lives. It was amazing primarily because we arrived at our meeting and eventual collaboration from very different origins.

He was a well-spoken, well-traveled Canadian of the world. His father had been a Royal Canadian Mounted Policeman who loved words and the sea. Robin had been an actor on radio and the stage and had written plays. As a journalist, he had covered wars and coups and rattles throughout Europe, Africa and Latin America. He had worked for Reuters, the Canadian Broadcasting Corporation, the BBC and NBC. He knew the difference between Bordeaux and Burgundy, and between a Bordeaux and a Burgundy. There was no restaurant menu he could not read, understand and parse.

I, on the other hand, spoke in a way that had not changed much since I had called the buses in Victoria. My international travel amounted to fourteen months in the Far East with the U.S. Marines, plus Mexico City and Acapulco with Kate on our honeymoon and maybe three other trips to Nuevo Laredo. I had covered Rotary luncheons, county commissioners' court, murder trials, governors' races, oil scandals and the Texas legislature for *The Dallas Morning News*, the *Dallas Times Herald* and the local public television station in Dallas. I thought wine came in three varieties—red, white and Portuguese rosé in a brown clay bottle. My eating habits covered the field from fried chicken and cheeseburger with everything to barbecue and Tex-Mex with everything.

What Robin and I had in common were important things. We both came from parents who wanted their sons to matter. We both wanted to matter as journalists. We both wanted to matter as writers. But what made it work was simply that we shared some basic beliefs about reporting and journalism.

We both believed that Getting It Right was the first rule of journalism. And the second, the third, the fourth, and all the way to the tenth. Sloppiness with little facts, items as little even as middle initials or titles, leads to sloppiness with the big facts, the big ideas and most everything else. Reporters and editors who use or permit imprecise language, imperfect sourcing, sweeping generalities, sarcasm, cheap shots and smug morality in straight news stories should be run out of the business on the tips of their copy pencils, on the sea of their videotapes.

We both believed the American people were not as stupid as some of the folks publishing and programming for them believed. We were convinced they cared about the significant matters of human events—war, poverty, corruption, government, politics and the other subjects that form the normal categories for news. And we were certain they could and would hang in there more than thirty-five seconds for information about those subjects if given a chance. And that, given enough information, they could even figure out on their own what to think.

But the most important belief we shared was that it had to be fun. We both agreed with Sticks Strahala of *The Victoria Advocate* that there was glorious joy in what we did for a living, that God had done some of his finest work when he created the occupation of reporter.

▪ ▪ ▪

The Watergate experience left Robin and me with two firm convictions:

A. Now was the time and PBS was the place for a serious daily news/public affairs program that dealt with stories in depth and at length.

B. We did not want to have anything to do with such a program unless we were in charge, unless we were the editors and we ran it. Otherwise, forget it. Neither of us was interested in spending every day in the energy-sapping game of mental

arm-wrestling that the intentionally muddled and muddy relationship between off-air producers and on-air correspondents
produces.

We realized that it was most probable B would always cancel
out A, so Robin went back to London. He had been on leave
from the BBC to work for NPACT during the 1972 elections
and had already extended his time. So he left. Both of us understood that we would always be friends but it was unlikely we
would ever work together again.

Life moves on. So be it.

I remained at NPACT, doing a series of programs that nobody much watched except the blood kin of those who appeared
on them. One of the programs, *Washington Connection*, took a
Washington story and attempted to connect it out into the country. It was a good idea, but we did not do it very well. Another
was *Washington Straight Talk*, a series of thirty-minute interviews
with Washington figures. I was not an accomplished television
interviewer. My questions were still highlighted by "you knows"
and fragmented sentences and thoughts. Many of them were
also much, much longer than the answers, because I would just
ramble on and on, from question to answer, incomplete thought
to irrelevant thought. Something like, "Is it true, as I know it is,
Mr. Strauss, that you are from Texas, which, of course, Richard
Nixon isn't, but he is president of all the states, and the question
is about the eighteen-and-a-half-minute gap in the tape, and who
do you think was responsible for that, and where exactly in
Texas did you grow up, anyhow, and why?"

Robert Strauss, whom I had known from my Texas political-
reporting days, was in fact one of our *Straight Talk* guests. He
was the chairman of the Democratic National Committee at the
time. One of the best things he had already done for me was
invite me to a large DNC holiday press reception. The place
had been packed with all of the familiar faces and names of
national journalism. My scrapes back in Texas with national
press people had been less than pleasant. On political trips and
other gatherings in the late sixties where I had come in contact

with them, I had always felt small and insignificant. Most of them ignored people like me, the local reporters. On press buses and planes, few of them would sit with us, speak to us or in any way acknowledge that we were even there. There were exceptions. Two in particular stand out, because they are still very much around and active—R. W. (Johnny) Apple, Jr., of *The New York Times*, and Jack Germond, then of the Newhouse papers, now of the Baltimore *Sun*. Both treated me and other "locals" as real people, and I have never forgotten it.

Neither was at the Strauss party, unfortunately. I had no one to talk to, so I mostly walked around and just listened. One conversation I overheard was between two of the biggest names in column journalism. One of them said something about a proposal then before Congress. The other columnist thought it was a lousy idea.

"The American people will never stand for that!" he fumed.

I looked at him carefully and listened a while longer, and realized this pompous ass wouldn't have recognized an American people if one had walked through the door. It made me feel good and even more arrogant about what I had brought with me from Texas to Washington. I left that party vowing to the Great God of Journalism that no matter what happened to me, I would never, ever stand around at a Washington cocktail party declaiming about what the American people would not stand for.

George Bush, also an acquaintance from Texas, was chairman of the Republican National Committee then. He didn't invite me to any parties, but he did appear on *Straight Talk*. I interviewed Strauss about his old friend John Connally, who was then under indictment for allegedly taking a bribe (he was later acquitted), and I talked to Bush about his president, Richard Nixon, who was on his way toward shame and resignation. Strauss and Bush are about the only two *Straight Talk* interviewees I remember with anything resembling fondness. I guess that is because I knew them, and so I was relaxed enough at least to be coherent.

A perceptive man in New Hampshire wrote to me after an interview I did with the then director of the FBI, Clarence Kelley. The viewer said few of my questions were comprehensible even on a basic how-are-you level. He was right. He said I did not follow up well and I was too soft. He was right. He wondered who I was and where I had come from and how I had gotten my job.

The worst thing about it was that I knew I was not doing well, but I was incapable of doing anything about it. I doubled my editorial cramming and preparation time, and even tried rehearsing questions. I did not get better. I still asked record-length, incomprehensible questions and let things fly by, and all of the rest. MacNeil was not there to counsel me. There was nobody else to turn to, no other professional I trusted or knew well enough to confess to that I was failing as a television correspondent, that I was sinking. It was a depressing, difficult time, and I began again seriously to consider returning to print journalism, the real world whence I had come.

Again, Richard Nixon intervened. The Oval Office tapes triggered the House Judiciary Committee impeachment proceedings. Paul Duke, who had come from NBC as Robin's replacement, and I anchored the PBS coverage of events that culminated with Nixon's resignation in August 1974. Paul, a good man and a terrific reporter, now moderates *Washington Week in Review* on PBS every Friday night in the studio next to ours at WETA-TV in Washington.

The awful highlight we shared during the impeachment hearings came when Barbara Tuchman, one of my all-time heroes, agreed to make an extremely rare television appearance as a guest analyst on our live evening coverage. We had expected there would be several lengthy breaks for analysis and insight from Ms. Tuchman, the Pulitzer Prize–winning historian and writer. But for some maddening reason, on this particular night there was only one brief recess. I introduced her immediately and asked if she would put what was happening to Nixon into some kind of historical framework.

Growing up in Kansas: one tough hombre.

At eight, with my brother Fred, the future Baptist minister, on the right.

At Victoria College, a busman, budding Hemingway, and editor of the school newspaper (I was the only one who asked for the job).

Grandfather Charles Lehrer *(seated, center)* and family: Thomas Edison's plumber—and a free-love socialist! That's my dad on the right.

Maternal grandfather Jim Chapman, general superintendent of the Nazarene Church, and a magnetic preacher.

Mom and Dad in the early 1960s.

A 1938 Flxible Clipper, the same model and year as
our Betsy, the mainstay of Dad's Kansas Central Lines.

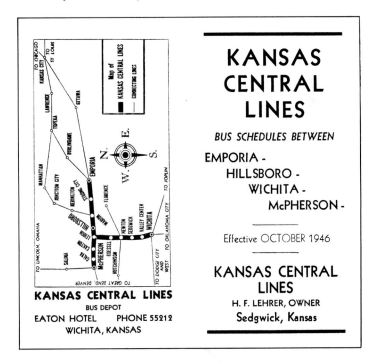

The Kansas Central and "connecting lines."
We lasted from June 1946 to July 1947.

Your Son's Devotion on Mother's Day. Freddie

The Marine Lehrers: Marine Dad *(top left photo, on left)*; Marine Fred *(above)*; Marine Jim *(left)*. A word of warning: *Never* correct a drill instructor if he mispronounces your name.

With *The Dallas Morning News*, 1960—the only foreign correspondent in American journalism who never left the city limits of Dallas.

Interviewing Jimmy Hoffa. I've got him on the run.

The hard-bitten city editor of the *Dallas Times Herald*.

Welcome to public television: *Newsroom*, KERA, Dallas, 1970–1972. We were white, black, Hispanic; male and female; long-haired; bearded. Some people went crazy and red in the face just looking at us.

From *The Robert MacNeil Report* to *The MacNeil/ Lehrer NewsHour*: free to make our own rules and our own mistakes. In Texas, it's called having a bird's nest on the ground—a terrific deal.

A bus of my own. Betsy II, a 1946 Flxible Clipper,
at home in West Virginia, and with its proud owner.

She began with an overview of the fourteenth century, about which she was then writing a book. That took all of the few minutes we had. I knew we were in trouble when she said, "Moving on now to the fifteenth century . . ."

And then I saw and heard Peter Rodino, chairman of the impeachment hearings, banging the gavel. I interrupted Ms. Tuchman, and that was that for her rare television appearance. We never even got to the sixteenth century, much less the twentieth, the one in which Richard Nixon had allegedly committed his high crimes and misdemeanors.

It was not her fault, of course. It wasn't even mine. Live television was simply not designed for the likes of Barbara Tuchman to put something like the Nixon impeachment into a historical context.

I left the studio that evening in a state of burning frustration, and further convinced that a life on television was not for me, even if, by some miracle, I did eventually get the hang of it.

There had been one hopeful development. Al Vecchione, a friend who was now managing NPACT, was working with the BBC on a historical retrospective about the Vietnam war. The two-hour program, called *The End of the Ho Chi Minh Trail*, featured an international cast of correspondents—the BBC's Julian Pettifer, Frenchman Olivier Todd, and me, the American. Julian, Olivier and I wrote and wove commentary around a compilation of war and political footage from the BBC news archives. It was all done over a ten-day period in London, in a pressurized atmosphere that was collegial, professional, difficult—and at times extremely tense. Linda Winslow, an NPACT producer, did a brilliant job of making any personality and editorial differences disappear. I left London exhausted, but feeling good about the program and about my own television work—for a change.

This was also a terrific experience personally, because Kate was with me the whole time on what was our first trip to Europe. Could I now say I was a foreign correspondent?

And that wasn't all. Robin, still in London with the BBC, told me at dinner one night that he might be coming back to America to do a nightly program for WNET, the public television station in New York.

All in all, a great ten days in London.

7

Something Called
The Robert MacNeil Report

Jay Iselin and Bob Kotlowitz did in fact bring Robin back to America—and to glory. They hired him to start something called *The Robert MacNeil Report.* It would be a nightly thirty-minute public affairs program on WNET that could and would be national and international in scope and reach, but would be broadcast only in New York City.

They agreed to make him the kind of boss over every detail he wanted to be. His title was executive editor.

How would you like to be my Washington correspondent? he asked me.

I'd love it, sir, I replied.

The program began with the deal that I was to appear two, possibly three, nights a week. NPACT had now been absorbed into WETA, the Washington public television station, and I was part of the absorption. Gerry Slater, who had moved from PBS to WETA as general manager, and Ward Chamberlin, WETA's president, were not happy about it, but they agreed to let me do the Washington end of Robin's program. MacNeil, meanwhile, had problems convincing some of the New York people that I was good enough for the new venture.

Who?

Lehrer. My old friend from Watergate days.

What's he been doing since?

He's been on public television. Your station included.

Oh?

The Robert MacNeil Report went on the air October 20, 1975. The first program was about the financial crisis in New York City, and that was about it for local coverage. The second night's was about the Middle East, and from then on there was no looking back at New York.

The programming concept was one story a night for thirty minutes. Bring guests into the studio in Washington and/or New York and ask them questions about that one story. The wrinkles came in how we arranged the order of the interviews, how we switched back and forth doing the interviewing, and most important, how we saw ourselves in our jobs sitting at our respective tables in our respective studios in Washington and New York.

We decided as an article of faith and practice that all guests were in fact guests and would be treated as such. We would help them get their positions or opinions out in a coherent and understandable form, so the audience could decide weight and merit. We would not beat up on our guests or embarrass them.

Those were our simple rules of the road. They grew out of our individual styles and desires, not out of any special goodness or even a what's-the-smart-way-to-go-about-this-in-today's-market conversation. Two other television journalist-interviewers starting a new program might have come up with an entirely different set of rules that fit their way of doing things.

The most important thing for us was that Robin and I were free to make our own rules. We did not have to become Mike Wallace or Walter Cronkite or anybody else in order to please some higher power, person or philosophy in public television. Whatever warts we displayed were going to be our own.

Two terrific things happened to *The Robert MacNeil Report* within only six months. It went national, and it got a terrific new title. The majority of the public television stations in the country, encouraged and led by the new PBS president, Lawrence Grossman, and others on the PBS executive and programming staff, bought us. They voted to help fund us and to broadcast us five nights a week as public television's first weeknight news/public affairs program. It was a big deal for us and for the system.

The new title was an even bigger deal. For me. It was the ever glorious and catchy *The MacNeil-Lehrer Report*. I have been known to joke that the title was the best one Robin's mother and mine could come up with. The real story is almost as interesting. Robin and I felt the title should have the PBS name in it somewhere. Maybe *The PBS Report, PBS Newsnight, PBS Nightline* or some such. But the leaderships of WNET and PBS at that time detested each other. The WNET people would not hear of having "PBS" in the title, as if it was something very personal. All of the generics—*Newsnight,* and so on—sounded strange by themselves, so finally Robin and I were urgently urged to please consider calling it simply *The MacNeil-Lehrer Report*.

It worked once for two guys named Huntley and Brinkley, so why not for you two? they said.

We said, Beware. You could end up creating two monsters.

They said, We'll risk it.

Okay, we said.

The MacNeil-Lehrer Report it became.

And I am certain there are people around who would argue that Robin and I have been proven right about our warning. But it's too late now.

The best thing about the coming of the new and glorious title was that it happened before my mother died. She loved the idea that her son was on a national television news program that also had his name on it. I was publicly aw-shucks embarrassed and privately delighted at the way she told everybody about me and what I did. Kate's mother did the same thing. She tended to do it while standing in grocery store checkout lines with her three granddaughters, however, which used to drive Jamie, Lucy and Amanda absolutely crazy.

Do you know who their father is? Kate's mother, whom we call GaGa, would say to some poor soul.

No, would respond the poor soul, shaking his or her head.

He's on public television and he wrote *Viva Max!*

Jamie, Lucy and Amanda would hide their faces as the poor soul would again shake his or her head.

At any rate. My mother moved to Lenexa, Kansas, a Kansas City suburb, three years after Dad's death. She wanted to be near Grace, her younger sister, who lived in Kansas City. Aunt Grace is a true pistol of a little lady. Full of energy and independence and stories and laughter and Jesus. She is a joy to be around, and it made sense that Mom would want to be near her.

One morning, after feeling bad for several days, Mom went to the local hospital for some tests. The doctors ran them and decided it might be an aneurism in her stomach. Or near her kidneys. Or something I did not quite follow. I flew out there. The doctors took me down into an X-ray room and showed me pictures of my mother's insides. One doctor said a shadowy figure was an obstruction and surgery was definitely called for. The other said he was not so sure and maybe it could be waited out.

It's your decision, Mr. Lehrer, they said.

I called my brother in Tennessee, and I called my uncle Paul, my mother's brother, who was a doctor in Los Angeles. The consensus among the three of us was, finally, operate.

Aunt Grace sat with me in the waiting room the night of the operation. The television was on. President Jimmy Carter was addressing the nation about the sad state of affairs in the United States of America in that year of 1979. This later became known as his "malaise" speech, even though he never once used the word. The memorable thing to me was that nobody in that hospital but Aunt Grace and me was watching. I made a mental note to remember that the next time I contemplated—as a journalist—the impact of crisis addresses to the nation by presidents of the United States.

But I was at the hospital as a son. The operation was supposed to take three, possibly four, hours. But in less than thirty minutes the doctor was out to say, Sorry, your mother didn't really need the operation after all. They closed her back up.

The other guy, in other words, was right.

She was taken to the recovery room and then to intensive care. And eventually the doctors told us she had pretty much had it. She was probably not going to recover.

From what? I asked.

From the operation, they said.

And I started commuting back and forth between Washington and Kansas City. Mom continued to deteriorate. Finally, the doctors took me into an office and said a decision had to be made. She was being kept alive now only by artificial means.

Did I want that to continue? Again, it was my decision.

Again, I called Fred and Uncle Paul. Again, the consensus was pretty much that it made no sense to keep her on a machine. But before I could transmit that decision to anybody, she died.

So, like my dad before her, my mother walked into a hospital and came out dead six weeks later.

Again, I allege no malpractice, no negligence. But I did suggest to everyone to avoid hospitals whenever possible.

■ ■ ■

I was no longer a son. I no longer had parents. No mother, no father. It was several weeks after Mom's death that I began to think about that startling development in my life, and I have continued to think about it a little bit at a time ever since.

I think about it particularly when nice things happen to me, such as when Jamie, our oldest daughter, got married, or when she and Lucy and Amanda graduated from something. Or when our grandchildren were born. They are the great-grandchildren Mom and Dad never saw or knew.

I even do so some routine evenings when the *MacNeil/Lehrer* name comes up on the video monitor in our studio.

Hey, Dad, look at that!

I see it, son, I see it.

Our name, Dad. That's our name on there.

I see it, son, I see it.

Oh, how I wish I had had that conversation the first night of something called *MacNeil-Lehrer*. He would have loved talking about it all to the drivers and the ticket agents in San Antonio and the big shots at the general office in Dallas. I regret very much that he never had that opportunity.

I regret very much this day and every day that I no longer have a mother and a father. They both believed in their sons, in their ability to do just about anything, their rightness, their smartness. There was never a time that I did anything of note, from getting an A on a report card to knocking down a pass in a B-team football game, that Mom or Dad did not tell me, Good job, son. You did that well, son. Nice going, boy.

My dad had a left eye that twinkled out of control when he was happy. Making that happen was a key motivator in my life until the day he died.

My mother smiled her approval and pride. She loved to read books, and she made damned sure her sons loved to read them, too. She was also a tiny bit of a snob, in the best sense, if there is a best sense. No matter how down-and-out we were at any given time, she made it clear to us and to all others that her family, and most particularly her sons, were better than just about anybody else. You just wait and see what they can do.

The day in May 1954 when my brother graduated from the University of Texas at Austin was the happiest and proudest and snobbiest I ever saw Mom and Dad, each in their own way. Look at our boy! There he is, a college graduate. Smart as they come, worked his way through school to get a business administration degree, never asked anybody for anything. Our son Fred.

That graduation day became a notable day in our family lore for the additional reason that there was only one dark blue suit in the family. Dad, Fred and I were about the same size, so we could all three wear it. Dad kept it most of the time, but we shifted it around among us according to need and special event. Fred needed it for his graduation. I had needed it the day before in Victoria for my junior college prom, so I wore it to Austin that morning on the bus. Fred and I switched clothes—I put on

his dark brown slacks and checked sport coat—in the men's
room of the Austin bus station, while Mom and Dad waited in
the terminal waiting room. Then we rushed up the hill to the
graduation ceremony.

At the end of the day, Dad and Fred and I did another switch,
because Dad was going to a big luncheon the next week in San
Antonio. He would be representing Continental Trailways and
the bus industry at some kind of travel-Texas gathering. This
time, I ended up with what Dad had worn to Austin. A gray
sport coat and dark blue slacks.

■　■　■

The MacNeil-Lehrer Report became a joy to do. It was the
ultimate in professional comfort and satisfaction. We were always prepared to scrap what we had on the books for a breaking
story, but we were also able to pretape discussions for major
holidays and take off some long weekends. The staff was small,
compact, and so were the decisions on what we would do on
any given Monday-through-Friday night. Robin and I were the
final authorities on everything. Not one piece of film or photograph or anything else went on the air that one of us had not
cleared first.

We had our live-television adventures.

A male university professor froze during an interview with
Robin about grain elevator safety. A female activist froze during
a discussion I ran about precinct caucuses. In both cases the
guests could not make the words come out. Their mouths
moved, their foreheads perspired, their minds crackled, their
souls convulsed, but no noise came. In both cases Robin and I
not only asked the questions but also answered them.

"Isn't it true, ma'am, that you are opposed to the use of the
caucus for nominating presidential candidates?"

Silence.

"Well, as you said in a speech two weeks ago in Orlando, it
is too exclusive a process. Isn't that right?"

Silence.

"You believe nominating presidential candidates should not

be left to a handful of activists who bring their self-interests to the caucus meetings. Correct?"

Silence.

A semi-prominent retired diplomat showed up in our Washington studio one night drunk. Smashed, juiced, pickled, soused. He seemed able, barely, to sit up in a chair and respond to questions, so we put him in his place. I asked him a question about the future of NATO or some such, and the little earpiece he had in his right ear to hear New York popped out.

It's all right, I said to him, because I am asking the questions right here in front of you right now.

He kept talking about the future of NATO and grabbed the earpiece. He tried to find his left ear to stick it back in.

He stuck it into his cheek. Then up around his nose. Below his ear and above his ear.

It's all right, sir. We'll fix it in a minute.

I asked him a follow-up about what we could expect from the Warsaw Pact just about the time he tried to insert the earpiece into his chin.

I said, Thank You, Mr. Ambassador, and threw it to Robin in New York.

One evening, during a hot discussion about abortion (all discussions about abortion are hot), an antiabortion Catholic priest was attacked by a huge fly. It landed right on the good father's nose and would not go away.

It's all right to swat it, I said to him.

He knocked it away, but after a second the fly was right back in the same spot on his nose.

The amazing thing was that the priest never missed a beat or a word. I recently had occasion to look at that segment (it's on an old Christmas-party gag reel) and I must say it was a most remarkable achievement. Discipline clearly is part of the training for the priesthood.

Every television operation has a green room, where guests go to wait for their entrance. Few of these rooms are actually green, and I have no idea where the "green" came from. At any rate, one evening two men there to discuss a Middle East topic got to talking while waiting for their joint appearance.

Before long, their voices were raised, their gestures were emphatic, and our staff had to pull them off each other. Each then refused to appear on the air with the other, and suddenly we had to substitute a tape piece.

On another occasion, a guest left the green room in New York to go to the bathroom and got lost in a stairwell that had only locked doors coming back in. He was found and liberated only after the segment had begun. We now have severe rules about where guests can go unaccompanied before airtime.

One night Vice-President Nelson Rockefeller gave me a short lesson in television interviewing. He had just returned, as all vice-presidents do, from an extensive trip abroad. He had come to tell us about it in a thirty-minute interview that Robin and I would split, alternating every seven minutes or so. There was some political news to ask about, in addition to the trip. Ronald Reagan had announced he was going to oppose Gerald Ford for the Republican presidential nomination. He had accompanied the announcement with some serious digs at Ford.

Rockefeller was in our Washington studio, so it was agreed that first I would question him about the politics and then Robin would question him about the foreign trip.

I said, Welcome, Mr. Vice-President, quoted what Reagan had said about Ford, and asked for Rockefeller's comment.

He sidestepped it.

I asked it another way. And then another and another, and finally the first seven minutes were up. Robin then went to the trip.

When it came back to me, I picked up the Reagan–Ford flap again, but with no luck. Rockefeller only smiled and either changed the subject or said something about "Republicans don't fight in public." Having this come from him, the original Republican combatant, was most frustrating.

In any case, he prevailed. Not only did he say nothing quotable or interesting about Reagan–Ford, he said nothing at all.

Nothing that anybody would have any cause to pay any attention to, much less remember.

So when the program was finally over and the lights were down and the microphones were dead, I said to him:

"No disrespect, Mr. Vice-President, but you didn't say a damned thing."

"That's right," he said, in that gravelly hi-fella voice of his. "I didn't come here to say anything."

I said something respectfully whiny about how hard I had tried to get him to say something—anything.

He said: "Look, fella, if people like you could get me to say things I didn't want to say, I wouldn't be here."

True, sir. So, so true, sir.

Another recurring problem was the guest who had had a conversion of some kind on the way to the studio. He had been signed on and preinterviewed as a left-wing fanatic about prison reform, but when asked the first question on the air sounded like a right-wing fanatic who believed all persons convicted of marijuana possession should be shot.

It happened to us in those early days, on a story about the Marine Corps, of all things. A Brookings Institution report on the future of the Corps had questioned the value to the nation of the amphibious warfare doctrine, and a recruit had died in training at the San Diego Recruit Depot.

We planned a full thirty minutes on "Whither the Corps." The first guest was the author of a new book that also questioned the present and future of the Corps. Robin would interview him in New York, and he was to lay out the rhetorical indictment. I had with me a two-star Marine general who would respond to the savage attack.

It was obvious after two questions, however, that the author had not come to criticize the U.S. Marine Corps. Robin tried everything he could just to get the man to say what he had said in his preinterview and his book. Nothing doing. He did everything but sing the Marine hymn and shout "Semper Fi."

It meant I had to play devil's advocate–plus with the general, which is not fun under any circumstances. My Marine heritage made it even worse. What was I going to do—ask the general about why that DI had harassed me about my name when I showed up at Quantico?

I got through it. But it was a long thirty minutes.

When it was all finally over, our reporter on the story gave the author a terrific blast. The man apologized, but explained: Look, it occurred to me coming over to the studio that the main audience for my book would be all of those ex-Marines out there in TV land. If I came on too strong on television, they might not buy it. So I decided to temper my remarks somewhat. Sorry.

We were able to indulge our special editorial interests and bents. I went to Cincinnati to interview Pete Rose on opening day of the baseball season in 1977. I rode the train to Harpers Ferry, West Virginia, for a piece on the financial future of Amtrak.

But some of our best work was about buses. We did a brilliant half-hour on the trials and tribulations of the intercity bus industry. It opened with me sitting behind the wheel of a Trailways Silver Eagle at the bus depot in Washington. Closing credits ran over the sound of my voice calling the buses at the Victoria, Texas, bus depot, just like it was 1953 all over again. We did an even more brilliant thirty minutes on the collecting obsession. The program opened with me standing against a wall in my own bus room, talking amiably, charmingly about my signs and badges and toy buses. And about how important collecting was to me and to many other normal Americans everywhere.

Roger Mudd, my friend who was then with NBC News, noted afterward that it was the first time in the short history of television that somebody had (1) opened a serious news broadcast from his own basement, and (2) tried to act like it made sense to do so.

We did programs we should not have done, about the sins and/or glories of artificial potato chips (a sociologist held a Pringles chip up to the camera and declared them to be "Crap-os"), turkeys, vegetarianism, lie detectors and truck driving. During one on tomatoes, Robin asked a tomato expert to cut open a store-bought tomato to demonstrate its limp awfulness. She cut it open and said it was a wonderful tomato. Surprise, surprise. On another program I tried to demonstrate how to operate one of the new electronic banking machines and could not make it work.

We should not have done these programs, because the one thing America did not need then—or now, or probably ever— was another serious television program trying to "lighten up" in order to "broaden the audience base" and do all of those dumb things people who don't know what they're talking about say about television programming.

It was a short and small lapse in judgment. We were mostly serious. As the first national commentator publicly to note our coming said, "They have the courage to be serious." Those early words from Thomas Griffith of *Time* magazine remain, in my opinion, the best ever said about us. Some critics have since edited them to say we have the courage to be dull and boring. To which I reply: True, and that takes even more courage.

Sometimes, like all good things, we went too far with our courage to be serious. The most monumental instance from those early days was in a 1976 interview with Rosalynn Carter, wife of the then Democratic nominee for president. We were to do a thirty-minute taped interview in our New York studio, one hour before airtime. I came to New York to do it with Robin. We spent all morning and much of the early afternoon reading and otherwise preparing. At around three, a reporter came to us with an AP story about an interview Jimmy Carter had done with *Playboy* magazine.

"He admitted he lusts in his heart for other women," said the reporter.

We immediately ordered the reporter to do whatever it took to get a copy of the full interview. We certainly did not want to ask Mrs. Carter about something her husband had said out of context. No, sir. Not MacNeil and Lehrer the Greats.

Within the hour, a copy of the magazine appeared. We were

down to less than an hour before taping. In a division of labor, it was concluded I would read the full interview and decide whether we should ask Mrs. Carter about it. There was no time for both of the Greats to read it.

I read it. I pronounced: "Robin, I think it would be a cheap shot to ask her about this."

"Fine," said my esteemed friend and colleague.

And we went to the studio and interviewed Mrs. Carter for thirty minutes on some of the great issues of the campaign and our time. But not a word was spoken about the *Playboy* interview.

When it was over, we took off our microphones and thanked her. Across the studio, somebody opened the door to the outside world, and from it came a storm of reporters, print and electronic. They started asking questions about the *Playboy* interview, which she answered pleasantly and effectively for several minutes.

Robin and I observed and listened to this from a position off to one side. After a few minutes, I turned to my esteemed friend and colleague and said: "Robin, esteemed friend and colleague, I think I made a mistake."

He did not disagree.

■ ■ ■

The major upside to the interview was simply that Rosalynn Carter had come. We had begun to arrive as a program. We had been there awhile and were now able to attract the biggest of the big-name guests. That was wonderful. In the beginning, our reporters would have to spend fifteen minutes explaining what public television was and then another fifteen explaining what we were, before they ever got to the question, Would Mrs. Carter—or the prime minister, governor, senator, pope, president, star, dog catcher—come on the program tomorrow night? But with the exception of a few, including Mrs. Carter, the guests who stand out in my memory are not the famous ones. They are the people like Ruth Lo.

Mrs. Lo, a native of Philadelphia, had met and married a

Chinese graduate student in Chicago in the 1930s. She'd gone with him to live in China and stayed there forty years. Now, in her seventies and a widow, she had come back to the United States to live. I interviewed her for thirty minutes on tape one afternoon in Denver, some thirty miles southeast of Boulder, where she had settled. She talked about how she had lived and survived during the various movements and revolutions in China. How during the Cultural Revolution, some neighbors had been scared into killing themselves, while others had been scared into killing their neighbors. I asked her about what it was like to be in America again after forty years. When the interview was over, I was moved to tears by what she had said. So much so that I could barely say, "Thank you, Mrs. Lo," and then turn to the camera and say, "Thank you and good night," to the audience.

I recently dug out a transcript of that program to see what she had said that had so touched me. It proved to be a good lesson about television.

At the very end, she had said about her return to this country: "The people here are so beautiful—these tall young people with their long hair, even their beards. I find them really astonishingly beautiful. The way they walk, and their friendly atmosphere. The first few days I was here, I went out for a short walk. I met absolutely strange young people on the road. 'Hi, Ma, how are you?' they said. 'Beautiful day, isn't it?' Well, it was such a change from the atmosphere of being very careful. 'Do I know this person? Dare I speak to that person?' It was just like a new world. And I loved every bit of it."

No, read like that in print it doesn't move. But spoken aloud by her in that Denver television studio that afternoon, it did. Her voice was melodious and strong and alive. It was the sound and bearing and force of personality of that gracious gray-haired woman as much as her words that did it to me. And to others. That interview drew more reaction in mail and phone calls than anything we had done up until then.

Another lesson about television? Could it be that the people out there really are not as stupid as the people in here who produce television programs think they are?

It was that belief that caused us to say yes when the PBS leadership came along in 1983, seven years after the beginning of the half-hour program, and asked if we would be interested in expanding to an hour.

• • •

The MacNeil/Lehrer NewsHour went on the air September 5, 1983. It had "Postcards," ten-to-fifteen-second shots of babbling brooks, majestic mountains, orange sunsets and other America-the-Beautiful scenes from around the country that we ran between major segments. "Bumpers," in TV production lingo.

It had book reviews by one of four regular book reviewers Robin or I interviewed.

It had cute profiles of small-town bandleaders and songwriters, hog callers and rodeo riders.

It had news stories sprinkled throughout the one hour, sandwiched between major studio discussion and/or documentary report segments.

It had a lot of new and exciting things.

But. Nobody but me liked the Postcards. Nobody but Robin liked the book reviews. Nobody but the subjects and kin of the subjects liked the profiles, and nobody much anywhere could follow what we were doing with the news of the day. Or why.

It was a mess. A well-intentioned, sometimes brilliant mess, but a mess.

The half-hour *MacNeil–Lehrer Report* had had a simple premise and purpose. One story a night for thirty minutes was the premise; a supplement to the nightly newscasts on commercial television was the purpose. Now, with the hour, it was several stories a night for sixty minutes as a direct alternative to the other newscasts. Once we had said watch us *after* you watch the others; now it was watch us *instead*. Everything about the program was a major change, not only in our concepts and purposes, but in our day-to-day, minute-to-minute way of doing things.

Every day was an exhausting, exhilarating adventure. Would we make it on the air tonight? And if so, with what? And in what order and shape?

Maybe open with a one-person interview about controlling

multiwarhead missile limits? Then a couple of news stories. And a hunk of Senate floor debate about the exclusionary rule. Three more news stories. Next, a profile of a left-handed bus driver who sings tenor at the Met. Then maybe a book review about a new deconstructionist novel. How about some more news stories? Then close with a four-person shouter about *Roe v. Wade.* Or gun control. Or peace in the Middle East. Or living wills. Or what really did happen to God.

Each new day seemed more than just a new day. With the rising sun came a new format, a new pattern, a new era, a new world. And we were there!

The man in the center of it all, the rainmaker, was Les Crystal, our executive producer. He had left NBC News after twenty years to organize, launch and run the new *NewsHour.* Al Vecchione, Robin's friend and mine from NPACT days, had been the executive producer of the half-hour program. He had moved on to become president of MacNeil-Lehrer-Gannett Productions, a company Robin and I had started with the Gannett Company to produce documentaries and other public affairs programs for cable and anyone else who was interested. It was a deal our agent and friend, Jim Griffin of the William Morris Agency, had put together with Al Flanagan, Gannett's chief broadcast man.

Linda Winslow, our friend from *The End of the Ho Chi Minh Trail* and one of the original two producers of the old half-hour *Report,* had returned to be the deputy executive producer of the one-hour program. She had already worked with us in drafting the proposal for the one-hour in her capacity as a vice-president of WETA. Dan Werner, who had come up through the ranks as a reporter, was the associate executive producer in Washington, which meant he ran things in Washington. With him, all things were and are possible for me and the program in Washington; without him, nothing would be.

Judy Woodruff had come from NBC to be chief Washington correspondent and to share substitute-anchor duties with Charlayne Hunter-Gault. Judy had begun her journalism career as a secretary in an Atlanta television news operation and had gone on to be one of NBC News' top correspondents. She was the Washington editor of the *Today* show and was covering the Carter White House when I asked her to lunch and laid out what we were hoping and planning with our one-hour. After no more than a couple of blinks she said, "When do I start?"

Robin, Les and I were stunned and impressed with her quick, gutsy willingness to give up life on a commercial network to come gamble with us. We have since become stunned and impressed with her professionalism and her goodness. She is a genuinely nice human being, a pleasure to work with and be around.

And on both of those scales, the professionalism and nice-person scales, she had a high standard to meet: the one set by Charlayne. I have neither met nor worked with anyone in this business who is more gracious than Charlayne. She also knows every joke ever invented. She came to us in 1978 from *The New York Times*, where she had worked as a reporter for fifteen years. Before that, her life had been marked forever by being one of the first two black students admitted to the University of Georgia.

Other new people had come also. Our reporting and producing staff had more than doubled its size. It had quadrupled in work load. At least.

At the low moments during the first three months, there were many thoughts about why we had gone to all of the trouble and anguish to expand so we could work so hard and so long this way.

And the official passing from thirty to sixty minutes had been one of much trouble and anguish indeed.

The PBS staff leadership, which had first suggested the idea, had run for cover when the initial response from the stations was not positive. It was the strong support from Jay Iselin et al. at WNET and Ward Chamberlin and his et al. at WETA that kept the idea and our enthusiasm alive. Al Flanagan, a tough, good man of Gannett, who had survived the bloody battle at

Peleliu as a kid Marine in World War II, was also with us, despite the fact that a one-hour would mean delaying any serious MacNeil-Lehrer-Gannett ventures. Al Vecchione, as always, was solid.

Two other major heroes were from AT&T: Charlie Brown and Ed Block. Charlie was the boss, the chairman; Ed, the executive vice-president and boss of the company's public affairs. AT&T had been the principal underwriter of our thirty-minute program. After a matter of minutes, it seemed, Charlie and Ed said they liked the one-hour idea and wanted AT&T to be the sole corporate underwriter. The projected budget was right at $20 million. The company's share would be half of that—$10 million; the rest would come from the stations and the Corporation for Public Broadcasting.

Throughout the difficult process of convincing a majority of stations to give the one-hour a chance, Charlie and Ed never blinked. Without them it would never have happened. Period. As the *NewsHour* finally has found its way and its place, a number of people have claimed credit for its coming into being. For the record: Charlie Brown and Ed Block, who to my knowledge have never claimed credit, are among the very few who could legitimately do so.

We found our way through trial and error. This is a polite way of saying we did many dumb things, eventually realized they were dumb, and then decided not to do them again.

It was the strength of a much-maligned system called public television that allowed us the freedom to do such a thing. And to survive and flourish.

The whole enterprise, however, was not helped by my having a heart attack.

8

What Happened to That Poor Fellow?

It started on December 11, 1983, at about four in the morning. That was when I woke up in my Washington bed with what at that moment resembled nothing more than indigestion. There was a dry tightness in my chest that I assumed I could swallow and burp away. Kate and I had been to a Mexican restaurant the night before with two other couples. Mexican food—Tex-Mex Mexican food, to be more precise—was my favorite food staff of life, but it sometimes extracted a price when I ate too much too fast, as I usually did and as I had done that Saturday night.

The swallowing and the burping did not make the tightness go away. I woke Kate up and got out of bed. I drank several glasses of water. Surely that would do the trick. It didn't.

"Let's call a doctor," said Kate.

"No, no," said I. "It'll be fine in a minute."

"A doctor, please! It could be something like, say, maybe even a heart attack."

"No way. It's the tamales and the beans and the enchiladas and the taco and the rice from last night. I will be fine."

After a while I got back in bed. The tightness did not disappear, yet eventually I did doze off. But it was not long before I was awake again. And up out of bed.

Again Kate said, Please, let's call a doctor. Again I said no. I made the point that it had not gotten any worse. Clearly, if it had been a heart attack it would have gotten worse. Where did I get that piece of stupidly incorrect information? I have no idea.

It was to be a busy day and evening. A holiday brunch, an open house and a downtown dinner were on our social agenda. At eleven o'clock we went to the brunch, at a friend's house close by. Our host was a psychiatrist, and the moment we arrived I realized there were other doctors of various kinds also present.

My chest was still tight. Was that a tingling I was beginning to feel in my left arm? Wasn't that also a symptom of a heart attack? I did not know much about heart attacks, because they were not part of my life or consciousness.

I had heard or read somewhere that chest pains plus tingling in the left arm were symptoms.

So why not say something to one of the doctors who were sipping Bloody Marys and egg nog and eating omelets, biscuits and other delectables? No. All they would do was say go to the hospital or something.

No hospitals, please.

I had a Bloody Mary and a plate of food and made small talk.

And after a while Kate and I went home. I turned on a Dallas Cowboys–Washington Redskins game on television. For Texas-heritage reasons, the Cowboys were mine as well as America's team then, and the Redskins were not. They were playing for the NFC division championship in Dallas.

The Cowboys were behind when we left for the next event, an open house. The hosts had TV sets on all over their house. I had nothing to eat and nothing to drink. I found a place in an upstairs room to stand and watch the end of the game. The Redskins, who were a big deal to most people in Washington except us, were winning. There were other people milling about. The man who milled up next to me to watch the game was Dick Cheney, then a congressman from Wyoming. We knew each other, and we exchanged a few words as the game wound down. I knew that Cheney had had a heart attack after he had left the Ford White House, where he had been chief of staff. My chest was still tight, my arm was still tingling. But I said nothing to him about my discomforts; I had no conversation like:

Hey, Dick, do a tingling arm and a dry tightness across the chest mean anything?

Hey, Jim, they sure do.

What?

A heart attack.

Oh. Hey, look at that pass into the end zone!

And before long Kate and I were on our way to the Madison Hotel for a dinner. Gannett, with which Robert MacNeil and I had recently formed our television production company, was having a small get-together of its broadcast executives and managers. Gannett owned several television and radio stations around the country. As a new member of the team, I was to come by and say hello. I said it, and Kate and I left early.

Kate continued to insist that we go to a hospital or, at the very least, call my doctor. I continued to insist that any minute everything was going to be all right.

No hospitals. Bad things happened to Lehrers in hospitals. They died.

Back home, I went to bed. I took a sleeping pill that was left over from a bout I had had with a back problem. It did not work. I remained wide awake. At midnight, I finally got scared. I decided that indigestion really did not last this long, that maybe I was having a heart attack, that maybe I should do something about it.

Kate dialed the phone number of my doctor in Washington. The woman who answered the phone made a mistake. She left some connection open and, with Kate listening, dialed the doctor. She told him a Mrs. Lehrer was on the line and had said her husband was having chest pains and his left arm was tingling. The doctor angrily told the woman—with Kate listening, please remember—that he was not on call, so she should call somebody else. Call somebody else! Before Kate could scream at him, he hung up. The woman said she would find another doctor and have him phone her. And in a few minutes, that is what happened. I described my symptoms to the doctor.

He told me go to the nearest hospital as quickly as I could.

I insisted on driving. I also insisted on smoking my pipe. I had a feeling my thirty years as an avid smoker might soon be over, one way or another. Probably the worst way. I was determined to go down and out with some tobacco smoke in my lungs.

One last smoke for a dying man.

Kate and I went to a small private hospital ten minutes from our house, Sibley Memorial. It was where our oldest daughter, Jamie, had gone for an operation on her foot. We had had no further experiences with hospitals in Washington. Why not Sibley?

There were no other patients in the emergency room. A nurse put me on an EKG machine. I kept hoping the tightness in my chest would go away, so I could get out of there before they killed me.

It did not. A doctor in a light brown suit said that he was not a cardiologist or even an internist, but that he and the other doctors who practiced at Sibley took turns on emergency duty. The hospital had a small-town warmth and casualness about it.

The EKG turned up nothing, but because the chest and arm problems persisted, the doctor suggested I stay. He sent me up to the intensive care room on another floor. Nurses there took some blood for tests and made me comfortable. I was given something to sleep, and sleep I did.

I awoke the next morning with the tightness and the tingling gone. Where they had gone and why they had gone, I had no idea. And neither did anybody else. Later in the morning, my regular doctor, who had been unwilling to see to my problem the night before, came by. He said it was important to find out why I had had the problem. He said a cardiologist friend of his would be looking in on me. Chemical tests were being run. Soon we would know, and all would be well, and wasn't that great?

My concern went from my health to my job. And it was some concern. The *NewsHour* was not working well. How could it be fixed and go on without me? Indispensable, incredible, wonderful me?

Kate called Robin and the others on the program to tell them I was in the hospital and why. But at my insistence she also told them that it was apparently not a heart attack and they could relax. Indispensable, incredible, wonderful Jim would return in a couple of days. Da-ta-ta-*ta!*

The cardiologist and my doctor decided it would be good for me to spend another night at the hospital as a precaution. Eventually night came, and Kate went home to get some rest.

I went to sleep with no trouble, and I slept until just after five in the morning, when I awoke with something crushing down on my chest. It had the weight and ferocity of a truck. My left arm was throbbing with pain, as if a knife were being scraped across and through it.

I sat up straight in bed.

I grabbed my left arm and doubled over. A nurse was there, and another nurse came. One stuck something in my left arm, and the other stuck her fingers in my mouth and forced something under my tongue.

I moaned and rocked back and forth. I heard one say something about morphine and nitroglycerine.

The truck kept rolling back and forth over my chest, and the knife continued to slice into my left arm. Sweat was pouring across my eyes and face. One of the nurses wiped it away with a rag. I felt heat and moisture all over my body.

I put my head down between my legs and threw my arms around my knees, and held on and squeezed and squeezed. I did not know what was happening, but I was sure it would never end.

I wanted to throw up. I wanted to scream. I wanted to cry. The nurses kept mopping me and talking to me.

And then it was over. The truck drove away. The knife disappeared. So did the heat and the sweat and the nausea.

I lay back down on the bed.

"You made it," said one of the nurses. They were both women in their thirties whose names and faces I do not know now.

Made it? Made *what?*

One of them said: "You just had a heart attack."

I knew it had to be something like that.

The good news was that at least I had beaten the Grim Lehrer Hospital Reaper. I was, in fact, alive.

But that was about it for good news.

■ ■ ■

One of the nurses phoned Kate and told her she should come to the hospital. There had been a development. It seemed to me that Kate was there in a matter of seconds. She stood there by the side of the bed while the nurses and I told her I had had a heart attack. I had survived and everything was going to be fine.

The nurses left the room, and Kate and I just looked at each other. I was still under the spell of morphine. I could barely speak, but that was no problem. I had nothing to say.

Kate got on the phone for help. The cardiologist who had been recruited the day before was too busy to come see me. Later, he was to tell me he had office appointments that had precedence over my problem. After all, I was in good hands in the hospital, he said. My regular doctor eventually showed up, but only to say very little that made any sense. He, too, seemed terribly busy and inconvenienced. He even told me that it was a shame we had come to Sibley, instead of a hospital that was farther north and thus closer to his office. Kate did not say anything to him about the late-night call he'd refused to take, but she essentially fired him.

With the help of Robin on the phone from New York and Dan Werner, our associate executive producer in Washington, arrangements were made to move me to Georgetown University Hospital and find a new set of doctors. Those already on the case clearly had more important things to do with their time and expertise than deal with me. They were the kind of doctor who gives the profession a bad name. Generally, the people we came across at all levels of the health care system were competent and terrific. But all lines of work, including most assuredly my own, have idiots in them like those two birds.

It was a long, frustrating, terrible day for Kate, which ended that evening with an ambulance ride in the rain from Sibley to Georgetown. It was only a few miles, but it seemed like a journey to a whole new world.

I was taken to a corner room in the cardiac intensive care section. Such a wonderful man in a white coat who said his name was Kenneth Kent was there. He was an important cardiologist on the hospital staff and the Georgetown University medical school faculty. His specialty was angiograms and angioplasties, I was told. Angiograms and angioplasties. It was the first time I had ever heard those words, along with all of the others that make up the language of heart attacks. Kate and I soon became proficient in that language and could speak it fluently with one and all. The important thing about Kenneth Kent—everybody, soon including us, called him Kenny—was that we were now in caring and competent hands. The heart attack was over.

Wasn't it?

Kate had already had some of the hardest part to deal with. She had called our two daughters who were away at college. Jamie was a senior at Vassar in Poughkeepsie, New York, Lucy a sophomore at Wesleyan in Middletown, Connecticut. They were both in the middle of exams, and Kate knew they would both be home soon. She told them I had had a heart attack, but she made it sound as if it was mostly like a bad cold, so they would go ahead and finish their work before scurrying home.

That lowball approach turned out to be impossible with Amanda, our youngest daughter. She was a junior at Sidwell Friends, a private school near our home in Washington. When she'd gone to school that morning, she knew that I was in the hospital, but she also believed that I had not had a heart attack and that there was nothing to worry about. Kate's mother was visiting from Texas. Kate had told her about the subsequent heart attack but asked her not to tell Amanda. Kate would come home and tell her herself.

But Kate's mother, understandably distraught, could not wait for Kate to arrive from the hospital. She blurted out the news to Amanda when she came home from school, in terms that made it seem much worse than it was. Amanda ran right out of the house. It was raining outside. But it did not matter.

She ran the seven blocks back to school to tell a teacher that a paper due the next day might be late. Her dad was sick. She broke down, and after a while someone drove her home.

Later that night, in my small room at Georgetown, Kate and I began to try to sort out what had happened. Kenny Kent had told the nurses it was all right for Kate to spend the night in the room with me, despite rules against such things.

Kate did not tell me what had happened to Amanda, or any of the other traumas of her day. I found out about all of that later. She reported only the good news, such as the fact that Cheryl and Don had dropped everything and flown down from New York to "run things" at home. Cheryl and Don Perdue, our friends. Cheryl had been my kid secretary at KERA in Dallas and had come with us to Washington and to PBS, and then gone to *MacNeil/Lehrer* in New York. Jamie, Lucy and Amanda felt as close to her as they would to a big sister, an aunt and a street-smart buddy all in one. She was from a small town in East Texas, and brought East Texas delight, wisdom and salty humor to everything and every person she touched. She and Don, one of the country's best professional photographers, had gotten married in our living room on the previous Valentine's Day.

Kate and I tried to talk about what it all meant, but there was really nothing either of us had to say. A heart attack. I had had a heart attack. What exactly was a heart attack? What did it mean for my life, her life—our life?

Neither of us knew. And we were both afraid to discuss our worst fears, our real thoughts. So we both cried. First I did, and then Kate joined in. I usually led the way in crying. I'd done it long before it was fashionable for men to cry. As Robin said, a good Lite beer commercial could cause me to tear up.

For once I had something real to cry about. I could see myself as a bent-over little old man shuffling around in brown imitation-leather slippers.

Oh, what happened to that poor fellow? somebody would ask.
He had a heart attack, somebody would answer.
Too bad.
Yes, too bad.
He looks vaguely familiar.
Yeah, he used to be on public television with Big Bird and all
of those animals and English people.
Oh. Are those white socks he's wearing?
Yes, I'm afraid so.
Too bad.
Grandfather Chapman and two of my uncles had died of heart
attacks. A third uncle had had one and survived. But I had never
connected any of those attacks to me directly, as being part of
what doctors call "family medical history," or even indirectly, as
a fellow human being who might want to be on the lookout for
chest pains and arm tingles.
So. In those first few hours and days it was left mostly to
my imagination to figure out what lay ahead. Most of what that
imagination could come up with were terrifyingly depressing
thoughts. I discovered it was not true what they say about a
person's whole past life flashing before him when he faces death.
It's the future, not the past, that flashes.
I was a dead man. Maybe I would live out the hour, maybe
the day or even the week or month, but it was only a matter of
time.
Poor Kate. Poor Jamie, Lucy and Amanda. They would have
to go through the agony of a funeral (keep the casket closed,
please) and then of life without me.
Money. The resale value of our house and our cars and my
shoes and shirts and socks and other worldly goods ricocheted
through my head. The bus collection. It was worth thousands.
Millions? Certainly. But to whom? Many people, thousands of
people, would come from throughout the world in their silver
jets to bid on my signs and toys and badges. An auction. Yes.
There should be an auction of the famous Jim Lehrer Bus Memorabilia Collection. Step right up!
But seriously. Would there be enough with the insurance for

Kate to see the girls through college? Insurance! How much did I have, anyhow? There was a policy I had bought in the service, and there was one in connection with AFTRA, the on-air broadcasters' union, plus another I had bought a few years back.

And then there was poor Robin. Poor Les, Linda and Dan. Poor Judy and Charlayne. Poor Al. Poor everyone at *MacNeil/Lehrer*. How could they possibly go on through journalism without me?

9

In the Ninety-eight Percent

I asked a nurse to adjust my hospital bed up to almost a sitting position. I opened a fourteen-by-twenty-inch sketchbook to its first, blank page, placed it on the portable tray table in front of me and picked up an artist's soft lead pencil and a plastic ruler.

I drew the state of Kansas, an almost perfect rectangle with its upper right-hand corner ripped off by the Missouri River. Then, underneath it, I drew a long, thin horizontal bar. And underneath that I sketched a half-circle, which I turned into half a sunflower. The state flower of Kansas, the Sunflower State. I lettered KANSAS across the bottom of the state and CENTRAL LINES in the bar beneath it. Then, with yellow and blue pencils, I filled it all in and finished it.

This was the logo of Kansas Central Lines, our late, great bus company. Dad had designed that logo himself, just as he had the bus line.

It was now the fifth morning after the heart attack. I had not been sure until now about what was going to happen next in my life. Or even whether there was going to be much of a Next.

Drawing a Kansas Central logo was my first real act of recovery. It was something real, although a bit crazy. I was no artist, of course. I had not drawn anything other than a doodle since I was nine years old.

I moved from art to making New Life lists in a small spiral notebook.

Healthy Things I Will Now Do

Never, ever smoke again
Never get angry again
Never again eat barbecue, pizza, hamburgers, french fries, chocolate fudge, Milky Ways, Butterfinger chips or Tex-Mex food
Exercise regularly and exhaustingly
Take a nap every day

Bus Signs I Will Now Go After

Overland Greyhound
Bowen Motor Coaches
Southeastern Stages
American Buslines
Dixie-Sunshine Trailways

Major Priorities I Will Now Live Every Day in Every Way

Love
Relax
Write

I had a long talk one afternoon with Dr. Kent about stress that eventually prompted another list.

Could this heart attack have been caused by stress? Could it be that I needed to get out of journalism and into something more peaceful and serene? Maybe join a monastic order? Or go back to bus-ticket-agenting?

It panicked me and scared me, and fortunately Dr. Kent saw this and helped me deal with it almost immediately. He said stress was only one of the major causes of heart attacks. Risk factors, they were called. I had all of the others, too. I smoked, I ate bad food, I did not exercise, I had some heart disease in my family.

So which, if any, actually caused my heart attack? There was no way to know for sure. But let's assume stress had something to do with it, he said. And he told me to make a list of all the things in my life that caused stress and anxiety.

Everything, Doctor?

Everything, he said.

The first entries were the easy ones:

> Riding the Eastern Shuttle to New York
> Making speeches
> Going to big cocktail parties
> Going to small cocktail parties
> Talking on the telephone
> Driving to work
> Listening to whining grown-ups

And we talked about my job. I had been in daily journalism for thirty years. What about all of those deadlines? he asked.

They are second nature to me now. Part of my life. No problem.

What about being on live television five nights a week?

It's no more stressful than any other line of work. I am aware of the potential for making an ass of myself, but it no longer causes my skin or my soul to break out in a cold sweat.

What about the people I worked with—and for?

Perfect. Absolutely the most perfect work environment possible. I told him about the unprecedented good fortune of being partners with Robert MacNeil, my best friend, a man who not only would never do anything to diminish me but went out of his way to help and enhance me. I was blessed to be exempt from the normal internal competition within television news organizations for airtime, and thus recognition, that holds friendship and trust to a minimum, and often turns normal, ordinary, nice people into abnormal, extraordinary monsters.

Pressure?

Yes, but not abnormal. The *NewsHour* change was difficult,

but nothing I was not used to. I had been involved in "new" things before. I loved it.

Competition?

Not really. We were held to a different standard because we were on public television. (MacNeil had the best line about ratings: "We pay absolutely no attention to our ratings . . . except, of course, when they're high.")

After several conversations, Dr. Kent said simply: Relax. There is absolutely no reason for you even to consider for a minute changing jobs or occupations. You are what you are. A direct quote: "I am sure that if I ordered you to go away and live on a desert island, within a week you would have organized some kind of newspaper for the natives." I did not disagree. Neither did Kate. We are what we are.

It helped. At least the idea of going back to work was viable. I did not realize that before. I know that sounds strange. But at the time, believe me, my fears of the unknown concerning heart attacks were overpowering. I had no idea what lay ahead.

Christmas came. Kate and the girls were there that morning in my hospital room. They gave me a giant puppet, which we quickly named Sammy Sue. Sammy Sue was a name I used a lot when interviewing people ("Yes, Senator, but is Sammy Sue Smith of McKinney, Texas, going to care about multiwarhead missiles if he has just been denied access to a hospital emergency room because he's poor?").

President Reagan had called me on Christmas Eve. No name-dropping intended, but he did do it. And his timing was absolutely perfect. A nurse had told me that the White House was going to be putting through a call in a couple of minutes. At that moment, Dr. Kent came in on one of his regular rounds to see me. We started talking. The phone rang. I reached for it.

"No way," said Kenny, looking distressed. "No phone calls. They should not be letting calls in here. I told them no calls."

I held up a hand. "It's all right. It's the president of the United States."

"Sure it is. No!"

I picked it up and said hello.

And then I heard the voice of Mr. Reagan.

"Hello, Mr. President. . . . Merry Christmas to you, sir. . . . I'm doing fine. Yes sir, I am." And we talked like two normal people for a good ninety seconds or so.

Kenny Kent was struck—and stuck. Was I faking this? Was he being put on? Was the president really on that phone? What in the hell was going on there?

I loved it.

And frankly, I loved it that President Reagan had called me. I know that the people in his communications office got him to do it and wrote it all out for him. So what? It was a terrific thing for him to do.

I was already being treated well there at Georgetown. But things got even better after that call from the president.

I went home a few days later with my head full of questions. They were all about what I was going to do with whatever time I had left to live. A morbid thought, sure, but one that focuses the mind.

My job was part of that. Stress and all the rest aside, did I really want to go back to journalism, to the *NewsHour*? What if I had, say, only five years to live? Would I want to spend them interviewing people on television five nights a week?

Fiction. I had to get back to my fiction. I simply had to. If it was five days, five weeks, five months, five years or twenty-five years, I had to do that. But could I do that and hold down my job? I had not been able to the last few years.

Did I want to live in Washington? What about going back to Texas? Or to Paris? Or the Fiji Islands?

Poor Kate. Now, finally, with the girls grown, she had had the time to get to her own fiction writing. She was well into a novel. Everything was clicking. Now this. Now she was going to have to take care of me. Damn, damn.

It was all in my head and in that little notebook. I left the hospital on December 28. It was five degrees, one of the coldest days Washington had had in years. But it did not matter. I was alive; I was ready to take some first steps toward real recovery. To make some real decisions and get on with it.

But it was not to be. Not quite yet.

■ ■ ■

First there was the coming of Oscar Mann, M.D. Because of his hospital and medical school responsibilities, Dr. Kent was unable to continue as my main doctor after I left the hospital. He would be available for consultations and any special problems that arose, but not as a principal private physician. Several people, primarily through Dan Werner at the office, recommended Oscar Mann. So did Kenny Kent. Oscar still is my doctor, and he always will be. Oscar, like Kenny, is the kind of physician everyone wishes for. He knows what he doesn't know, he cares, he is accessible. He even makes house calls.

But even Oscar couldn't make it be over. I started having chest pains again. At first they were small, only barely noticeable. But they were terrifying. They came when I walked downstairs from our second-floor bedroom in the morning, and when I went back upstairs in the late afternoon. For the first few days at home, that was all I was allowed to do. I was so afraid I would have another heart attack that I dreaded going back up the stairs at the end of the day.

I also had to be knocked out with a sleeping pill once I got up there and in bed. I was afraid to go to sleep, because I was afraid I would not wake up.

Some courage came after a few days. I widened the walking route to include several turns around our living room, and loops through the dining room to the kitchen and back again. And again. The chest discomfort came and went.

Finally, on about my tenth day home, Kate, who seldom left my warm side, ventured with me out of the house. I was going stir-crazy, among other things. It was still very cold, but we thought it would be terrific to walk the two blocks up to the Washington cathedral and then walk around inside. Referred to by many as National Cathedral, it is the majestic "first church" of Washington. It is here that prominent Washingtonians are formally sent to their makers, where presidents and vice-presidents go on inauguration Sundays, and where, I have been told and choose to believe, spies from the many nearby embassies and chanceries go to exchange secrets and treachery. It is my single most favorite Washington building. I defy anyone to walk in there—anyone, of any religious faith or nonfaith—and not be moved by the simple fact that human beings are able to conceive and construct things of beauty and grace. Manmade does not always have to be awful, in other words.

At any rate. We never got to the door. On the incline coming up from the street, I had those chest twinges again. We turned around and went back home. Ever so slowly.

And that evening Oscar came by to see me. He took my blood pressure and listened through his stethoscope and asked a lot of questions.

"I think we'll put you back in the hospital," he said, when it was over.

So. The next morning I was saying, Hello again, wonderful cardiac nurses and attendants and interns and residents of Georgetown University Hospital.

I was happy and relieved to be back, but there remained that nagging Hospital Reaper thing. I knew I was risking it again, but I figured, Better to die here in a hospital than going up the stairs in my own house. Or in my own bed on my own sheets.

Over the next few days, much blood was drawn, many tests were run. And finally Oscar and Kenny said I was on the verge of having another heart attack. We think you should have a bypass operation, they said. Open heart surgery, it's called.

Open heart surgery? What did you say? Open heart surgery! You mean go in there with a knife and actually cut open my heart? Like it was a can of tuna?

No, that was not what they meant. But they might as well have. I didn't know any better. I didn't know anything at all.

Again, it fell to Kate to sort it all out—to deal with the emotional trauma, hers and mine and the girls', as well as the real-world task of determining what in the hell to do. Sure, she—we—trusted Oscar and Kenny. But she quickly realized that having a bypass operation was no longer considered always the right and only thing to do.

She called Bryan Williams, an old friend in Dallas who had been my doctor years before and was now a dean at the University of Texas Southwestern Medical School in Dallas.

He was on an airplane to Washington a short time later and was soon standing at the door to my hospital room, saying, "Damn it, Lehrer, I taught you better than this."

Bryan looked at the angiogram pictures of the blocked arteries leading to my heart and talked to Oscar and to Kenny. And he took Kate to dinner and discussed the options.

He also helped her check out the designated surgeon. His name was Robert Wallace. Georgetown had hired him away from the Mayo Clinic in Minnesota, everybody said. He was top-notch, everybody said. He had a good reputation with other heart doctors, said Bryan.

The doctors who worked on my mother and father had also had terrific reputations.

Wallace came to see me. Like all surgeons, he did not travel alone. He came with an entourage of young surgeons who walked and listened in admiring proximity, like young priests around the pope (or the Cardinal of St. Louis). A man in his fifties, he had the walk and manner of somebody whose time and energy were precious, whose confidence in himself was both supreme and justified. I was certain that he would be a quarterback if he ever played football, a pitcher if he ever played baseball, a baritone soloist if he ever sang opera, a recon scout if he was ever in the Marines, the point gunman if he ever robbed banks.

"What is your win-loss record?" I asked him.

He was both annoyed and amused, but I liked him immediately and could tell he even liked me. Although maybe not so immediately. His young-surgeon admirers seemed astonished at my questioning tone. I had the feeling I was the first person ever to ask such a question of Bob Wallace.

"Generally, it's ninety-eight percent," he said.

"Ninety-eight percent of what?" I asked.

"Ninety-eight percent of all bypass operations are successful."

"Successful?"

"The patient survives the operation."

He turned to leave. I was keeping him. There were people waiting to be cut open somewhere.

"What do you mean 'generally'?"

"Of all bypass operations done in this country. It's a routine operation. Like having your tonsils out."

"This is not routine for me, sir," I said. "What is your record?"

I could tell he was not used to this, but I could also tell that he really did not mind. I had the feeling he wondered why everyone didn't ask such questions. I was certain he would be asking them if he were in my place.

"Same as that, ninety-eight percent or better," he said. "You'll live."

Yes, sir.

He gave Kate a booklet on open heart surgery for us to read. And left us to make our decision.

Despite our anguish—again, more for Kate than for me—there was really not much of a decision to make. Of course, we would do what everyone said we should do. Of course, we would let this man Wallace who had been enticed by Georgetown from the Mayo Clinic cut open my heart like a can of tuna.

No, no. It wasn't going to be like that at all. The heart wasn't opened. The chest was opened with a saw, so the surgeon could attach some veins transplanted from the leg to bypass the clogged arteries.

Right. To us, as they say in politics, it was a difference without much of a distinction. Either way it sounded terrible.

And it was.

■　■　■

I was moved to another section of the hospital. A nurse came in and terrified Kate and me with the details. Somebody would come tonight and shave off some of my bodily hairs. Somebody would come in the morning and take me away. Somebody would give me an anesthetic to put me to sleep.

After the operation, somebody would take me to a recovery room.

And on and on until I was perfect and cured.

Assuming I was still alive.

Roger Mudd and his son Daniel came by to see me. Daniel told me New Corps Marine stories. He had just spent four years as a lieutenant in the Marines, including some time in Beirut. He had gone in on his own after college, for his own reasons— he'd thought it would be a terrific experience, he'd thought his privileged education and life required him to give something back. Now he was about to go to the Kennedy School of Government at Harvard.

My three incredibly wonderful daughters hung in there with Kate and me for a long, long day of nervous talk about everything except what mattered and what was on all our minds.

Hey, kids, I love you. You are terrific. If I die, please try to keep the bus collection together. The most valuable pieces are the signs. The heavy porcelain-enamel ones. Give them to Uncle Fred.

Hey, Honey Kate, we had a great life together. With the insurance, you'll be fine. At least for a while. I hope to hell you don't have to sell the house. I love you!

I love you! I love you! I love you!

Nothing even remotely like any of this was said, of course. Why is it that at the times when large talk is required, we fall into the smallest of talk?

The big surprise for all of us came when suddenly there at the door we saw Robin and Donna MacNeil. When Kate had called them to tell them of the decision to move quickly on the operation, they'd driven from their weekend house in Connecticut to an airport and flown to Washington. They came bearing words of love, comfort and encouragement—and two Milky Way bars. Donna knew that Milky Ways were my all-time favorite food. She simply knew there was nothing I wanted more on this night. Particularly if it was going to be my last.

I did not believe for one second that I would be in the ninety-eight percent, either generally or in Wallace's league.

We Lehrers died in hospitals. They'd missed me the first time, but now they'd get me.

▪ ▪ ▪

Uncle Fred, my brother, called me from Tennessee the next morning. I was already beginning to get groggy from Valium or something. He wished me luck and said a prayer to me.

A prayer. Fred was still preaching the gospel according to Southern Baptists. He had long ago given up on making me see the same light and lights he did. It had been a hard decision, because he was so full of what he himself believed, he could not understand why his brother did not believe the same thing. I had not enjoyed the treatment, and eventually voices and emotions were raised before everything cooled down and we went about our spiritual lives, each in our own way.

But now Fred prayed for me in his own way, and that was just fine with me.

And something went wrong soon afterward that made me think Fred knew I was going to need some extra prayer this morning. My Hospital Reaper pessimism, in short, was right on target.

The main anesthesia did not work as quickly as it was supposed to, or it was given to me later than planned, or the operation began earlier than planned. Whatever, something was slightly out of whack, and I was not completely unconscious and out of it when I was wheeled into the operating room.

So. I saw bright overhead lights and heard people laughing and talking about things that made no sense. I felt darkness coming and tried to stop it all. I tried to scream: No! Wait a minute! I'm not ready yet! I'm still awake, you idiots! I'm going to die! Stop this! No! But no sound came out of my mouth.

For weeks afterward, that scene came back ever so vividly

right before I went to sleep at night. The scene included those silent shouts.

But the important thing that morning was that I *was* in the ninety-eight percent—both generally and for Dr. Wallace. I survived.

Coming awake in a cardiac recovery room was a joyful experience. I was unable to say much because of tubes down my throat, but I could see and listen as Kate and then Jamie, Lucy and Amanda and the doctors each came down into my sight and said: It worked. It worked fine. You are fine.

You look great, Daddy.

All is well, Jim.

I had escaped the Hospital Reaper again.

Except when I coughed and hiccuped, as I did a lot the first hours and days after the operation. Each time it happened, it felt like a knife—or to be more precise, a saw—was careening down my chest.

Now the real recovery finally began.

■ ■ ■

I weighed 153 pounds when I went home. That was two less than I weighed when I had gotten out of the Marines in 1959, and twenty less than when I had gone into the hospital the night of December 11.

My face was drawn and wrinkled, there were gigantic bags under my eyes. My skin was yellow from the loss of blood during the operation—a condition that in pre-AIDS days would have been routinely corrected with a blood transfusion. I looked worse than the little old man shuffling around in brown slippers and white socks. I looked like a little old man who had just been released from Devil's Island with some kind of exotic disease. Probably venereal. And then run over by a truck. Or in my special case, a bus.

Probably a Flxible Clipper.

I had a truly ugly scar down the center of my chest. It looked exactly the way a chest should look after being sawed open from just below the neck to just above the navel. There was another, less gruesome scar down the inside of my left leg from the crotch to the ankle. That was where the vein for the bypass had come from.

To one who had never before had so much as a serious cut on his body, intentionally or otherwise, it was not a pleasant sight. I assumed the worst. The scars would be red and sore and grotesque for the rest of my life. It would mean never, ever doing anything in public that required removal of any clothing. I would adopt the dress code of a monk.

I avoided looking in the mirror at any of my parts, including my face, and set about trying to do all of the right things.

There was the smoking. I really thought I could not live without smoking. I had smoked heavily for about thirty years. I had smoked my first cigarette with Willie Porter at the Victoria bus station in 1954. It was a Camel, which from that day forward I would, like the man in the commercial, gladly "walk a mile for."

I relished opening a fresh pack, tapping out a cigarette, lighting it with a Zippo, drawing in the smoke, blowing it out, mashing the butt in an ashtray or on the floor or wherever when it was finally all over. The ritual of smoking a cigarette was about the only constant one I had in my life, in fact. It was part of me and what I did.

At Missouri I'd never thrown away a cigarette butt. I'd kept them in a small shoebox so that when finances got close, as they often did, I could go back and get the last two or three puffs out of them. In the Marine Corps, I'd learned how to light and smoke a cigarette in driving rain, in hurricane-force wind, in any and all kinds of situations. Semper Fi.

For years, I had lit a cigarette the second I got up in the morning and put out the last one of the day just before putting out the light. Cigarettes went with coffee, sex and all matter of things and pleasures. I smoked between courses at restaurants, sometimes even between bites.

I followed all of the trends. I went from nonfilter Camels to Winston filters and then to True menthol filters, from regular size to king size, from soft pack to hard pack, from the real thing to low-tar-and-nicotine. And eventually I went from cigarettes to cigars, little cigars and a pipe.

Kate did not smoke, and never had. She had a ticklish nose. My smoke bothered her. So she complained about it a lot and I tried to accommodate her by smoking less around her.

Then she and the Surgeon General started the health thing. So I switched to the filters and on down the road, each time swearing that I would never again return to what I had just given up.

I lied.

It was only at home that I smoked a pipe or little cigars or whatever. I continued to smoke cigarettes at work and on all other occasions when I could sneak them.

The only times I smoked cigarettes in front of Kate were when we traveled on airplanes. She was—is—a white-knuckle fearful flyer, so I said I didn't go much for flying myself, but smoking would make it easier. It had to be cigarettes, because cigar-smoking and pipe-smoking were forbidden on planes. She bought it. The deal was always that I would quit once we landed. But I was usually able to delay the public switch back to the whatevers for a day or two.

Once the girls got old enough to know about smoking and to scream bloody murder at their father, they joined the attack. It takes supreme addiction and determination to continue to puff on a cigarette with four people crying and/or shrieking at you about dying and lungs and cancer.

I surrendered. I agreed to quit, but I never really accepted my decision as final. I assumed it was only for a short time. I put my long-term faith in the Woody Allen movie bit about the guy who came back to life after being dead (or was it frozen?) to discover that while he had been gone, scientists had concluded smoking was actually great for your health.

I quit cold turkey several times, often crumpling up a pack of cigarettes dramatically and throwing it out of a moving car, or some such thing. I always did it in front of Kate and the girls. It was a good show.

I tried nicotine gum. I even went to a hypnotist in Washington who got me off tobacco for a few months. But it eventually wore off. Nothing worked. It came back. It always came back. Probably because I never really accepted the fact that it was over.

And I simply continued to cheat and lie about it. It also created a lot more tension between Kate and me than either of us realized at the time. I always wanted a cigarette when I was around her, and she was the one who was keeping me from getting it.

At the time of my heart attack I was in a standard double-life routine—pipe at home or with the family, cigarettes everywhere else. I kept cigarettes under the seat of the car, in my office desk drawers. They were everywhere except at home.

I had smoked that pipe with a special enthusiasm on the drive to the hospital with Kate that December night. I remember wishing I had a cigarette and wondering whether there were any in the car. And did I dare reach under the seat and smoke one? Why not? This could really be it this time. Through either death or disease, I really might never, ever smoke again.

My concerns after I got home from the hospital were all false alarms. Not only did I not smoke anything, I did not want to. Not so much as once. Maybe there were two parts to the smoking addiction, one physical, the other psychological. It was several days in the hospital before I came enough to my senses even to think about something like smoking. By then the physical addiction was gone, real cold turkey. When I did think about it, I thought also of why I was in the hospital. And so the psychological addiction went away, too.

Clearly, I had happened on an easy way to quit smoking. Have a heart attack.

10

Romper Room

On Oscar Mann's orders I enrolled in the cardiac rehabilitation unit at Georgetown Hospital. Dr. Sam Fox was the man in charge. Chuck Crocker was his main assistant. Grace Hoeymans and Karen Sanders were among the others.

Every Monday, Wednesday and Friday morning at seven, I went to their basement workout room at the hospital. My pulse and weight were checked, and then for an hour or so I rode an exercise bicycle, walked on a treadmill and did other horrible, sweat-inducing things designed to rebuild the strength of my heart and body.

Work was done there also on rebuilding my soul. Two men named Harry and Charlie were in charge of that. Harry Smith, an international lawyer, and Charlie Berman, a homebuilder, were fellow patients. They, too, as we often joked, had faced down their respective makers and convinced him/her to buzz off for a while.

As we often joked. That was mostly all we did. Harry knew—knows—more obscene jokes than any man alive, or at least any man alive I have ever known about. And that includes some I came across in the Marine Corps who were world-class garbage-mouths. I have never been a big fan of that kind of humor, but I laughed like a high school sophomore at Harry's jokes and obsessions.

Charlie's specialty was morbidness. Most every twinge, ache or pain felt by any of us brought some sour crack from him about some awful certainty. A cough was always terminal lung cancer or a Far East pneumonia, which had been caused by a leaky kidney valve that could be fixed only by a transplanted liver or something-or-other. The success rate was minus two percent, and the operation would cost $125,000, none of which was ever covered by insurance. If you could even find a doctor to do it. Most of the ones who could do it were dead. Or in prison for income tax evasion. Or animal rape.

The important thing about being with Harry and Charlie those three mornings a week was that it was the only time I could say and think out loud the really grim things that were always hanging around in my head. Kate and our daughters did not need that kind of thing from me. They had enough real worries of their own. So did Robin and other friends I might otherwise have talked to.

But with Harry and Charlie and the others who came to our class, anything and everything went. We talked about weird things to do at each other's funerals, where to send various parts of our bodies for science, where to send various death-wish bombs for vengeance, how long we would be comatose before our respective wives would have the respirator turned off. We often said good-bye at the end of class with lines like, "If I make it through another day, I will see you on Wednesday." Ha, ha, ho, ho.

We also talked about stupid things we had done as kids, and about politics, journalism and baseball. Charlie had played pro ball briefly after college and had been on the roster of the Brooklyn Dodgers (my favorite team) and even gone to spring training at Vero Beach. Harry beat up on me for everything he didn't like that he read in any paper—particularly *The Washington Post*, which he loathed—or saw on any television program. I didn't mind. Nobody minded anything. We were like people who had shared a ride on the *Hindenberg*.

Chuck Crocker did his best to maintain some kind of order, but it was clear he knew the value of our talk to each other. He and Sam Fox were even occasional targets of our child's play. Sam, like Oscar and Kenny, was a real-world doctor, a man who understood the point of practicing medicine. Then in his sixties, he was in perfect physical shape, and brilliant. He knew everything about heart disease and rehabilitation, treatment and surgery, diet and exercise. To ask him a question was to get a full answer, at times, thought some, a little too full. But that was Sam. He believed in taking everyone seriously, even giggling middle-aged heart patients.

Harry, Charlie and I would occasionally say something to Sam like: "Is peanut butter good for the heart?"

And Sam would take a deep breath and respond with something like: "Well, there are four important studies extant on that, and they reveal some differences between chunky and creamy. There is the famous Hertzberg study, done in Vienna in 1949, where they took eighty-two middle-aged male mice and fed them nothing but chunky peanut butter for seven years, and another eighty-two middle-aged male mice and fed them only creamy peanut butter for seven years. The results were interesting but inconclusive. Eighteen percent in the chunky group had had heart attacks within the seven years, but only twenty-five percent of them died. While in the creamy group, sixteen percent had had heart attacks, but twenty-seven percent of them died. So does it mean chunky is worse for the heart than creamy? We simply cannot be sure. There was slightly better data gained from the Victoria College study of 1978. In that one, they gave smooth, creamy peanut butter to a family of eight left-handed monkeys. . . ."

And on and on it would go. As Charlie, Harry and I listened with fake rapt attention while walking on the treadmill or pedaling the exercise bike, trying always to keep from breaking up.

Charlie began referring to it as Romper Room, after a well-known children's television program of an earlier time. He had it about right.

■　■　■

There was the food problem. The eating thing. I had had the eating habits of a pimply-faced fifteen-year-old. My daily preferred diet was drawn from a preferred option list of Fritos, Cheez Whiz, chili, pepperoni pizza, Milky Ways, Butterfinger chips, peanut butter (chunky); hamburgers with fries, tuna-salad sandwiches with fries, bacon-lettuce-and-tomato sandwiches with fries, fried chicken with fries, barbecue ribs, beef and/or sausage with fries; Dr Peppers, chocolate chip ice cream, butter brickle ice cream, real potato chips, cottage-fried potatoes; scrambled egg with melted cheese, green peppers and onions; chocolate milk shakes, corn dogs, chili dogs; biscuits with butter, waffles with hot maple syrup and butter, pancakes with hot maple syrup and butter; salt, fudge, black coffee, and pastrami sandwiches with mayonnaise.

Ah, pastrami sandwiches with mayonnaise. If I had in fact died from that heart attack and somebody had ordered up an autopsy, I am sure the pathologist's knife would have cut into a body of ninety-eight-percent pure pastrami sandwich with mayonnaise. For reasons that I do not remember, and which probably would make no sense if I did, I started eating pastrami sandwiches with mayonnaise for lunch when *The Robert MacNeil Report* went on the air, and I had continued to do so on an almost daily basis. There was a deli kind of place near our office that supplied them, although Monica Hoose, the staff person who went after them, usually had to withstand some abuse from the deli people when ordering.

Pastrami on rye with mayonnaise. Is that what you said?

Yes, sir. It's not for me. It's for a guy in my office.

What kind of nut is he?

Your regular kind.

Somebody should tell him it's mustard that goes with pastrami. Not mayonnaise. Never mayonnaise.

I'll tell him. Thanks.

Now I had to give it up. Not just the pastrami sandwiches, but literally everything else I ate. There was nothing in my regular diet that was sanctioned for a Recovering Heart Attack Patient. I did not like or eat fruit. I did not like or eat green vegetables. I hated everything about fish, from their goggle-eyed and scaly look to their smell and their taste. Except for tunafish salad. I loved tunafish salad, most particularly the way I made it. That was with a lot of diced apple, sweet pickle, lettuce and tomato, packed and covered and owned by a smooth, creamy mixture of mayonnaise and lemon juice.

Again, as with smoking, I had no choice. Again, as with smoking, I went cold turkey from pastrami with mayo et al. to all of the good things et al.

Carrot and celery sticks with a nonfat yogurt dip. Melba toast. Vegetarian baked beans. Cute little cups of raspberries and strawberries and blueberries. Apples. Great glasses of orange juice. Decaf coffee. Water cornbread. Green beans. Peas. Peas! Spinach casseroles. Caffeine-free diet soda pop. Unbuttered, unsalted popcorn. Toasted pita bread. Oatmeal. Oatmeal!

Poor Kate had the terrible jobs of arranging for such boring food and then making damned sure I ate it.

The only good thing that happened was bread. I had always thought bread was bad for you, and so apparently did everyone else. But shortly after I started down the new roads toward the world of good eating, it was revealed in a glorious new scientific study that the carbohydrate in bread was terrific for the heart and other body parts. I did not know how many left-handed monkeys or aerobic white mice it had taken to establish such a delightful finding, but I was grateful for their sacrifice.

It gave me bread to eat, but mostly it gave me hope. Maybe there was another team of scientists in Harlingen or Brownsville, Texas, running some blind study with placebo tacos and enchiladas, who would soon report in *The New England Journal of Medicine* that Tex-Mex was better for you than celery and carrot sticks with nonfat yogurt dip.

Hope was everything.

■ ■ ■

I spent most of each day watching movies on television and reading and answering the mail. Many people, some of them complete strangers, wrote to me. They said warm and encouraging things and wished me well. I was astonished at people's concern and generosity. I could not imagine taking the time to sit down and write a letter to somebody I did not know just to say: I'm worried about you, please take care of yourself.

I started a nap routine. It was Kenny Kent who suggested it. Every day, he said. Do it. It will help you mentally as well as physically. A physical feeling of tiredness can lead to a psychic feeling of depression, he said. A smart man.

Roger Mudd came by to walk with me. He brought stories from his wars at NBC News, and books about English buses.

Other neighbors and friends dropped off other books and food and flowers.

Robin called me from New York every afternoon after my nap. *Every* afternoon. I watched the *NewsHour* every evening with much pain. I felt guilty for not being there at its time of supreme need. And the more I watched, the more aware I became of how supreme the need was. Something about it was not right. The program was not working. The mix was slightly out of kilter. It made me uneasy. It made me think about getting back to work. But Robin and I never discussed the program or any other thing serious. It was always light and personal and about me. How was I doing? Like the good boring invalid that I was, I answered by telling him in detail about my walks and my movies and my letters. And my aches and pains.

He always faked keen interest. He was my friend.

I went to work on my Bus Signs list.

"Bowen," I had written. Bowen Motor Coaches. Back in the fall, a man in Dallas who dealt in old signs had told me about a man who lived "somewhere near Jacksonville in East Texas" who had a sign from Bowen, a long-gone Texas company that had been one of the forerunners of Trailways. He refused to tell me the man's name or even exactly what town he lived in, on the grounds that he, the dealer, would work on it. He had already tried to get the man to sell the sign and he had said no.

I called the Jacksonville, Texas, Chamber of Commerce. They gave me the names of two antique dealers in the area. I called them. The second was a helpful woman who was intrigued by my basic pitch.

I am looking for a man who has an old bus depot sign from Bowen Motor Coaches.

Is he a dealer?

Probably not, but I don't know.

She gave me the name of a man who might know. He traveled around a lot looking for things like that.

Bingo. He knew exactly who the man was.

I called him. He was home. And he was stunned at the fact that a man from Washington, D.C., was on the phone asking about a bus depot sign he had hanging in his barn.

Would he sell it? I asked.

No.

Not for any price?

Try me.

I tried him.

Sold, he said.

And a week later a UPS man delivered a magnificent little red-white-and-green enameled sign. It said BOWEN across the top and BUS STATION across the bottom. In the center—I could not believe my eyes—was a Flxible Clipper. A 1939 Flxible Clipper not much different from Betsy of Kansas Central. Across its side, under the windows, were the words "Bowen Serves Texas."

It was a happy day.

I also scored on Overland. Here again, a man in Colorado had told me about a guy he knew who had a sign from the old Overland Greyhound Lines, which had run from Chicago and Kansas City west through Iowa, Nebraska and Kansas to Denver, Salt Lake City, San Francisco and Los Angeles. But the owner had not been ready to sell it when I first talked to him. I called. Now he was. The deal was made.

And in another few days, another UPS man came, with a red-white-and-blue OVERLAND ROUTE bus depot sign in the shape of the Union Pacific Railroad shield. The Union Pacific had started Overland and owned it until it was sold to Greyhound.

Two up, two down.

But it was a strike-out on the next item, Southeastern Stages, an Atlanta company that had run from there to Savannah and Charleston, South Carolina. A woman who had been the Southeastern agent in Denmark, South Carolina, had told me she had an old sign. I had located her by calling literally every agency Southeastern had on its system. I had called her repeatedly about it. She'd been too busy to talk or unable to find the sign or unwilling to part with it.

This time I said I was going to send her a check for the sign. She didn't say anything much. So I sent the check. And in a few days she sent it back. She said there had been a fire in her garage and the sign had been destroyed. I did not believe her. But I had nothing else to believe. So that was that.

And I turned my full attention to number four on the list—American Buslines.

American was one of those rare and special creatures of intercity bus travel. It had been a one-route operation that went from New York to Los Angeles, through Pittsburgh, Columbus and Indianapolis to St. Louis. There, it had picked up Highway 66 though Missouri to Springfield and Joplin and gone on to Tulsa and Oklahoma City, where it had turned straight south to Dallas. From Dallas it had gone west along Highway 80 out through El Paso to Arizona and California. American had been independent from both Trailways and Greyhound and had operated out of its own depots everywhere. And it had been independent in spirit as well. Its fares had been slightly cheaper than those of the other two companies, but it had frequently offered specials such as free pillows and meals, or penny-a-minute refunds if the bus was late. The company had gone quietly out of business and completely disappeared in the late 1950s. A drivers' strike had shut it down, and Continental Trailways took it over.

I had a American Buslines cap badge in my collection, but I had no depot sign. I was determined to find one. So I got out an old *Russell's Official National Motor Coach Guide* and started calling depots all along the old American Buslines system.

Hello, I am calling with a strange question.

Yes?

Do you happen to have or do you happen to know of anyone who has an old bus depot sign from the old American Buslines? That really *is* strange.

Well?

No.

That was how it usually went. But a woman in Big Spring, Texas, remembered one in the garage behind the depot. She went out and looked. It was gone. A man in El Paso thought he remembered seeing one hanging in an antique store. He described the store, and I located it through information. No. The store did not have one and never had had one.

Somebody told me that a restaurant in Pauls Valley, Oklahoma (on the Oklahoma City–Dallas leg), was the American depot. Might there be a sign in its basement? I phoned. No.

I must have made at least fifty calls, including several along an American spur line from Kansas City down through Springfield, Missouri, to Memphis. American had bought it from another company, Mo-Ark Trailways. Nothing. I put an advertisement in *Antique Trader*, a weekly tabloid that goes to just about everyone in the antique business in the country. Under "Miscellaneous Wanted," I advertised for an American Buslines sign, as well as one from Dixie-Sunshine Trailways, number five on my list. And I said a small prayer.

Ten days later, the mail brought a letter from an antique dealer in Nebraska City, Nebraska. A Polaroid was included. Was it . . ? Could it be . . ? Yes, yes. Yes!

It was a picture of an American Buslines bus depot sign, red, white and black. AMERICAN BUSLINES, it said. BUS DEPOT, it said. To the left was the figure of a woman in a kilt doing a Scottish dance. That had been the American Buslines symbol in the early fifties. It stood for cheap fares. (I'm sure such a thing would now be considered an ethnic slur against the Scots for their supposed parsimonious habits. Right, Mr. Robert MacNeil?)

I read the letter. The dealer had seen my ad in *Antique Trader*. Was this what I had in mind? If so, it was mine for seventy-five dollars. However. It was not the enameled metal type I lusted for (I have always lusted in particulars when it comes to bus signs). It was a small glass light-up sign. I would take what I could get. I called Nebraska City immediately.

The sign arrived a few days later. It was only twelve inches wide by eight inches tall. But it did say and show all of the right American Buslines things. And the electric part and the light worked.

I chalked it up as a semi-bingo and resolved to continue the search for the enameled metal sign.

I still had nothing working on Dixie-Sunshine. This had been one of the original Continental companies that had run all through East Texas. I had no leads, no ideas, no one even to call. The ad had brought in nothing.

But the American Buslines success had given me hope. Someday, someday, even a Dixie-Sunshine would come my way.

11

We Need You

Les Crystal took care of the Great Work Dilemma. While I was still gingerly and privately and achingly thinking about whether I would return to the *NewsHour,* and if so, when and how, Les called with a suggestion: Why not plug in by phone to our morning editorial meetings?

We need you, he said.

We need you.

Those were the magic words. Words I would commend to anyone and everyone interested in focusing the mind of a sick, worried, indecisive person.

A couple of days later, and then again every weekday morning at ten o'clock, my phone rang. Through the wizardry of a conference call, I became the third station on the daily Washington–New York meeting about what would be done on *The MacNeil/ Lehrer NewsHour* that night.

Those daily meetings were open to all members of the staff. The New York folks gathered in Robin's office, the Washington staff in mine. After a quick run-through of the news since the previous night's broadcast, all of the senior producers laid out stories they thought we should do that evening, and ways they could—and should—be done. There was also a lot of pre-meeting conversation and planning, but it was at the ten-o'clock gathering that it came together. Or at least began to.

At first, on the phone now at home, I did nothing but listen. I was reluctant to say much. I was out of it on the news, but I was even more out of it on how it should be executed. I was not comfortable suggesting things the actual doing of which would have nothing to do with me.

But I got over that. Before long I was putting in my many cents' worth, just like old times.

And I started thinking it wouldn't be too long before I might even be able to go into the office for the meetings. Still not do anything on the air, just hang around for a couple of hours in the morning and then go home at nap time.

Les, without ever saying what he was doing, had shown me the way back to work.

And I, without ever saying it, even to myself, had followed.

■　■　■

Then one Monday morning I woke up and decided I would go to the office. Unannounced and unbugled, I would just show up. Instead of doing the morning meeting by phone, there I would be, in person.

There were proper shocks all around. Not only at the fact of my being there, but at my appearance. I still looked yellow and sick and invalidy. Exactly, in fact, like the little old man in the shuffling slippers whom I feared turning into. I could avoid looking at myself, but the people in the office could not.

Gosh, you look great, Jim, they lied.

I felt strangely out of place sitting at my desk, talking on my phone, looking at the bus signs on the walls. Nobody had known I was coming. The place was a mess. There was dust on everything, as if the owners, people from far away, had been gone for the season and were not due back for months. Maybe years.

Maybe never?

We had the morning meeting. The senior producers did their respective numbers on what we should or could be doing that night. I was sitting in the seat where I had always sat. Had Judy sat in my chair when I was gone? Had a new seating routine come about in my absence? All groups of people who meet regularly eventually work out regular seats. Commuters do it on Dallas buses, New Jersey trains, Seattle ferryboats. *MacNeil/Lehrer* people do it at the morning meeting. I have seen more than one senior producer get red in the face when some visitor from the New York office, say, inadvertently took the producer's chair around the table of power.

I tried to imagine what it was like in my office, around this table, at this meeting without me.

I couldn't.

I came back the next day. And the next and the next, until it was part of my daily routine that also and always included a long nap, at least one long walk and at least one movie on television.

After a couple of weeks, I decided, again without telling anybody, to stay at the office and take my nap. There was a couch in my office that Ward Chamberlin had donated to me when he had renovated his office. I lay down on it. And soon I was fast asleep.

It was the beginning of the first good habit I had ever had.

■ ■ ■

One afternoon, the doorbell rang at home. I was ready, as I was every day, to watch the four-o'clock movie on television. But I did not watch it this day. There on the porch stood Paul Tsongas, the U.S. senator from Massachusetts. He and his wife and three daughters lived down the street. He had just been diagnosed with lymphoma, a deadly cancer of the lymph nodes. He had decided to quit the Senate and go home to Lowell, Massachusetts, to die or be cured, whichever the case turned out to be.

He told me he was out walking and had decided to stop by. Come in, I said.

We went into the living room, sat down and started talking. We talked, and even joked, about our respective states of infirmity. Who would ever have picked the two of us out of the

Grim Reaper's lineup for early demise? Why us? Neither of us had ever thought about being sick, much less being dead. People like us didn't do that kind of thing. Not now, at least. Not yet. I was forty-nine years old, he was even younger—forty-three.

We discussed priorities. However much time he had left, he did not want to spend it fighting with senators and interests over legislation that meant so little to so few. I was reminded of the story he had told me one evening at a neighborhood cookout. He and Sam Nunn, another Democratic senator, and been working for months on an amendment to a foreign aid bill, and they had been short one vote to get it to the floor. They went to a senator with a reputation for stupidity and self-adulation and asked for his vote. Yes, he replied. On one condition. That you change the name of the amendment to mine. It had been called the Nunn–Tsongas Amendment. Take your name off and put mine on, he said. Tsongas and Nunn wanted the amendment passed. So they agreed.

I could understand why he would want to go home to Lowell.

However much time I had left, I found myself saying to Tsongas, I wanted to spend it doing pretty much what I had been doing before the attack. I loved my family life and my work. I needed a few modifications and adjustments here and there, but basically it was going to be full speed ahead just at that moment. Right then, right now.

He left after an hour. I had never had a conversation with another person about death. I had never been with someone who was dying before. Not someone this young, not someone who could speak real words about it. I was shaken by the fact that he saw me as a kindred spirit. As someone who was in it with him. As someone who was also very sick.

As someone whose life was also suddenly a matter of uncertainty.

I wanted to say, No, Paul. You've got it wrong. I am not going to die. You may. But not me. No, sirree.

But as we shook hands and said good-bye at the front door, I was moved by all that we did have in common. We were both sick. We had public lives to sort out. We had great private lives, with wives and children we loved and respected to help get us through it.

There was a huge difference, though. A very serious one. In the sixty-plus minutes we'd spent together he'd gotten worse, while I'd gotten better. That was the difference between a creeping progressive disease, such as his cancer, and my heart disease, against which the body's natural healing processes were always at work.

It was definitely a difference with a distinction.

I felt so, so sorry for Paul Tsongas, the dying man, as he walked down the sidewalk. And I felt so, so happy for me, the healing man, as I waved after him.

I had it all wrong, of course. As all followers of the 1992 race for president of the United States know, not only did Paul Tsongas not die, his cancer went into remission and he came out of the whole ordeal more alive than before.

■　■　■

One morning in late March, I showed up in the office wearing a coat and tie. What's up? everyone asked. This is the night, I replied.

Robin knew it. So did Les, Linda, Dan, Charlayne and Judy, but no one else did.

And at six P.M. Eastern Time, three months after my heart attack, there I was. Robin opened the program the regular way, and instead of saying, as he had for three months, "Jim Lehrer is off tonight," he said simply, "Jim."

I went ahead and did the program the regular way, and then some sixty minutes later, at the end, said something about how terrific it was to be back, and thanked everyone who had expressed concern. And that was that.

In those first few days, I started a routine that I follow still. It is built around my nap. Kenny Kent and Oscar Mann both insisted that I keep taking one every day, even after returning to work. They said I was going to get tired faster than before. And since I had to be at my best and freshest at the end of the

day, when I went on the air, a nap made even more sense. I
found from that first day that it was easy to close the door to
my office sometime after twelve-thirty, lie down on Ward's old
couch and conk out until two o'clock or so.

I had to endure some abuse from MacNeil, Mudd and others
("When Snookums wakes up and is out of his jammies, would
you have him call me?"), but I remained steady.

From the nap rule came a no-lunch-out rule. I would never
ever again eat lunch in a restaurant. No more doing business
over the noon meal. Ever. I established a habit of eating a turkey
sandwich with mustard, lettuce and tomato in my office that was
almost as rigid as my habit of pastrami with mayo on rye had
been before.

Good habits. They were a whole new thing to me.

The fact that I had had a heart attack and might have another
one any second was always there. Always right there in the front
of my mind, all of the time. *All* of the time. Literally every
second of every minute of every waking hour.

Then, after a week or two, like a glorious gift from on high,
a few seconds would go by without my thinking about it. A
whole few seconds. Then a whole minute, then a couple of
minutes. Two whole minutes.

I remember how delighted I was to realize suddenly I had not
thought of my heart problem in almost thirty minutes. Thirty
whole minutes! One half of one entire hour!

The thoughts, when I did have them, were always about having another heart attack. A whopper. Not in the intensive care
unit of a hospital but while walking down Wisconsin Avenue.
Or typing at my word processor. Or talking on the telephone.
Or driving down Rock Creek Parkway to the office. Or munch-
ing on a carrot stick.

Or interviewing a senator on live television about the North–
South dialogue over grain credits.

I was certain that whenever or wherever it came, sudden death
would come with it. I had been lucky once. But what about
Number Two? What if it happened some evening at dinner at

DeCarlo's, our favorite restaurant? Or while I was driving along a country road in Texas? Or sitting on an airliner? Or brushing my teeth?

With a serious heart attack, you have five to ten minutes to get something going before it's too late. Five to ten minutes is not a lot of time, particularly when you are not prepared.

I would be prepared.

I never went anywhere in Washington without plotting at all times the fastest route to the emergency room and my friends at Georgetown Hospital. I never went anywhere out of Washington without casing the place for the nearest hospital. I even checked the yellow pages for cardiologists in every city and town where I stopped or spent the night.

I talked to Dan Werner about what to do at the office. Okay, if I have a heart attack and am still alive and awake, get me to Georgetown. If I have passed out or am passing out, forget Georgetown. It was at least twenty minutes away from our office, which was in the Shirlington section of Arlington, Virginia. Take me across the interstate to a closer hospital. With an ambulance, or with whatever gets me there as fast as possible.

Some of the other psychological fallouts were trivial. Before, I had been careless about fastening my seat belt in cars. Not now, no more. The idea of having my sawed-open chest thrown up against a steering wheel absolutely terrified me. I could hurt just thinking about it. And I thought about it a lot.

I also became an obsessive reader of the obituary page in *The Washington Post*. I was looking not for names of people I knew, but for those of men who had died of heart attacks. And then for how old they were. A good day for me began when all of the heart attack victims were over seventy. A bad day, and there were a lot of them, was when they were in their early fifties and had died "while at his office," "while on a vacation trip to Rome," "while walking his dog," "while eating in a downtown restaurant."

■ ■ ■

I began to think I might want to do a documentary on heart attacks. Something that would be personal but also general and informational enough to help others. I could call it something like *My Heart, Your Heart.*

Great idea, said Robin. Terrific, said Al Vecchione. Al mentioned it to Mary Delle Stelzer, who worked at AT&T. Wonderful, she said, and we'll underwrite it.

I began making some notes and putting some thoughts together, and Al started thinking about a staff to produce it. But within a few days I got cold feet. I was concerned about turning my heart attack into another career, and becoming known primarily and forevermore as That Guy on TV Who Had the Heart Attack. In short, doing a hell-and-gone television special about heart attacks hardly fit an agenda for putting it all behind me.

Then I changed my mind again, because of a conversation I had on the phone with a man who had just had a heart attack. We had been only casual acquaintances (he worked for one of the networks), but he was desperate for some information. He threw question after question at me.

Why did I have a bypass instead of angioplasty?

Was I scared of having another heart attack?

Did I still eat Tex-Mex food?

Did I have nightmares?

Did I wake up crying?

What was my LDL cholesterol count?

Why did I decide to go back to work?

What about eggs?

What kind of running shoes did I wear?

As he talked—and as I talked over the next few weeks to Charlie, Harry and others at Romper Room—I realized another basic truth about people like me: The best information and advice on how to learn to live with the experience of a heart attack came from those who had been through it themselves. Doctors, particularly good doctors like mine, had their crucial roles to play. But so did real people who had woken up one morning with a tightness in their chest and not known what in the hell to do about it. I decided, too, that if I handed out the right preventive information I might even be able to help somebody avoid those pains and all that went with them.

So. In a few weeks I was at work on the documentary with Larry Pomeroy, a friend and former CBS producer with whom I had worked before on a public television project. Larry and I both did the writing: I did all of the personal things involving me, and Larry did the bulk of the rest, on the basis of general research on heart disease he and his team had done.

The resulting one-hour program was broadcast on PBS the evening of February 27, 1985. It opened with the sound and image of an ambulance screeching through traffic on a rainy night. Then my voice came on to say: "I had a heart attack and a double bypass operation. My name is Jim Lehrer, and over the next hour I will tell you about my experience and what I've learned since about heart disease—why it kills more of us than any other disease, and what you and I and medical science can do about it."

After some opening credits, I appeared on screen sitting on the side of a bed in the coronary care unit at Georgetown Hospital. For the next hour, my story was woven through and around a lot of straight information. And it ended with me in Romper Room saying to the camera:

"I feel better now than I did before my heart attack. I have more energy and more stamina, my brain seems to work even better now than before. Why? I don't know for sure. Maybe I was in a decline before the attack. Maybe not getting good blood circulation or something. Maybe it's because I no longer smoke and eat bad food and do all of my exercising in a chair with my feet on a desk. Maybe it's because of the bypass. Maybe it's because I'm working at combatting stress and conquering some of those items called Type A behavior. I don't know. But there's one thing I do know: It wasn't worth it. It wasn't worth having a heart attack and open heart surgery and all the rest, even to feel this good. My doctor said I might not have survived that attack if I had not been in a hospital intensive care unit when it happened, and it is likely the damage would have been worse if I had survived. If I knew then what I know now, of course, I would have gone to the hospital sooner that December day. Of course, I would have stopped smoking and junk-eating and started exercising sooner. Of course, of course—there are all kinds of things I would have done differently if only I had known.

"The reason for this program was to pass on what I know now, hopefully before 'then' comes for you or someone you care about. I'm Jim Lehrer. Thank you."

I had never been one to doubt or belittle or even question the power of television. But if I had been so inclined, the response to *My Heart, Your Heart* would have forever put it to rest.

Hundreds of people rose from in front of their television sets and did good things after watching that one hour. They quit smoking or started jogging or threw away greasy foods. Or they went in for physicals and stress tests.

Some actually had their lives saved. I heard from several people who said they had felt a twitch and a dry tightness or something similar in their chest, and because they had seen *My Heart, Your Heart*, they had gone quickly to a hospital.

The most stunning story was told to me by a woman in Washington. She came up to me at a high school lacrosse game, introduced herself and said I had saved the life of a woman in her office.

"She had had chest pains off and on for several weeks," said the woman. "But she had never done anything about it until one morning a few weeks ago. It happened again, and this time she came over to my desk and said: 'I'm having those chest pains again. That man Lehrer on public television said not to fool around. Would you drive me to the hospital?'

"I drove her over to Georgetown. She got to the door of the emergency room and had a full-scale heart attack. She collapsed right there in front of me and everybody.

"She survived. And the doctors said she did with about four or five minutes to spare."

I have spent thousands of hours on television doing various things and will spend thousands more before I sleep. But it is certain that I have never done and will never do anything on television with the importance or impact of *My Heart, Your Heart*. I am grateful to all who worked with me and supported me in doing it.

12

Risks

A few weeks before my heart attack, I had been given an offer I could not refuse. Vassar College, Class of 1984, had invited me to be the speaker at its May commencement. The special thing about that class was Jamie Lehrer, one of the graduating seniors. Our Jamie. So certainly I would make the speech. I would do so with pleasure and with humility, I wrote back to Vassar President Virginia Smith. I did not say I would do so also with absolute fear and petrification. There are fewer things more difficult than making a commencement address. Having a child in the audience and graduating class raises the difficulty two or three powers. Minimum.

It wasn't until late February, after I had returned to work, that I remembered that May commitment. The last thing I wanted to do was write and deliver a speech of any kind, much less one as important and perilous as a commencement address to a class to which one of my very own belonged. There is simply no way for any child of any commencement speaker to do anything but sit in frozen fear while a parent makes a commencement speech. What if nobody laughs at the jokes? What if everybody does laugh—but at the wrong places? From the parent/speaker's point of view, the potential for grief and destruction is enormous. Nothing could be worse than being a cause of embarrassment to your child on graduation day—one of the most important days of your child's life.

So. Why not duck it? Making formal speeches was one of the things on the new No, Never list, and there was no question in my mind that Jamie and President Smith and all other interested parties would understand if I said, Well, you know, with the heart attack and everything maybe it would be better if, well, you know . . . And then they would finish the sentence by saying something like, I understand. Certainly, Daddy. Certainly, Mr. Lehrer. You are off the hook. Next time.

But. There would be no next time for Jamie. And I was determined not to let the heart attack get in the way of the things I wanted to do. That was the whole point of the new list. Eliminate all of the things I did not want to do, in order to have time for the things I wanted to do.

I made the speech. And I am glad I did. It was a gorgeous day in Poughkeepsie that May 20. The students and their parents and other family and friends received what I had to say about as well as could be expected for any commencement address. I have always believed that the most irrelevant person at any graduation is, in fact, the speaker. Few people in the audience come to hear the speech, and even fewer will remember anything that is said. Everyone's attention—correctly—is on the individual graduate each attendee has come to cheer and choke up over. The graduates themselves are understandably wrapped up in the real business of the day, their being graduated and sent off to the cold world of work or graduate school or whatever. I have been to countless—hundreds, maybe thousands—of graduations of various kinds through the years. I do not remember a single word spoken by any of the commencement speakers, or even what any of them looked like, mostly.

That is not completely accurate. I do remember one commencement vividly. Back in Dallas, Lucy, then four years old, graduated from a day school run by the Dallas Health and Science Museum. The commencement was held in a classroom one morning. The speaker was some poor guy connected with the museum. He had decided to give the graduates and their parents a small lesson on the solar system or some such, and he spoke from a lectern on a small platform. The twenty or so beloved graduates were assembled in chairs behind him. He had barely started talking, when the kids began to wave to their parents out in the audience. At first, none of us would wave back. We all frowned in disapproval. But before long a father, and then a mother, returned the wave, and soon we all were waving adoringly at our marvelous children. The poor speaker was forgotten, and it wasn't long before he figured it out and wound down his explanation of why Mars is farther from the sun than Earth is, or whatever. And we got on to the serious business of the morning: the handing out of diplomas and a short production of *Little Red Riding Hood*. The latter was a particular highlight for us, because Lucy played the title role.

But back to Vassar. There was one additional problem I've forgotten to mention: Meryl Streep, a Vassar graduate, had been the commencement speaker the year before. As I noted right at the beginning of my speech, I was aware that the members of the Class of '84 might very well be saying to themselves at that moment: "If I had been born a year earlier, I would be listening to and watching Meryl Streep right now, instead of this boring guy from boring public television."

But a terrific thing happened as a result of my speech. My main pitch and advice was to take risks. I'd put it in the speech at Kate's suggestion. After I had finished writing a draft, I'd read it out loud to her. She'd said all of the right things, but then said maybe it needed a bit more "body"—a euphemism for "substance."

Like what? I asked, about two-thirds annoyed.

Like telling them what you really believe about risk-taking, she said.

So I did. I told the graduates that to search for a safe place is to search for an end to a rainbow they will hate once they find it. I urged them to put their mind and their spirit, their money and their energy, their stomach and their emotions on the line. To do otherwise, said the wise old man at the lectern, is to live no life at all.

I even recounted two examples from my own life: how I had walked out of *The Dallas Morning News* when it wouldn't run my civil defense series, although Kate and I had no money, and a baby on the way; and how Robin and I had decided to take *The MacNeil-Lehrer Report* to an hour. I did not want the Class of '84 then, nor do I want anyone now, to think I believed these events to be of a heroic nature. I do not. But I do believe—as I told these graduates and as I have told anyone who would listen ever since—that the soul needs risk-taking in order to grow and flourish. And that applies to personal relationships as much as the workplace. The world is full of people—I know plenty of them personally—who have spent their lives standing away, keeping others away, protecting themselves from emotional commitments. They do it in the mistaken belief that to expose the nerves and the soul is to risk being hurt. And who needs that?

I believe that being hurt is a healthy by-product of risk and commitment. Traveling through emotional peaks and valleys, hilarious laughing and hell-and-gone sobbing, is what humans do. It is also all right to yell and scream a little bit from time to time. It's a sign that we care enough about another person, a conviction or anything when we draw real, gut-wrenching spiritual blood.

So that's pretty much what I told Jamie and the other graduates, and my fellow parents and loved ones, that May morning in the sunshine at Poughkeepsie. I finished by telling them that I knew none of them would ever remember a thing I'd said, but that was okay. I understood. And that was that. Thanks to Kate, I had delivered a message that meant something, to me at least. Who can ask for anything more than that?

The story is not over.

Late one night a few months later, the telephone rang at our home in Washington.

"Is this the Mr. Lehrer on television?" said a young male voice.

Half awake, I muttered yes. I assumed the worst. A guy in Pomona or someplace else in California, probably drunk, who thought it was only nine o'clock, calling to tell me how lousy I or some guest on our program had been. Or to offer his services as a guest or an essayist. Or to make a suggestion about a story we should cover. Probably in Central America.

"I was in that graduating class at Vassar," said the young man.

How nice.

"You remember what you said about taking risks, sir?"

Umm-huh.

"Well, sir, I had taken a job with a Wall Street brokerage firm and was supposed to go to work on that next Monday in New York."

Mmmmmm.

"But I really didn't want to do that. I really didn't. I had a business idea of my own I wanted to try. Some other guys and I. So I listened to what you said. And I thought to myself: Why not scrub the New York job and do my own thing? So I did. Sitting right there listening to you, I decided. I told my folks right after the procession what I had decided. . . ."

I was now completely awake.

"They thought I was crazy, and they were a little upset. But I told them I was going to follow Mr. Lehrer's advice."

Oh my God!

"I did, and it worked, and that is why I'm calling you."

"What happened?" He had my full attention.

"I went into the business of making a special kind of sunglasses rim. They're made of clear hard plastic tubing. And you can change the colors with tiny colored BBs that can be dropped into the rims. So if you want pink one day, you fill the rims with pink BBs. If you feel like blue, put in blue. There can be combinations, like red, white and blue for the Fourth of July."

"It's working?"

"Yes, sir. That's why I'm calling you. We're going to be on *The CBS Morning News* tomorrow, talking about them. I owe it all to you, Mr. Lehrer, and I wanted you to know."

I accepted his appreciation. Especially since I had already started taking some new risks in my own life, this time in my writing.

Writing. Another major item on the list.

■ ■ ■

I had not been doing very well with the writing before my heart attack. I hadn't done very well with it since *Viva Max!*, to tell the truth. *Newsroom*, then PBS, then NPACT, and then *MacNeil/Lehrer* had sapped my energy, psychic as well as physical. So had the business of being a husband, father and normal person outside and beyond my work. There simply was not enough left in me to write—at least to write anything that amounted to anything. This could all be a giant rationalization, of course.

What is incontrovertible is that what I wrote was terrible.

Immediately after the glow of *Viva Max!*, I wrote a novel about a preacher who tried to shut down a house of prostitution operating in his small Texas town. My brother, Fred, then a real-life Baptist preacher in the real Texas town of Schulenberg, west of Houston on U.S. Highway 90, had told me about a real house of prostitution in the neighboring town of La Grange. It was called the Chicken Ranch. In my story, it was the Chicken Coop, which was also the title of the novel. If it all sounds familiar, it's probably because of the world-famous musical and movie, *The Best Little Whorehouse in Texas*. They were the creation of my good and dear friend from Texas, Larry L. King. There was absolutely no connection between what I did in 1970 and what he did a number of years later. In fact, unless he reads this book (the one you are reading now), he will never know about it. I have never told him that I, too, tried to do something about the Chicken Ranch but could not bring it off. He lives five blocks from me in Washington, and we see each other quite a bit. Maybe someday I'll embarrass myself by telling him.

Hey, Larry. You remember that whorehouse story you wrote?

Sure. It changed my life.

Well, I wrote one about the same whorehouse before you did.

What happened to it?

Nothing.

That's too bad.

Thanks, Larry.

I also wrote one called *Revolution Man,* about a CIA man who between assignments lived under deep cover on the beautiful beaches of Padre Island, in the Gulf south of Corpus Christi. His assignments involved going to foreign countries and overthrowing their governments. I was still very much a pure-boonie Dallas reporter at the time. I have no idea where the idea came from or how I thought I knew enough to write such a thing.

Next, a political book. I divided Texas into five states, in accordance with an agreement worked out around the time Texas had become a state in 1845. The idea of five Texases, with ten senators, five state legislatures and five of everything else, good and evil, appealed to me. I can't even remember what the specific story line was or who the central characters were.

Then I did a novel about the perfect church. It was a glass skyscraper in the shape of a cross. It had its own football and baseball teams and publishing company and golf course and tennis courts.

None of these novels was published. None of them even drew any real interest from anybody who might have published them. Later, in the early days of *MacNeil/Lehrer,* I updated the glass-church idea by superimposing a newspaperman hero on it. It didn't work, either. After that, I drafted a sixty-page proposal for a novel-dash-movie about a national television correspondent who makes up a story in order to confess all later, and thus establish himself as a celebrity villain, à la boys of Watergate, who wrote books and went on the lecture circuit to confess their sins in the name of God, repentance and cash. Nobody was interested in publishing that novel, either.

I did finally write a book that was published, by Atheneum in 1975. It was nonfiction, the story of the one year of Kansas Central Lines. It was titled *We Were Dreamers.*

Now that I was at home and recovering from the heart attack, the time had come to try fiction again. It was one of those burning things about which I ended up having little choice. Back in that hospital room, when I had begun thinking about what lay before me, "Write" had been on the most important of the lists. And it was there to stay—at least until I proved once and for all that I did not have what it took to be more than a one-novel writer. And that one novel a book that mostly only Peter Ustinov and I knew about. And he didn't much care.

But even just the idea of starting a novel made me tired. A. C. Greene had made me such a nonbeliever in short stories that they seemed out, too.

Once again, it was Kate to the rescue.

Why not write a play? she said.

Fine. The only problem is, I don't know how. I haven't even thought about writing plays since college.

Learn, she said.

Learn, I said.

And set out to do so by reading every play I could find to read, and attending performances of every play I could find to attend.

Before long, I had an idea for one I might write. How about something set in a bus depot in South Texas in the fifties? The main characters could be a young white ticket agent, his girl-friend, a redneck terminal manager and a older black porter.

It would be about friendship, love and life in a bus depot.

What a terrific idea!

■ ■ ■

I called the play *Silversides Thruliner*, as in, "May I have your attention, please? This is your first call for Continental Trail-ways Air-Conditioned Silversides Thruliner to Houston and Dallas . . ."

It required a simple set that included the ticket counter, a few unkempt black vinyl waiting room chairs and two water fountains, one marked "White," the other "Colored." The main character was a kid named Bobby Earle Masterson. He was a ticket agent, but he wanted to be a newspaperman and writer like Robert Ruark, whose column he read regularly in the local

newspaper. He was going to junior college in the daytime and
working at the bus station at night. The other characters were
Honey, his girlfriend, who worked in a nearby bank; Harold,
the depot manager; and Willie, the porter. There was also Sleeping Man, who mostly slept in one of the vinyl chairs, because
he could never get up his courage actually to get on a bus, and
a bus driver named Ice Cream, so named because ice cream was
all he ate.

The play opens with Bobby Earle calling a bus on the PA
system. It closes the same way. In between there are ninety or
so minutes of pure dramatic dynamite. Will Harold fire Willie
for tearing down the "Colored" sign over the water fountain after
hearing news of the *Brown v. Board of Education* school deseg-
regation decision? Can Bobby Earle persuade Harold, a genuine
but well-meaning 1954 redneck, to change his mind? Will Bobby
Earle go away to the University of Missouri to become Robert
Ruark? Will Honey go with him? Or will they both stay right
there in their small Texas town and live their lives happily ever
after as man and wife, ticket agent and bank teller? Will Sleeping
Man ever get on the bus? Will Ice Cream ever eat anything
besides ice cream? Whew!

Roger Mudd and his wife, E.J., came over to our house one
evening for a reading. We split up the parts—I played Bobby
Earle—and read it out loud. E.J. said there were too many "god-
damns" in it, but otherwise she thought it was terrific. So did
Roger and Kate. So did Robin, who had written plays seriously
before going into journalism, and a New York actor friend, Dion
Anderson. So, of course, did I.

Through my friend Jim Griffin at the William Morris Agency,
a reading with real actors was arranged at the Manhattan Theatre
Club in New York City. The actors did a terrific job, but the
real hero was a young woman from the theater's front-office staff
who sat in the audience and laughed at every line. *Every* line. I
wanted to purchase her and take her with me to all things I did
from that point on in my life.

I quickly wrote another play, *Cedar Chest*. It was based on a real letter I had received out of the blue from a woman in Sedg-wick, a small town in Kansas where we had lived during the early days of Kansas Central. She said my mother had left a cedar chest with her when we had left town in 1947, and now there was a dispute between her and a neighbor over ownership of that cedar chest. It got me thinking, and soon I made up a story about two elderly ladies in a small town in Kansas. One of them is giving up her drugstore and moving to a nursing home, and has decided before she leaves to take revenge on the other lady, her best friend since childhood, and anyone else in the town who wronged her during her life. The central dispute re-volves around who is the rightful owner of a cedar chest. I won't ruin the excitement by telling any more, but it does not give away too much to say that there is also a character named Smithy who comes in and out of the drugstore throughout the play, and always says weird things, followed by "if you know what I mean."

For instance:

"You can't see your shadow for the trees out there this morn-ing, if you know what I mean."

"What America sings, it don't always see, if you know what I mean."

"Haven't you got to go to neutral before you go to reverse? If you know what I mean."

In the final line of the play, one of the ladies even picks up the habit. She says: "There's no telling a dime from a nickel in a popcorn bag after a tornado comes and goes, if you know what I mean."

Well, *I* knew what I meant. I was so exhilarated that I im-mediately wrote another play, without even waiting for reaction on the first one. It was entitled *The Defections of Andrei Gromyko*, and was about Gromyko, then the foreign minister of the Soviet Union, defecting to the West because he had a failing heart and needed one of those mechanical hearts that were going around at that time, particularly in Louisville, Kentucky. By the end of the play—five years later—Gromyko is sitting in a chair, his body attached to noisy machines, with piles of videocassettes all around. With him are a former Soviet ambassador to the United States and a CIA agent, and they have run out of movies. They are watching *Bus Stop* for the tenth time. What are they going to do? Oh, now there was a cliff-hanger if I ever saw one.

Two William Morris playwright agents sent the plays around to theaters all over the country . . . and around. No one was interested. After a while, I had trouble getting the agents on the phone. They became increasingly low-key and quick to hang up when I got through.

Eventually, the word came to me from my very sad friend Jim Griffin that the two agents thought I was writing too much, too fast and not well enough. What? The story of two high-level Soviet defectors watching *Bus Stop* not good enough? A fight between two little old ladies over a cedar chest not good enough? The dilemmas of the people in a small Texas bus depot in 1954 not good enough?

Why in the hell didn't they tell *me*? I asked Jim.

They were afraid it might give you another heart attack, he replied.

It was the first time I had heard such a thing. And it startled me. Was that going to be my new identity, my treatment now and forevermore?

Lehrer did a lousy interview with Secretary Weinberger.

Yeah, but we can't tell him.

I know.

It would give him another heart attack.

Right.

He's also four years behind on his Exxon bill.

Yeah, but we can't tell him.

I know.

It would give him another heart attack.

And somebody just stole his car.

Yeah, but we can't tell him. . . .

What I said to Jim Griffin about those two agents is Marine Corps unprintable. But it made me even more determined to be a playwright. Or something like that.

■ ■ ■

It was a stop at a Dairy Queen in East Texas that began to make that a real possibility.

Between the 1984 Democratic National Convention in San Francisco and the Republican in Dallas, I took a week off from work. It turned out to be one of the most important weeks of my post–heart attack life. Post–heart attack life. That is a difficult phrase, because it means the rest of my life.

At any rate. Much of that week off was spent in North Texas, where Kate was tending to her mother, who was ill. As a form of relaxation and release—escape, too, I am sure—I drove off one morning, to wander for a couple of days. I headed east from McKinney, Kate's hometown, to Greenville and other places in East Texas, with no particular destination in mind.

I was driving down U.S. Highway 69 between Greenville and Mineola, when I decided I wanted a cup of coffee, so I pulled into a Dairy Queen on the highway outside Emory, a town of a thousand. In many small towns throughout Texas, Oklahoma, Kansas, and I assume elsewhere, Dairy Queens have replaced the small drugstore lunch counters as the place to eat, meet and talk.

I asked for my coffee to go. As I was waiting for a waitress to pour it, I heard a male voice next to me say: "I gave you a twenty-dollar bill."

"No, you didn't," said a female voice. "It was a ten."

The waitress was a woman in her late forties, all dressed up in a Dairy Queen uniform. The customer was a man of twenty-five or so. His hair was long and dirty, as were his blue jeans and leather jacket.

"I know it was a twenty," he said. "That was all I had."

"It was a ten," said the waitress.

"It was not!"

"It sure was!"

The guy slammed his fist down on the counter. "I want my twenty-dollar bill!"

"Well, you ain't getting it!"

"I ain't leaving here till I do!"

My waitress brought me my coffee. I paid for it with exact change and got out of there.

It was only after I was almost to Mineola, twenty miles away, that I started the what-ifs. What if neither backed down? What if it turned violent? What if the police were called? What if some shots were fired? What if this, what if that?

I turned the car around and drove back to Emory and the Dairy Queen. I was prepared to drive up on anything. A bombed-out shell. A police-hostage standoff. National Guardsmen at the ready. Ambulances and police cars. Action Central Radio News reporters on the scene.

Nothing was happening. I went inside. There had been a shift change. Two other waitresses were now on duty. There was no sign of the young man, and no sign of a struggle or anything violent.

So I left, and was left with my imagination.

The play I wrote after this brush with real real-life was called *Dairy Queen*, and it ended up being the first play of mine to be produced. But by then it was called *Chili Queen*. I had to change the title, because a Chicago lawyer for Dairy Queen wrote me a letter threatening to sue me if I did not. It was one of those unreal-world letters that help give lawyers a bad name. I wrote the guy back and said so. But it was a blessing, because in changing the title to *Chili Queen*, I brought a lot of good chili-related things to the play.

On November 15, 1986, *Chili Queen* opened in New York at Hartley House on West Forty-sixth Street, very near Broadway physically, but way, way off it otherwise. Hartley House was an old settlement house with an auditorium that seated 150 people on folding chairs. The production was by Playwrights Preview Productions, a nonprofit organization of actors and directors founded and run by a marvelous woman named Frances Hill. With Frances directing, and a cast of terrific actors working for nothing on their own time, we workshopped and sweated over that play for eight months before it was done for real. *The New York Times* gave it a favorable review, and we all thought we were onto something—and somewhere.

Washington, D.C., was our first destination. Roger Stevens, the head man at the John F. Kennedy Center for the Performing Arts, came to a staged reading of the play at a small theater in Washington, and put it in the Terrace Theater at the Kennedy Center for a four-week run in the summer of 1987. Frances was already working on a plan to bring it back to New York off-Broadway after that. Real off-Broadway!

It did not happen. The *Washington Post* reviewer trashed us, all of us. The play, the directing, the acting, and me in particular, for even thinking a TV anchorman could write a play. All future plans for the play went down the tubes. It has not been produced since, and probably never will be. It was a devastating experience in every way. The scars are as deep inside me as those down the outside of my chest.

I was saved from myself and my self-pity by the Sundance Institute's playwrights' workshop, and by Eudora Welty and Jane Reid-Petty. If it had not been for Sundance and those two ladies of Jackson, Mississippi, I am sure I would never, ever have gone to another play, much less tried to write one.

I had already made the commitment to go to Sundance, outside Salt Lake City, in July, to workshop a play called *The Great Man*. I left Washington two days after the *Post*'s crush and spent seven good days with actors and directors and others in the theater. I told them what had just happened to me, and they did their best to help me get through it. Thank God I had Sundance as a place to go.

Meanwhile, Jane Reid-Petty was running a professional theater in Jackson, the New Stage. She was also its leading director and actress, as well as a close friend of the city's leading lady, Eudora Welty. I had met Miss Welty a few years before, through our shared friend and literary agent Timothy Seldes, and had discovered to my delight that she was a devout viewer of *The MacNeil/Lehrer NewsHour*.

I'll never forget the excitement Robin and I bathed and floated in when I told him.

If Eudora Welty watches, that means we must be doing something right, said Robin.

Miss Welty, a member of the New Stage board and the namesake of its Eudora Welty New Playwrights program, told Jane I was writing plays. Jane called me and asked me to send her some. I did, and she staged readings of none other than *Silversides Thruliner* and *Cedar Chest*. Afterward, I sent her a brand-new one, *Church Key Charlie Blue*, which was about a down-and-out former pro football player dropping in on a group of men watching a Monday Night Football game in a bar in a small East Texas town.

Jane liked the play, and a deal was struck to stage it in January 1988. All of that had been set before the *Chili Queen* tragedy, and it was there to do when I finally stuck my head and soul out of the wreckage.

The reviewer for the Jackson *Clarion-Ledger* did not give the production a terrific notice, but that did not matter. It was a great experience in every possible way for me.

I spent two weeks in Jackson for the rehearsals, most of the day with Miss Welty, whom I now called Eudora with all of the love and friendship I could muster, sitting by my side. In the evening, she and Jane and I would have dinner, usually at a Greek restaurant that she liked very much.

I began to consider every minute I spent with Eudora a special minute in my life. I never tired of listening to her talk about literature, her life in Mississippi and elsewhere, or anything else. She brought warmth and perception to every topic, every thought, every sentence. *Genius* is a word soiled and ruined by misuse, but it is no misuse of it when I say she is one, without question. And she's definitely the only genius I have ever known well enough to call by her first name.

No matter what happens, I will always look back on the time I spent with Eudora Welty as the highlight of my checkered life as a playwright. No reviewer's whacks can ever take those away

from me or make me regret having followed up on Kate's line:
Why not write a play?

That experience also highlighted how fortunate I was to work
with a man named Robert MacNeil.

President Reagan ordered a bombing strike against Libya
while I was in Jackson the first time. I called Robin in New
York.

"I guess I should come back and do the program tonight," I
said, after some preliminary talk. "It's an awfully big story."

"Let's think about that for a moment," said my friend. "How
many people are there out there who can come on television
and deal with the American bombing of Libya?"

"Oh, ten thousand or more, probably."

"How many people can sit in a theater with Eudora Welty
while their play is being developed?"

"I think I'll stay here," I said.

"Only a fool would do otherwise, my friend," said my friend
Robert MacNeil.

That evening, Eudora went home from the theater early. "I'll
watch the program for you," she said, "and give you a full report
at dinner."

At the Greek restaurant two hours later, speaking from
notes, Eudora gave me a rundown on what had happened on
MacNeil/Lehrer. Her report included not only the substance of
what had been said by the deputy secretary of state and others,
but also minute and original descriptions of their style, tone and
body language.

"Robin, I could tell, seemed most uneasy at some of the answers," she said.

"What did he say?" I asked.

"He did not say anything," she replied. "But I could tell."

I was sure she could. I was sure she could tell most anything.

■ ■ ■

Meanwhile, The One-Eyed Mack had also come into my life.
Mack is the hero of five novels I have written. Twenty, possibly
even thirty, more are yet to come. He is now the lieutenant

governor of Oklahoma, but when he started he was a nobody kid in Kansas.

Mack was born during the Fourth of July holiday of 1985. Robin was on vacation that weekend, and I went to New York to coanchor the program so I could go to a reunion of my dad's family across the river in New Jersey. Jamie and Lucy were away, but Kate and Amanda were there for the reunion. The Fourth itself fell on a weekday, which meant there was a program to do. But a major discussion had already been taped and it was a dead news day, so there was very little for me to do to get ready for the broadcast.

I was in Robin's office on West Fifty-eighth Street, sitting at his desk in front of his office computer. Why not play around with something?

For reasons I cannot explain, I started thinking about somebody who had had an eye torn out by a can. A can that had been kicked in a kick-the-can game. A boy. In his teens.

I began writing in the first person. The kid is outside watching some smaller kids play the game. Suddenly the can is kicked. It flies up toward him. He ducks. Too late. It hits him in the left eye.

Where is he? Why not a small town in Kansas?

The next thing he knows, he's at a hospital. His father is there. His father? What does he do? A Kansas highway patrolman. A trooper. The kid, who is sixteen and a half, has dreamed of someday growing up to be a trooper like his dad.

It is his only serious dream. The Trooper Dream.

Now his dad tells him, "It takes two eyes to be a state trooper, son."

That is one more than our hero now has.

What will he do with his life now?

That was about where I ended it. But what was it? I was still writing only plays, mostly the kind that nobody wanted to produce. Maybe this one-eyed kid could be in a new play. Maybe what I had just written could be a monologue of some kind in that play.

I took what I had written back to the hotel that night and asked Kate to read it. It was only three or four manuscript pages.

She pronounced it terrific and said, Keep going.

Going where?

Wherever it leads.

A play? A short story?

Whatever. Enjoy yourself.

So I kept going. The kid puts a black eyepatch on his left eye and tries to go on with his life. He loves the patch, but his dad thinks an artificial eye would be better. The kid goes to the local junior college and then gets ready to go to work. Where? Why not at the bus station? Yes. He has always been fascinated by buses. And while with just one eye he cannot be a bus driver, he can certainly be a ticket agent.

The depot manager will not hire him. The kid is sure it is only because he has just one eye. He is the victim of discrimination.

So what is there in the world for a one-eyed kid to do? Be a pirate. One day he hops the Santa Fe doodlebug train, throws away his false eye and replaces it with the black patch, and heads south for Galveston, Texas, a place the town librarian had told him was on the Gulf of Mexico, a kind of ocean.

On the train, he meets up with a small-in-stature small-time hood named Pepper. Pepper asks the kid what his name is. What is his name?

Mack.

Mac?

Mack as in truck. M-A-C-K. I'm The One-Eyed Mack.

I had by now decided it would be a long short story. Maybe a novel.

Mack and Pepper become friends and traveling companions. They have many adventures, several involving buses. While Pepper sleeps, Mack is brought to a sexual climax on a bus between Galveston and Beaumont by a prostitute named Lillian. Later Mack and Pepper steal a bus from a depot parking lot and end up in a small town in Oklahoma I christened Adabel.

I titled the book *Kick the Can,* and with hardly a breath went on to the next. It was *Crown Oklahoma,* and was about how Mack married Pepper's widow—Pepper had joined the Marines and been killed in Korea—and then found himself elected lieutenant governor of his adopted state, almost by accident, and had to thwart the evil deeds of a national television news correspondent who made up a terribly negative story involving Oklahoma.

The Sooner Spy was next—I had always wanted to write a spy novel, though this one hardly qualified—and involved such characters as a Russian spy who lived in Oklahoma but did not spy anymore, and a young man who said he had been inspired by a commencement address Mack had made at a small state college in southeastern Oklahoma. The address had been about taking risks.

Lost and Found featured five former Marine lieutenants who served together on Okinawa in an outfit they called the One-Nine; now, thirty years later, each for a different reason has decided to run away and try to recapture the magic of those days. Mack must track them down, while simultaneously attempting to solve the mystery of a Continental Trailways Silver Eagle bus that has crashed through a railing on a bridge over the Red River, killing twenty-seven people, including the driver.

Finally (so far), Mack book number five, *Short List,* chronicles Mack's adventures as he suddenly finds himself on the Short List to be the Democratic nominee for vice-president of the United States. How he got on the list, and what happens then, is what the book is about, and I drew heavily on my experience covering national politics to write it. I have drawn heavily on my experience in writing all of the Mack books.

That, of course, would be obvious to anyone who has paid attention reading this book—the one you are reading now. Buses, always buses. And usually Marines and the press. But I also found a way to use my Vassar commencement address. In fact, I have Mack say word for word some of the things about taking risks that I said to Jamie's class. (No, it is not plagiarism if the material stolen was originally written by the thief himself.) I thoroughly enjoy writing about Mack. He takes me back to where I have been and allows me to tinker and imagine and feel good about my life in ways I never thought possible. Writing will always be a scratch-and-worry endeavor for me, but Mack has brought pleasure to it.

I cannot imagine these recovery years without him.

It is probably not a stretch to suggest that creating a character with a physical infirmity grew out of my heart attack. My own resolve to go on, to hang tough, to take some new risks, was in my mind as I wrote about this kid trying to find a life with only one eye.

I know for a fact that my growing annoyance with a system of journalism that could permit an ambitious, greedy TV correspondent to make up a story and get away with it led to *Crown Oklahoma*. Other annoyances with my line of work and the general world of news and politics were right in the front of my mind and my throat when I wrote *Short List*. No question about that.

What truly came pouring out was my impatience with the starch of pomposity that has crept into some of the practitioners of journalism. Some of them never quite got over being recognized in a 7-Eleven store for the first time, or the print equivalent, which is being asked for their opinion by some important person. It went to their heads and their judgment about themselves. Now they believe they are more important than the people on whom they report, and definitely more important than the readers and/or viewers—the people they report for.

All of us in journalism should be concerned about the fact that people have begun to see us all as one. Simpson and Totenberg. Biden and Rather. Metzenbaum and Will. Sununu and Lehrer. We are all peas of the same pod. Anything goes, in the pursuit of our careers and our smears.

And without question, my understanding of a desire among responsible adult people to chuck it all and run away from home made it easier to write *Lost and Found*.

I am not through. There are many understandings and annoyances, and other material, still waiting to be used in a Mack book. Look at the possibilities:

Mack and C. (his friend C. Harry Hayes, the one-eared director of the Oklahoma Bureau of Investigation) are summoned to the bedside of a dying man living as a recluse on a farm in a desolate part of Oklahoma. He wants to confess. He claims he was part of the John F. Kennedy assassination team. He was to have driven Oswald out of Dallas, but Oswald was captured before he could. Mack believes the guy, C. does not.

The Democratic presidential candidate who did not take Mack as his running mate comes away with a soft spot in his heart for this one-eyed guy. He gets elected president (we're talking fiction here, please remember) and appoints Mack ambassador to Tunisia. Mack has adventures that include either making peace between Arabs and Jews or thwarting an attempt to disrupt that peace. C. might come over as his legal attaché, as FBI agents do. Or maybe Mack gets waylaid in the confirmation process and never makes it to Tunisia.

Mack, at a civic banquet in Oklahoma City one night, tells a woman that his dream since boyhood has been to take a cross-country bus trip. The woman asks if he would be willing to auction off such a thing for the upcoming fund-raising auction of the Oklahoma Museum of Art. A kind of Ride the Bus to Philadelphia with the Lieutenant Governor item. Mack, wanting to be nice and to help art in Oklahoma, casually agrees. He ends up having to take the trip—maybe to New York or Boston or some other place, like Philadelphia or Wilmington—with an unreformed juvenile delinquent. The wealthy buyer of the "item" donated the trip to a home for bad boys. A trip like that would be good for a kid who has nothing and will never be able to travel otherwise, they tell Mack. He and the kid have quite a trip.

And.

Mack goes to Washington or some place for a meeting of the National Lieutenant Governors' Association. He faints and ends up awake in a hospital intensive care unit twenty-four hours later, having been given an emergency heart bypass operation. By mistake.

How about a murder mystery where several members of the Oklahoma legislature are killed, one at a time, each in a different and bizarre way? Maybe an investigation of something like Abscam is involved. Maybe it turns out some rich Oklahoman has bought the legislature—not just a few of the members, but the whole thing.

I could even have Mack and C. try to make peace between a plumber who opens a free-love socialist commune in southwestern Oklahoma and a Nazarene preacher who wants to shut it down in the name of Jesus. The dramatic highlight could be a watermelon-eating contest between the plumber and the preacher.

13

Crazy Questions

That trip through East Texas in the summer of 1984 was important because it led to *Chili Queen*. But that was only part of it. It also got me started on a new and blessed thing in my life. The aimless driving through the small towns of Texas, Oklahoma, Kansas and anywhere else.

On that same East Texas trip, while I was at the Holiday Inn in Lufkin, the seed for another play, *Church Key Charlie Blue*, got planted by an advertising flyer urging everyone to join the crowd in the motel bar that fall for Monday Night Football. In Lufkin, I also came across a statue of a World War I soldier, which later turned up in *Kick the Can*.

I found and bought an old Continental Trailways ashtray in Gladewater. I got a couple of leads on a Dixie-Sunshine Trailways depot sign in Tyler. A woman in Henderson refused to sell me an old picture of a Missouri Pacific Trailways bus, but trying to buy it was truly fun. (She kept saying, "No, you don't want that." And I kept saying, "Yeah, I do.") I had the same good experience but no luck trying to get a woman in Jasper to part with a small CONTINENTAL TRAILWAYS, JASPER, TEXAS sign.

Moving slowly down the two-lane highways, stopping and starting with jerks and whims anywhere I wanted was freeing and exciting—as well as freeing and relaxing.

In Newton, Kansas, I went to a cab stand in part of what had once been a huge depot for Santa Fe trains and buses. Amtrak still used a small space in it. In the forties, our Kansas Central buses had crossed over the tracks nearby on the way to our own stop up the main street at a flower shop.

I was there now because I had been told Trans State Trailways used to stop at the cab stand. Trans State had gone bankrupt after unsuccessfully trying to replace some of the Kansas routes abandoned by Greyhound and Trailways in the late seventies and early eighties.

I popped the question to a young woman behind a desk.

"I have a crazy question to ask you. Do you by any chance happen to have a sign from the old Trans State Trailways still around somewhere?"

She laughed pleasantly, as if I had said something funny, and said, "We sure do. It's back in the back."

"Well, it may sound strange, but I collect old bus things like that. Is there any way I could persuade you to sell that sign to me?"

She laughed pleasantly again, confirming that it did indeed sound strange, and swung around in her chair. She called a man out of an office. He was clearly one of the drivers. About forty, short hair, clearly a good man of Kansas. She told him my story.

"It's all right with me," he said, "but it isn't mine to sell. The boss is gone for the rest of the day. You come back in the morning."

I explained that I was just passing through. Would he mind calling the boss?

"He'd think I was crazy," said the man.

"Oh, come on," said the young woman, a wonderful person. "Just give the sign to him. It isn't worth a thing to anybody around here. Let him have it."

She and I watched the driver think. He went back into the office, and in a few seconds he came out with the sign in his hands. It was about twenty-four inches long, twelve or fourteen high. On white metal in large red letters was painted TRANS STATE

TRAILWAYS, and below it, in smaller letters, BUS STATION. That was all. Nothing fancy. No enamel finish, no pictures of old buses in art deco circles. Hardly a museum piece.

But I wanted it. I really wanted it.

"Can't let you have it without talking to the boss," said the driver.

"Then call him," said the wonderful young woman.

Okay, okay, gestured the driver, and he picked up the phone. He told the story about this man who had come and wanted to buy the old bus depot sign, said he was just passing through and everything. He took the phone from his head and said to me:

"How much?"

"Thirty dollars," I said.

He repeated it into the phone.

"Fifty?" he said back to me, obviously relaying the amount from the boss.

"Forty," I said.

"He says, How about forty?" the driver said into the phone. He listened for a second and then said to me, "Deal."

I gave him two twenty-dollar bills and took the sign.

"I cannot believe this," said the young woman. "It's not worth a thing. I cannot believe it that he would let you pay him forty dollars and you would pay it. All it is is some words painted on some tin."

I let it go. There was no way I could expect her to understand. Poor thing.

That sign hangs on the inside of one of the doors to my bus room at home. I can see it, in fact, from where I am sitting now writing this on a word processor.

It's a lovely reminder of the lovely pleasures I get from my solo drives. Since my heart attack, I have made more than two dozen such trips to and through parts of Kansas, and just as many or more in Oklahoma and Texas.

Most of these trips are tacked on either end of or squeezed in between other travel for business or family reasons. There is seldom a plan to it. Usually I get in a rent-a-car at the airport in

Wichita, Oklahoma City or someplace, and just start driving. I seldom know where I will be spending the night. I carry with me a pocket-size tape recorder and a thirty-five-millimeter automatic camera that requires only that the user be alive for the pictures to be in focus.

That Trans State sign is only one of several great items I have picked up this way.

At a Rexall in Clifton, Texas, I turned up a one-of-a-kind Waco-Cisco Coaches sign, as well as a newer one from Central Texas Bus Lines. In Louise, Texas, I picked up a Continental Trailways sign I had never seen before—and I've never seen another one since. I happened on a wrecking crew in Hugo, Oklahoma, tearing down the old depot and headquarters building of the defunct Jordan Bus Company. I left with books of old tickets, as well as a small sign that said "To Buses." In Ottawa, Kansas, I got a Trailways and a KG Lines sign. In Leavenworth, one for Trenton–St. Joseph Coaches. And many more.

It's not just bus things I'm on the lookout for. I pick up talk and sights and other bits and pieces that might find their way into a Mack book or a play, but most are simple happenings that never find their way into anything.

Like what happened after I had the Mexican plate—a cheese enchilada, a tamale, rice and beans—in Abilene, Kansas.

The sign outside the motel-restaurant said "Tex-Mex, Italian and American Cooking." Nothing on the menu was in keeping with my new diet. But Sam Fox, my doctor of everything at Georgetown, said it was all right to blow it occasionally. It was bad for the body, he said, but good for the soul.

The enchilada and the tamale and the rice and the beans had no real taste. They could easily have passed for Italian or American food (whatever that is). When I finished eating, the waitress gave me a check for less than five dollars and told me to pay the motel front desk. She pointed me through an open door right there next to the restaurant.

A man of fifty or so, also in a regulation short Kansas haircut, was behind the desk, talking on the phone. Off in a corner were a couple of clean but ratty lobby chairs and a television set. An old cowboy movie was showing.

On top of the TV set was a homemade sign. In black letters on white posterboard was written: JESUS IS WATCHING.

The desk clerk hung up the phone, and I took out my camera.

"I've never seen a sign like that before," I said to the desk clerk.

He looked up and I nodded toward the TV.

"I hadn't seen one, either, till I went to work here," said the man. "It was the owner's idea."

"Mind if I take a picture of it?" I said.

"Whatever pleases," he said.

I took a couple of pictures.

The man gave me my change and we exchanged thank-yous.

"He is," he said.

"Sir?"

"Jesus *is* watching."

"Yes, sir," I said, and left.

Jesus is watching what? I said into my tape recorder later, in my room at the Best Western across the street. Is Jesus watching the man behind the desk and me? Is He watching all people who watch that television? Is He watching to make sure nobody watches any dirty movies on that set? Or does it mean Jesus is watching *also*? He, too, likes cowboy movies?

Like I said, a simple happening.

Many of the places I have gone—and continue to go—are where I have been before. Towns and neighborhoods and streets where I lived growing up, schools I attended, stores I shopped in, depots I passed through. I have driven the Kansas Central route three or four times, walked into the lobby of the Eaton Hotel in Wichita twice. The white frame building of the Marion Hotel in Marion is still there. But the Warren Hotel in McPherson, scene of the great pinball incident, is now a parking garage.

Willie's and my bus depot in Victoria, Texas, is gone, a fancy bank building in its place. I was stunned to see on a recent trip that the old rooming house five blocks west where we had rented two rooms has been rehabilitated, restored and painted a pale green, in keeping with the Victorian motif of Victoria's historic district. Only one of our rooms there was a bedroom, which meant I had to sleep on a screened-in porch. When it was cold, I moved inside or slept on the porch with gloves and socks on.

Lawrence Stadium in Wichita, once home of the national semi-pro baseball tournament, is still there, as Lawrence-Dumont Stadium. I have stopped by several times to see games in the last few years. I also have been to see the Oklahoma City 89ers play. They are a Texas Rangers farm club in the Class AAA American Association. I never go to baseball games anywhere else—only on my travels in Kansas, Texas and Oklahoma. That was where I experienced baseball and where it still exists for me.

Baseball is all through most of the Mack books. Mack's son, Tommy Walt, pitched semipro ball for a while for the Buses, the team sponsored by Oklahoma Blue Arrow Motorcoaches. He had to quit because he was not good enough. His fingers were too small to get a good hold on the ball. He could not hit a curve or judge high fly balls in the field, so there was no other option but to quit the game altogether.

That all came to me quite naturally one evening at Lawrence-Dumont Stadium in the summer of 1988. A Wichita team was playing one from Arkansas City. I watched a kid shortstop for Wichita go through the closest thing to hell there is for a young man trying to play baseball.

A ground ball was hit right at him. He misjudged the big hop, and it bounced off his chest. The runner was safe at first.

Crack! The next batter hit one to the shortstop's left. He made a great move, caught it at his shoetops on the run and then swung around with a skip just right to make the throw to first. He couldn't get the ball out of his mitt! Finally, when he did, he threw it wild over the first baseman's head. Now there were runners on first and second. Both there because of his errors.

Another *crack!* This time a fast grounder to the second baseman. It was cleanly fielded, and tossed underhanded to the shortstop for the first of two. A chance to make it up!

The kid shortstop made the play and the pivot, but threw the ball into the dirt. It bounced by the first baseman. All the runners were safe, and the man on second scored.

It was stunningly tragic. There weren't more than 150 of us in the stands, but everyone was quiet. I yelled, "Hang in there!" and immediately felt like an idiot. My heart was breaking for the kid.

And so was his for himself. He walked to the edge of the infield and faced left field, fell to his knees and looked up to the sky. Then he leaned forward and put his hands on his knees.

I couldn't see his face, but I hoped for his sake that he was not crying. Please, kid, try not to cry!

The third baseman came over to him and patted him on the back. And said something. It's okay, Pete? Scooter? Pee Wee? Joe? Billy?

In a few seconds, the shortstop was back on his feet and in position for the next pitch. Eventually, two more outs were made. And nothing else was hit to him.

He was the first batter up. It never fails. The Baseball Gods— I assume there are more than one—always seem to bring the fielding hero or goat of the previous half-inning to bat first after his great or awful performance.

Here he was, that poor kid shortstop, close up. I could see he was probably nineteen or twenty, with the good build and good looks all shortstops should have.

"Show 'em what you can do, Short!" I yelled. A few others in the stands also shouted words of encouragement.

But I knew what was going to happen. And it did. He swung and missed at the first pitch. The second one was down the middle and he did not swing. Called strike two. Then two balls, one inside, the other outside. And finally a fastball right down the middle, where it should be. The kid swung and missed. Strike three.

He turned back toward his dugout, that bat in his hand. He started to throw it. I felt that if he had, the emotional energy alone would have made it fly all the way to Kansas City, almost two hundred miles away.

But he thought better of it. Instead, he took the slow walk back to the dugout.

Hell. I had been witness to a young man in hell. What would he do about it? Would he now quit this team and this game? Would he get drunk tonight? Would he tell his parents and his girlfriend? Where were they, anyhow? Oh my God, I hope not here in the stands!

Several minutes later came the final humiliation. His team made the third out in the inning and returned to the field. But somebody else went out to play shortstop.

Had the manager benched the kid? No! No manager could be that heartless and stupid. Maybe the kid himself asked to be taken out.

Please don't make me go out there again, Coach.

Nobody likes a quitter, son.

Please!

If I don't, then you're off the team.

If I do, then I'm off everything.

■ ■ ■

William Least Heat Moon, Charles Kuralt and others who travel the back roads of America have passed on their hints and suggestions for travelers. Without suggesting any kind of likeness-of-league, here are a few of my Rules of the Road.

Stay at Best Westerns. They are all locally owned; their relationship to each other is strictly in a collective advertising name. So they have names like Prairie Inn–Best Western, Sand Dollar–Best Western. No two are alike physically, but they are all clean and cheap, and most have free coffee and doughnuts in the lobby in the morning.

Stay off interstates, except in areas of majestic mountains, great prairies and other gigantic sights that must be seen at a distance to be appreciated. It is on the back roads—the blue highways, Heat Moon calls them—that the people and places of interest are. The best of those are the abandoned U.S. Highways. Some are hard to find and are no longer marked, but driving them is like driving through America in the 1940s. There's a stretch of old U.S. 40 from Junction City to Abilene, Kansas, that is typical. Grass grows between the concrete highway sections. Artifacts of motels and cafés and gas stations that were once the center of attention sit alongside the road, ignored and unattended. It is not hard at all to imagine scenes from the forties and fifties of ACF-Brills and Aerocoaches and Flxible Clippers roaring down those old roads.

Go alone. Why go to all of the trouble of getting away to another world if you'll have to carry on a conversation the whole time? (There are exceptions. A. C. Greene, my writing-mentor friend in Dallas, went on a day's drive through near West and Central Texas with me. He was with me when we found the Waco-Cisco sign in Clifton, in fact. My daughter Lucy also went on one drive through South Texas with me. She was great company, too.)

Don't turn on the car radio. Most local radio disc jockeys and news broadcasters and commercials sound alike, no matter where you are. And the music they play is almost always the same, no matter where you are. The sounds that are important are the ones the people and the vehicles and the animals and the vegetables and the minerals around you are making.

Don't turn on the television in the motel room. Read or write or sleep. You can watch TV at home. (If you feel you have to watch something, make it a news or public affairs program on public television. Maybe one that lasts an hour.)

If you live in Washington, D.C., or New York City, don't tell anybody. Lie. Say you are from New York or Washington, and that is all people will talk to you about. First, they'll want to know how in the world anybody could live there. You explain that, and then the conversation turns permanently to the idiots in Congress, street crime and other things you do not want to talk about, or you would not be in some place like Paola, Kansas, or Ardmore, Oklahoma, or Palacios, Texas.

If you are stopped for speeding by any kind of police in any town, city or state, say you are sorry. Do not argue, do not

explain. Just apologize. Admit you are somebody from somewhere else who was not paying attention. (And by the way,
Officer, could you recommend a nice place to get lunch? Nothing fancy. I hear the cheeseburgers around here are dynamite.)
I have found that most cops will let you go with a warning if
you're from out of state, if you're nice about it. I have found also
that if you are not nice, you will be stuck.

Don't speed, anyhow. What's the point of going all the way
to the middle of Post Rock country in western Kansas, say, and
then speeding up U.S. Highway 183 from La Crosse to Hays
and not really seeing anything? (Post rock is white shale that
European settlers in the 1800s dug up to use as fence posts.
There weren't any trees and they needed something to hold up
the barbed wire. Some of the pieces weigh more than three
hundred pounds. They are still out there and are still being used
as fence posts.)

Don't travel by itinerary. Don't have to be somewhere at a
certain time. It prevents you from following a "Train Museum"
sign down a road or taking an impromptu afternoon nap on a
picnic table in a city park.

Ask questions. It saves time, and it's a good way to stretch
the legs and talk to people. Where is the art museum? The
library? A McDonald's? The post office? The bus depot?

Yes, the bus depot. Once you find it, check it out carefully
from the outside. Is there a "Buses Only—No Parking" or other
sign hanging out front that you do not have? Check around
back. Anything old and discarded lying around that might be
collectible? Then go inside. Always enter the place with a Jimmy
Stewart smile and gait. Say to the first person you see, "Hi. I
have a really crazy question to ask you." The person smiles
back. You say, "You know that old Trailways sign around back?
I was wonder if I might buy that." Or, "Do you happen to have
or know of anybody around here who might have a depot sign
from the old Southern Kansas Greyhound lines?" Or whatever
is appropriate. Then . . .

Oh, never mind.

14

Skivvy Shirts

I had not been back to work in full swing long before Robin, Les and company began talking to me about the real world they had kept from me. The program was in trouble. Not just on the air. There were already rumblings from some station managers and others in the PBS system about returning us to thirty minutes. By force.

We started talking about what to do. Fortunately, watching the program many weeks at home had given me a most unique view of what *The MacNeil/Lehrer NewsHour* was—and wasn't. What seemed to be working and what was not, what should be thrown out and what should be retained, and so on.

The most important thing I learned was that we were producing the program on a false, stupid premise, and that was that people would go to their TV sets when we came on the air and sit there for the full sixty minutes. It was arrogance on our part, of the first—and worst—order. Nobody does that. People dip in and out of television programs, particularly those like ours.

Hey, Gladys, *MacNeil/Lehrer* is doing multiwarheads and their influence on the North–South dialogue again tonight. Let's watch *Wheel of Fortune* for a while and then come back to *MacNeil/Lehrer*. They've got an interview with the deputy defense minister of Upper Volta coming up I really do not want to miss.

But the way we did it every night, it was impossible to dip in and out with any certainty of where you were or what was coming. News stories of varying length and importance were sprinkled throughout the program. Soft stories were here, there and everywhere. Hard stories were there, here and everywhere. Nothing was labeled. There were no internal "promos" about what was still to come. If you didn't happen to catch the beginning, you would never know the terrific Upper Volta interview was even coming up. It was a program arranged primarily for the most rabid of the *MacNeil/Lehrer* fanatics and for the families of the participants and a few others who might sit glued to their chairs in front of the TV set from the time they heard our ever popular theme music at the top until they heard it again at the bottom.

We were also trying to do too much. Serious discussions about arms control, the economy, politics, medicine, science, foreign affairs, the law, the media, business, labor, the environment, the arts, crime, urban affairs. Plus hard-nose documentary reporting in all of those areas. Plus book reviews. Plus profiles of offbeat people stunned to be profiled. Plus the Postcards. Plus, plus, plus. We were stretched too thin trying to do too much, and the thinness was showing up in just about everything.

We set out to examine everything we were doing. And we did it with the sounds of the posse coming our way from over the hill. The manager of public television in Oklahoma (of all places) began a public and private campaign to undo us. He recruited stations in the South, plus others in Ohio and elsewhere, to join the effort. Resolutions were passed at various public television meetings around the country urging us to return to the half-hour. And there were a lot of public television meetings to pass such things. Jim Day, who managed the stations in San Francisco and New York, is famous for having once said, "Public television is a series of meetings, occasionally interrupted by a program."

The going got rough, very rough. Again, it was AT&T that made the difference. Charlie Brown and Ed Block, joined now by Mary Delle Stelzer, an assistant of Ed's assigned to our account, held fast. So did the people at WNET, WETA and Gannett. Ward Chamberlin, one of the really good people of this world, called me to say that if the system turned us out, he would leave public television, where he had worked most of his adult life. He wouldn't want to be involved with something that dumb, he said.

The crucial time came in June 1984. Robin addressed a luncheon of PBS program and station managers in Seattle. Mary Delle spoke at the same luncheon, pronouncing loud and clear AT&T's commitment to the program. At a difficult session where some of the program managers were openly and aggressively hostile, Les Crystal laid out the changes we were going to make in the program.

They were:

Lead the program every night with a summary of the day's news. Close it every night with a recap of the news.

After the news summary, concentrate, with either a discussion or a tape, on a major news story of the day.

Good-bye, book reviews.

Good-bye, Postcards.

Good-bye, profiles of offbeat Americans.

It seems like such a simple list. It is unfortunate that we had to go through so much anguish to get there. But at the risk of sounding like a PBS superpatriot, I have to say that is exactly what public television should be doing. Let people try things. And then let them move on if they do not work. That is what happened to us, and I am forever grateful.

There are limits to my gratitude, obviously. Some extremely deep scars were left by it all. The most severe for me were from the way the people in charge of my old station, KERA in Dallas, actively worked and voted against us. Bob Wilson and Ralph Rogers were long gone to other things by then, and the new management did not support the idea of giving us another chance. It hurt, because it helped others say, "Look, Lehrer's own station isn't even supporting him."

But even that has almost flowed under the bridge. Almost. As a prominent Oklahoma politician says a lot, "Show me somebody who can't tell his friends from his enemies and I'll show you somebody who's going to end up with no friends." The people at the stations in San Antonio and Austin, for instance, stood with us all the way. There is nothing I would not do for them. The same goes for the many station program managers who worked with us in analyzing our problems and carrying our message to their colleagues in the system.

Scars aside, the important thing is that when the stations voted that fall, we were renewed for another year. The margin was thin, but the fact of it was not. We asked for another chance and the good people and stations of public television gave it to us.

And we went about the business of keeping our end of the bargain.

■ ■ ■

Going to work every morning became a pleasure, and even more important, so did going home every evening. I left the studio—most of the time, at least—liking what we had done and how we had done it.

We still made mistakes, including the biggest ones of all: having the wrong people on the wrong night talking about the wrong story, devoting twenty minutes to something that really deserved only about five, or five to something that merited twenty. And we still made the normal mistakes that go with the territory of daily journalism.

But the *NewsHour* began to work as a television program. Our new mix was clicking. Our return to basics, to the hard side of the news, felt right, was right.

So was our Skivvy Shirt Rule.

The rule says (more or less): If MacNeil comes on the air in his skivvy shirt and says, "Good evening. Leading the news this Friday is peace in the Middle East," most sighted members of the audience would not hear a word said about the Middle East. They would be staring with concern and wonder over the fact that MacNeil is sitting there in his skivvy shirt.

Hey, Gladys, look! MacNeil's doing the news in his underwear!

Hey, Harry, you're right! Look at him!

The same would be true of other items of personal hygiene,
such as uncombed hair or a tie askew. But it goes much further
than that. Everything the viewer sees and hears must pass the
Skivvy Shirt Rule test. Nothing should be noticed or absorbed
except the information. Nothing else should be memorable.
There is no such thing as a pretty slide, a zippy piece of
music, a trendy shirt, a dynamic set, a tough question, or
anything else, if it deflects even a blink of attention from the
information. Those few seconds while the viewer admires or
retches over the gaudy green tie or the red-white-and-blue-
flashing map of the drought belt can destroy the whole point of
the exercise, the transmitting of information.

Hey, Gladys, look at that swell pink-and-white background
behind the secretary of state!

Hey, Harry, yeah! Wow!

What was that? What did he just say?

I think he said something about bombing Havana, Harry.

Gosh. We missed it.

Full-screen videotape in a news report or documentary is not
exempt from the rule, either. Moving pictures certainly have an
important place on a television news program, but only when
they portray an event worth reporting. Spectacular footage of a
fire that caused little damage to person or property should not
be broadcast simply because it's Spectacular Footage of a Fire.
It happens. Marvin Kalb told me CBS killed his analysis piece
the night of the Soviet invasion of Czechoslovakia in 1968 because some Spectacular Footage of a Fire in Little Rock, Arkansas, came in at the last minute. There were no injuries in
the fire, and only one small building was affected. But the pictures were great!

Look at those flames, Gladys!

They're gorgeous, Harry!

Is that downtown Prague, Gladys?

No, it's downtown Little Rock, Harry.

The Skivvy Shirt Rule has applications beyond what is normally considered visual or graphic. The most important has to do with the "all-powerful journalist" concept of American journalism. Robin and I do not believe in it.

We see our function as a quiet one. We believe journalists can have a professional and adversarial relationship with the people they cover that does not have to be mean or confrontational. We do not see ourselves as Mr. District Attorneys, with the job to prosecute publicly within the limits of the law all persons holding public office or public opinions. Our job is to question public figures about their actions and views, but to do it in such a way that our audience can judge their veracity or worthiness.

We, the journalists, are not judge and jury any more than we are prosecutors or defense attorneys.

In other words, like the set and the slides, the interviewer/journalist should be mostly invisible. If one of us loses our temper on the air or steps over the line of civility, we detract from what is important. It is not important to prove to our audience how tough we are. Our journalistic/interviewing manhood is not on the line every night.

Hey, Gladys, look at Lehrer beat up on Gary Hart!

Yea, Harry, Lehrer is one tough guy.

Wow!

Wow.

Unfortunately, that particular Harry–Gladys exchange is not a complete figment of my imagination. I have violated the Skivvy Shirt Rule many times, and probably will many more times before I go away. But the worst so far did involve Gary Hart, the former Colorado senator and Democratic candidate for President.

It happened in December 1988, right after he reentered the race for the Democratic presidential nomination. He had dropped out seven months earlier because of the revelations about his relationships with Miami model Donna Rice and other women who were not his wife. His decision to come back had been met by derision in the newspaper editorial pages of the

country. He came on our program live from New Hampshire
thirty hours after his reentry announcement.

I asked him what he thought of the reaction.

"The response has been great," he said.

That made no sense to me. So I said: "In what way has it
been great?"

He cited the personal reaction of voters on the streets in New
Hampshire and Maine. I asked him about the high school kid—
it had been on everybody's news program the night before—who
had asked him about Donna Rice. He said he had had a lot of
questions about serious issues before that came up.

I asked if he felt the issue of his judgment raised by the
Donna Rice episode had been adequately addressed. There was
then this exchange.

He said: "Yes, I do. I said I made a mistake, and I said yesterday all I want is the votes of all the people in this country
who themselves have made mistakes."

"And you think that's all that needs to be said about it?"

"No. But that's all I intend to say about it."

"Let me read to you what *The Washington Post* said in an
editorial this morning: 'Gary Hart got back into the Democratic
race on Tuesday, seeming neither to remember nor to be especially interested in the reasons that he had got out. We expect that if he can, he still has to address directly and plausibly
those questions having to do with his behavior and his candor
with the public before he can hope to get anywhere. This, the
newly reinstated candidate most emphatically did not do yesterday.' "

"Well, they're entitled to their opinion. What I want to know
is what the people of this country think."

I then asked for a further explanation of the Rice business.
He said he would answer no more questions about it, because
it was not anyone else's business.

"Why is it not anyone else's business?" I asked.

"Because it isn't. It hasn't been the business of the American
public for two hundred years, and it isn't today," he said.

I felt some warmth rising in me. This man is sitting in the middle of a rainstorm denying that he is getting wet. It's absurd.

I kept at him.

"You don't think it speaks to the question of judgment as to what a person would do as a candidate for president of the United States?"

"Well, Jim—may I call you Jim?"

"You may."

"Let's reverse the logic. All right? Does it suggest because Ronald Reagan used poor judgment on Irangate that therefore he's unfaithful to his wife?"

"I don't understand what you mean."

"Well, it's exactly the reverse of that logic that you're suggesting."

It went on more or less like that for nearly twenty minutes.

Afterward, there were angry calls and letters. I was accused of being hostile, unfair, and of using a double standard by stepping over our own line of civility and dispassion in the way I went after Hart. Without reviewing the tape (that's important), I dismissed the criticism. I responded to my critics by simply declaring them wrong. I had stepped over no lines, done nothing different with Hart from what I had done with anyone else.

And I went my righteous way about the interview until more than two years later. Robin and I were being interviewed by our friends and commentator colleagues David Gergen and Mark Shields for a PBS special on the fifteenth anniversary of *MacNeil/Lehrer*.

(Hey, Gladys, get in here! MacNeil and Lehrer are talking about how wonderful they are!

I'm busy, Harry.)

Mark asked me about the Hart interview. He said some people thought I had been tougher on Hart than was warranted and than was normal for *MacNeil/Lehrer*.

Again, I defended myself, denying that I had been unfair in any way.

But then several weeks later, I watched the fifteenth-anniversary program. It included an excerpt from that December 1988 interview. I was appalled. The critics had been absolutely right! It was not so much in my words but in my demeanor. I came over as angry with Gary Hart for what he had done and what he was saying. You could sense it from my facial expressions, tone of voice and all the rest of my body language.

It stuck out as obviously inappropriate as if I had been wearing a skivvy shirt.

Sorry, Gladys. Sorry, Senator.

• ■ •

I consider interviewing people on live television the ultimate risk in daily journalism. And Skivvy Shirt Rule problems are only part of it. I wish I had a nickel for each time something stupid has come from my mouth that I wanted to reach out, grab and stick back down my throat before anybody heard it.

Or for each time I should have asked a question in a form that was not totally incomprehensible.

Well, Senator, if Gorbachev does scuttle the Soviets' land-based intermediate-range nuclear missiles as was announced last week after President Bush's agreement as he had said earlier he might but the announcement wasn't it a surprise in light of what has been happening in the Middle East and with Yeltsin but maybe not because of their economic problems?

Well, Jim—may I call you Jim?

You may.

Could you repeat the question, Jim?

No, sir, I couldn't.

Or for each time I should have reread a preinterview or article or book chapter so I would have better understood a certain subject or a guest's point of view before I went into the studio.

So, Professor, you believe strongly that animals should be used in medical experiments?

No. It's just the opposite. As I said in my book, *Never Use Animals in Medical Experiments*, I am opposed to that.

Or for each time I've lost my concentration for a split second and missed what a guest has just said.

Should we sell grain to Cuba, Senator?

Yes, we should, Jim. But first we should bomb Havana.

What kind of grain, Senator?

Concentration is at the top of the list for anyone who interviews people on live television. My powers to concentrate have been finely honed by the fear—and the reality—of doing something like that grain-bomb exchange. Much of the ability to concentrate comes from preparation. Anyone, even someone fresh out of the Texas newspaper business, can write down questions to ask. The trick is to know enough to understand the answers, to be secure enough in your knowledge to be able to concentrate on what the guest is actually saying, the words that are actually coming out of the guest's mouth. There is a tendency to be thinking always of the next question, out of fear of the embarrassing sound of silence. It was this problem that I later realized was at the heart of my early *Straight Talk* difficulties. I was not confident enough to listen, to engage the guest, rather than merely to sit there and ask questions.

I am so honed now that even a fire above my head would not stay me from swift completion of my appointed interview rounds.

I boast from experience. I was interviewing Beryl Sprinkel, chairman of President Reagan's Council of Economic Advisers, and had just asked him something regarding what he proposed to do about interest rates or some such.

There was a loud *pop!* right above our heads. I knew it was one of the hot studio lights. It had blown. I also knew Mr. Sprinkel probably did not know that.

We both blanched. He looked right at me. I held his eyes. And re-asked the question.

He began his answer.

I got a whiff of smoke from over my head. It was clear from his eyes that he, too, smelled smoke. It was also clear that if I looked up to see what was going on, he would also look up. And that would be the end of the interview.

I assumed that neither of us was in danger, or someone on the camera crew would have done something—like maybe stopped the proceedings and gotten us out of harm's way.

So the interview continued. As did the smell of an electrical fire.

We finished in another three or four minutes. It seemed much, much longer.

I thanked him for being with us. The program switched to New York for Robin to introduce another segment, and Mr. Sprinkel and I both looked up at the ceiling. There, about twenty feet above our heads, a television light was ablaze.

Mr. Sprinkel and I congratulated ourselves for our courage under fire, as members of the crew raced about the studio like firemen just arriving at a shopping mall blaze.

There was an even more dramatic incident in 1991 that taxed both Robin's and my powers of concentration.

In the middle of a three-guest discussion, the picture from New York suddenly did a jump or two in my monitor. Dan Werner said in my earpiece that I could no longer interview the one guest in New York because of "a disturbance in our New York studio."

I passed this on to our audience and continued the discussion, not knowing what in the world was going on in New York. Disturbance? What kind of disturbance?

I went on with the discussion for a few more minutes. Then Werner said in my ear: The disturbance is over. You can go back to your New York guest.

Fine. But first I asked Robin—on the air, so everyone could hear—to please tell us what had happened.

He reported that several men had come into the studio and handcuffed themselves to his desk. They were members of ACT-UP, an AIDS activist group. Their purpose was to call attention to the need for more attention and resources devoted to AIDS issues. It turned out similar assault teams had gone to CBS at the same time.

The men who had come into our New York studio were arrested and removed, but not charged. Some ally on the inside at WNET had apparently let them in the building one at a time during the day, to lie low until that evening when we went on the air.

There are indeed perils in live television. . . .

■ ■ ■

Within a year of our doing it our new way, the public television system moved solidly behind us. The management of stations in Oklahoma, Dallas and elsewhere gave up trying to put us out of business or take us back to thirty minutes. The television critics, with one irrelevant exception, usually wrote nice things about us.

MacNeil/Lehrer continued to get stronger. Under the leadership of Les Crystal, Linda Winslow and Dan Werner, the daily design of the elements in the program improved, as did the quality of our tape pieces, the staff organization, management and allocation of our fixed, limited resources. The use of reporting contributions from public television stations was increased and enhanced. Gergen and Shields came aboard as our regular political analysts. We added essays as a regular feature, the first essayist being Roger Rosenblatt, the writer-editor-playwright-monologuist. We paid more attention to running hefty excerpts from congressional hearings, news conferences and other events that had happened during the day. Another Roger friend, the one named Mudd, joined us, first as an essayist and then as our Capitol Hill correspondent and substitute anchor. He came to us directly from a train-wreck situation at NBC. Robin said often, and accurately, that Mudd was one of the best writers and the single best reader-to-camera anchor there was in the business. I never understood the failure of CBS, and then NBC, to grasp and use him and his talents properly. But that was their problem. There was only one Roger Mudd, and we had him.

He added strength to what had become the strongest correspondent corps in television news. There were Charlayne and Judy, and now Roger, plus three major field correspondents, Kwame Holman, Elizabeth Brackett and Tom Bearden, and our man of the international world, Charles Krause.

We had, and have, people who detest us and what we do, and we always will. It has to do with the basics of our program. Am I sitting across from our guests to judge their answers to my questions as right, wrong, insane, great? No. I am there to help these people get their positions, opinions or whatever across in a way that the audience can understand and judge. That is it. I have no other functions.

There are people who believe it is not enough for journalism merely to dish it out without placing a judgment of some kind, to help the viewer figure it out. I agree that judging is a legitimate journalistic function. Newspapers and magazines have commentators of all stripes who do that, who say: You have heard the arguments; now here is the one I think is correct. That is not what Robin and I signed on to do or want to do. And we believe there is a place for what both our most devoted fans and our severest critics call our rabid even-handedness. MacNeil and Lehrer, Messrs. Bland and On the Other Hand.

The people we truly drive nuts are the righteous ideologues and activists who believe there is only one side to every question—their side. After the Persian Gulf war, a left-wing pro-Palestinian group issued a press release accusing us of being toadies to the Israelis. A few days later, an Israel-first weekly-magazine editor accused us of being toadies to the Palestinians. We questioned hundreds of people on our program over the course of the buildup to the war through to its conclusion and aftermath. No view of any stripe, foreign or domestic, went unheard. That's what drove the critics from both sides crazy. The avid pro-Israeli editor did not want the position of the pro-Palestinians heard at all, and vice versa. Harry and Gladys, fortunately, feel otherwise.

We do need criticism. All of journalism needs it. Right now, the only regular criticism we get comes from ideological organizations from the left and right. They care not about sloppiness or anything else having to do with the quality of reporting. They care only about their own political slant on the news. They have no credibility except with their own cheerleading squads, and thus they have absolutely no impact.

The most important development in those post-1984 years

for the *NewsHour* was the way our audience, our Harrys and Gladyses, grew and flourished with us. Even when some of the issue pros didn't quite get it, the people who watched us knew and understood what we were up to.

They knew our secrets, too. They knew there was nothing special or startling or earth-shaking about taking the news seriously, and presenting it in some detail with people representing all sides, all opinions, all perspectives on it. And they knew there was nothing special or startling or earth-shaking about MacNeil or Lehrer or anyone else connected with our program. It takes no particular brilliance to decide, say, to interview the secretary of defense for twenty-five minutes after the invasion of Panama, or to devote the full hour every night for weeks to the Gulf war or, later, to the coup in the Soviet Union or the fight over the confirmation of Clarence Thomas to the Supreme Court.

What we brought to it was simple luck. We had the good fortune to come along at a time when there was a need for a nightly program that went beyond the headlines, and when public television saw and acted on that need. And most important in personal terms, saw fit to turn the acting over to us.

We have been allowed to function as journalists in the freest atmosphere possible. Never has an executive of public television sought to interfere in or influence what we do. Neither has anyone from AT&T, PepsiCo or any of our other corporate underwriters. Our mistakes are all our own. We have been given the right to be wrong, the right to function in an atmosphere restricted and restrained only by our own imaginations, abilities and judgments.

It's what in Texas is called having a bird's nest on the ground. Translated: a terrific deal.

It has given me the opportunity to be present. To drive home in the evening feeling as if I were there when something important happened, even though all I did was interview some of the participants or observers or whatevers.

Where were you when the Berlin Wall came down, Lehrer?

I was there.

You mean there at the wall itself?

There in our studio in the Shirlington section of Arlington, Virginia, in suburban Washington.

Wow.

Well, it has been a terrific wow for me. And it goes beyond simply interviewing famous and/or important, smart and/or articulate people about big events. I have no list of favorite or least favorite guests I have interviewed. The only list I have—and it is in my head only—is of rude and pompous and otherwise unpleasant people. They come from all parties, all wings, all genders, all ages, all races, all religions, all interests, all professions, all countries.

As in the case of Ruth Lo, the woman who had returned from a life's experience in China, the interviews I remember most from more recent times—since the *NewsHour* began—are not those of awful people, or even of cabinet ministers, senators, dictators, princes and the like.

They are of people like Jacqueline Jackson-Quinn, a woman I interviewed on her front porch just before the 1988 presidential election.

My introduction to her interview on the *NewsHour* of Tuesday, November 1, 1988, said it all:

"Next, a conversation with somebody you've never heard of. Her name is Jacqueline Jackson-Quinn. She is a thirty-seven-year-old widow with four children who works as a teacher's assistant in Denver, Colorado. She was one of several voters I talked to recently, for a segment in a special program to be seen on public television next Monday night, election eve. Ms. Jackson-Quinn's thoughts about the next president, be he Dukakis or Bush, seemed to us to deserve a fuller hearing than the special will afford. So and thus—I give you Jacqueline Jackson-Quinn of Denver, Colorado."

She spoke about how Americans had just stopped dreaming, and how we didn't teach our children to dream anymore.

"Can a president help us dream?" I asked.

She answered: "Sure. Kennedy gave us dreams. You saw what

happened there. Johnson had dreams that he was able to pass on to the country. Even Nixon had a couple of dreams. The whole point of it is, Congress does what it wants, but the president can give the country a feeling of what we can be again, that we don't have to be second-rate to any other country. Our children can be the best-educated children in the world. And it doesn't take a lot of money. It just takes commitment. It just takes a commitment to do and use what we have to the fullest.

"Everything goes back to education, you know, and when children aren't educated, when they don't have dreams, when they don't have hopes, when their expectations aren't high enough for themselves, and the community's expectations aren't high enough, then you get street gangs, and you get children who are the products of such people. I mean, these children's parents failed in school, to a large degree. And so there's a big push on from the secretary of education about parent involvement, but the parents you've got to go out and get are the very parents who the school systems failed, to a large degree. These are the people who have no faith, because they know that they did not get it, so to speak, and their children—there is no push for their children to excel. And it's the whole thing of where the money is, with street-gang kids, and the whole idea of what makes you a man or what makes you a woman.

"You know, in this country it's money, there's no two ways about it. You can't deny it. And it's a matter of: What value system are you going to give your children, are we going to give the American system, to get that money? It's pretty hard when you're raising kids, and especially when you've got older teenagers, and you're saying to them you work hard, you're honest, you give it 150 percent and you'll get your reward—and the kid knows. You're driving a secondhand car, down the street's a pusher in a BMW.

"Kid's aren't dumb, you know. We hauled up a value system that says you must have the money—you know, this is one way of showing that you've made it in America—and who's got the money in these neighborhoods? The pushers have. The most

visible people with money, let me put it that way, are the pushers. I'd much rather see visible people that work for what they
have, that sacrifice for what they have, the way we're all taught
you did it in America. You know what I'm saying?

"It's really funny to hear a president talk about money for the
contras, because of the great danger from the Sandinistas.
The Sandinistas are not killing children in Denver; crack is. The
Sandinistas are not destroying homes in this country. If we're
going to throw some money at something, if we've got that
money to use, let our armies protect us from our real enemies,
and that's drugs coming in. Put them out there and let them
protect our borders against the enemies that are really destroying
our children.

"The other thing I'd really like to see him do is to start rec-
ognizing the people who have the most influence on American
children, because when you talk about crime, you're talking
about the failure of a system to give children a value system
that's workable, and that comes out of the schools. Teachers
have our children six to seven hours or more a day. What I'd
really like to see is a national pay scale for teachers. If the government wants to support something on a national level, have a
national base for teachers' salaries, basic teacher's competence,
which I know is something teachers don't like to hear. But the
bottom line is, until we educate children and give them a value
system where they feel that their education will get them where
they want to go in their lives, we'll have the problems of crime.

"It doesn't make sense for a child to go through eight years of
school before he can get into a summer reading program. Generally
speaking, summer schools take place in high school, to get those
credits you need to graduate. Well, Jesus Christ, the kid has stum-
bled through for eight years. You know, put the money where it's
needed. We're not talking about a lot more money. We're talking
about just deciding where money needs to go to be the most ef-
fective. Elementary schools are ignored, almost. We get the hand-
outs, you know. We get what's left. And then for eight years, here's
a child muddling through with one social worker in a school with

475 children, maybe one psychologist who comes a couple days a week, and then all of a sudden, high school, you've got these terrible problems with street gangs and stuff, because you've ignored this kids for eight years and given him just enough to make him look good on paper or to satisfy your budget requirements or whatever. Put the money down there, give personnel when these kids are young, when they're impressionable. Most Americans my age grew up with Sky King and the Lone Ranger, who never killed anybody; and it may sound utopian, but Jesus, those were my values. That's where I got them from. You know, the Pledge of Allegiance, that was there. And there were teachers, who, for whatever reason, put their all into us, and that's where we got our values from. Now they're worrying about their money, they're worrying about the budget, they're worrying about equipment. They shouldn't have to worry about this.

"The first eight years in school will give us what we want. We can cut down on crime. It's not going to happen overnight. And that's another thing. The president, any president, needs to stop putting Band-Aids on things and get seriously into dealing with problems realistically. I'd like to see the president just be a president, be a leader. It's hard to tell kids about ethics and how to think logically, and that if you do the wrong things, somebody's going to call you on it, when the politicians are doing the wrong things and they're getting away with it. You know, the other day my son missed a football practice, so he can't play Saturday. That was the rule. He'll live by it. But when he looks up and he says, I can't play football Saturday because I missed a practice, and then you've got a person who's becoming a national hero because he defied my Constitution, that's a load of bull. How do you do this with children, when they're constantly seeing our leaders circumventing the Constitution—but he can't play Saturday because he missed a practice? It's like he says, 'Mama, you know, there's two sets of things going on here. You're telling me to live one way, and the people who run my country, they do what they please and they get away with it.'

"And this is what kids are seeing. Children are not dumb.

There are no stupid children in this country. Even with the mediocre education they're getting, they're not stupid. They see what's going on. And those are the people they're going to look to as role models."

We were inundated with comments about what she said. We have had her back on several occasions since.

Finding Jacqueline Jackson-Quinn, listening to her, realizing how special she was, and then having the simple editorial authority to put her on the air for however long we wanted: this is an example of the supreme pleasures and privileges—a top wow—of doing what I do for a living, of having a bird's nest on the ground.

15

Hello, Betsy

And one day it came to pass that the Voice of Buses Past spoke to me.

Jimmy Charles Lehrer, it said, buy a bus. A real bus. One that has real air brakes that go *sssssss*, real seats that recline, and a real motor that purrs and pops.

What kind of bus should it be? I asked.

A Flxible Clipper, of course.

Where would I keep it?

In your barn in West Virginia.

What would I do with it?

Play with it.

Kate and the girls and everyone else will think me crazy.

Ignore them, Jimmy Charles. Ignore them.

. . .

A Flxible Clipper. Of course.

I recalled one my bus friend Fred Rayman had told me about a couple of years earlier. Fred was a driver for Oklahoma Transportation Company in Oklahoma City who also collected and coveted bus memorabilia. The Flxible he mentioned was a 1949 twenty-one-passenger model—called a Baby Flex in the business. He had come across it on a used-car lot in Houston.

I called Fred. He said he would call a friend in Houston to see if the bus was still there.

Does Kate know about this? Fred asked.

I declined to answer.

In a few days, he was back with a name and a phone number. The Baby Flex was now owned by a man who lived near Bristol, Tennessee. Bristol was on the border with Virginia. There were in fact two Bristols—one Virginia, one Tennessee. I had driven through them several times in the early days, when Kate and the girls and I had gone back and forth between Washington and Texas.

It was only a six-hour drive from Washington.

For two weeks, I got nothing but a ringing telephone. Then, when I finally made contact, my hopes and dreams were immediately dashed. The man confirmed he had the little Flxible, but it was not in that good a shape anymore. He had torn out all of the seats and interior baggage racks in preparation for turning it into a mobile home. I could have it for $3,000, as is.

I expressed my disappointment and started my good-byes. I was not interested in a bus with no seats or baggage racks. No, sir.

"I've got another one that still has everything," the man said. "She's the standard larger size, and inside she is just like she came from the factory. Twenty-three reclining seats. One row of single seats on one side of the aisle, a row of doubles on the other. Five across the back."

How old?

"She's a 1946."

Why is she in such good shape?

"She was bought by a hotel up in the Pennsylvania Poconos to take people from the train station to the hotel," said the man. "Then a man bought her and kept her in a garage for more than fifteen years. I bought her from him. She's never been in regular line service."

Does she run? Does the motor and all of that work?

"You bet it does."

How much do you want for her?

"Sixty-five hundred."

That was more than I was thinking of spending.

"You'll never find one in better shape. Never."

I asked him to send me photographs of both of the Flxibles.

In a few days, a packet of photos arrived. Even at a glance, it was clear the 1946 was something very special. She was painted two tones of blue on the outside. There were traces of rust here and there, but nothing that terrible. Inside, it was pure magic. The seats, the racks, the windows, the driver's seat, the steering wheel, the dashboard, the door levers—everything was exactly right, proper and perfect.

It was as if the Voice had had her in mind when it spoke to me.

Flxible Clippers had been in and out and through my life for years. When we had moved from Beaumont to San Antonio, it was on a Trailways Flxible Clipper. They had been standard equipment for all of the runs out of Victoria, except for the Houston–Corpus Christi through route, which had used the larger ACF-Brills.

Flxible Clippers had even been involved in my fiction life. It was on a Flxible Clipper between Galveston and Beaumont that The One-Eyed Mack had his illicit sexual experience. And later it was a Flxible Clipper that Mack and Pepper stole from the bus depot parking lot in Lufkin, and drove to Houston.

But the main connection was a real one. The year of that bus was also the year of Kansas Central. If, in the summer of 1946, Dad could have afforded to buy a brand-new Flxible like this one, instead of our 1938 Betsy, who knows what might have happened? Now I could have the bus he could not buy.

I made a full presentation to Kate, complete with the it's-for-Dad line and photographs.

"I knew this was coming someday," she said calmly. "I can only be grateful that it has taken this long in coming."

Why she knew it was coming was Piedmont, an eighteenth-century house we had recently bought outside Charles Town,

West Virginia, an hour and a half from Washington. What was special about the house was its history—George Washington had had dinner there one night in 1771 while on his way to spend the night with his brother Samuel down the road—and its terrific condition. The previous owners had not screwed it up. It was in perfect shape for restoration, and with the help of our friend and architect Hugh Newell Jacobsen, we had set out to restore it.

But there was another thing about the house that made Kate smell a bus rat. There was a marvelous barn on the property. A barn that was the ideal size for a bus. An old intercity bus. She knew it. Anyone who saw it would know it. It was a natural.

Now with Kate's warm, enthusiastic endorsement, I called the man outside Bristol to make the deal. It was not easy. He wanted twenty-five dollars extra for a Flxible name plate he had recently bought and attached to the front of this bus—my bus. I wanted him to drive the bus to Roanoke, which was three hours up Interstate 81 closer to our place in West Virginia. I would drive down in a car with someone and meet him in the parking lot of a shopping center or some such place. The car and the someone would then follow me up to West Virginia.

The bus wasn't legally registered, he said. It doesn't have papers anymore. They expired. Come and get it here at my place.

I offered him an additional three hundred dollars if he would drive it to Roanoke. Well, okay, he said, but I may have a problem with the registration.

He had problems with the registration all right. It took him several trips into Bristol to get a temporary permit to drive the bus. I could not help but wonder what he thought I would have done had I showed up at his place believing I could simply drive it away. But I remained silent and we set a date. Two Saturdays from now, around eleven A.M., in the parking lot of the Sheraton Inn–Roanoke on I-81.

"Have you ever driven a bus before?" the man asked.

"No, sir," I replied.

"Well, it won't be hard to learn. She's easy."

■ ■ ■

I could see her seconds after we turned off the exit at Roanoke. A blue Flxible Clipper, identifiable a mile away by the distinctive air scoop in the back, which helped keep the motor cool. The One-Eyed Mack had described that Flxible scoop as resembling an upside-down comma.

It was ten-forty in the morning. Annette Miller was with me in the car. Kate was away seeing her ill mother in Texas. Jamie, Lucy and Amanda were each in their own way out of town or out of the country. Roger Mudd, who had volunteered to come with me, could not do it that Saturday morning. Neither could Bob Beard, a friend and real bus driver for Trailways out of Washington. So it fell to Annette, the *NewsHour*'s Washington news editor, who had also offhandedly volunteered to help me on this fateful day. We had left Washington at seven. I was sure she was having second thoughts, but she had kept them to herself, and I appreciated that.

As we circled around to the parking lot, my heart sank a bit. The blue paint was more faded than I had been able to tell from the photo.

I pulled the car right up to the side of the bus. The rust spots were more noticeable than I had noticed in the photos. There was also some rust color around the glass of the side windows, called Edwards Sash by bus people because they were made by a company with that name.

But. There she was. A 1946 Flxible Clipper. And she was about to be mine.

The man was sitting behind the steering wheel. His wife and teenage son were also on the bus.

I stepped up into the stairwell. I was hit by the most marvelous smell. The smell of a bus in 1946. A mix of stale cigarette smoke and mohair and machine oil.

The owner had not exaggerated. The bus was in pristine condition inside. The chrome tubes of the overhead baggage rack gleamed. I walked up the aisle. Fluted lights by every seat, art deco ashtrays. The seats were in immaculate condition. So was the flooring and the ceiling.

The transfer of power took less than fifteen minutes. I gave the man a cashier's check for the full amount. He signed over the title. Then he said:

"Now get in here and let me explain about the gears and all."

I slipped in behind the wheel and knew beyond any doubt that I was doing the right thing. There to my left were the spotlight and a rearview mirror. There to my right were two small fans, and the hand lever for opening and closing the door. Straight ahead above was a mirror for keeping an eye on the passengers. Below that were the curved windshield, and the dashboard, full of well-designed little pull-out chrome switches that turned on lights and heaters and buzzers.

I put my hands on the steering wheel and gently pulled it to the left and then to the right.

Look at me now, Pop.

"It has five gears," said the man. "Plus reverse."

Five gears? Plus reverse?

He stood up by me and grabbed the gearshift lever that came out from the floor. It had a round, hard black rubber knob on top.

"First is down there." He moved it. "You try it. Put the clutch in first. The motor's not running, so it's all right."

I stepped on the clutch with my left foot and grabbed the gearshift lever. It would not budge.

"You'll get the hang of it," he said. "Up here is second." He moved the lever up to second. And then to third and to fourth and finally to fifth.

"Reverse is all the way toward you and then up to the left—hard."

I tried to get it into second. I couldn't. But I did move it around awhile until I got it down into third. Or maybe it was fifth. And I got it from there up to reverse.

I felt ready.

"Crank her up," said the man. I pulled out the ignition switch and pushed in on the starter button.

There were a couple of *pops* and then a *clack* and some real noise. It was running. I gunned the accelerator.

"Why not take a turn around the lot here?" said the man.

Good idea.

Everyone else got off the bus. I worked and pulled and jerked and finally got it into first gear. Slowly, ever so slowly, I accelerated and began releasing the pressure on the clutch. It moved. My bus, with me behind the wheel, moved.

I turned toward the back of the lot, which fortunately was mostly unoccupied. I crept twenty yards and stopped. *Sssssss*, said the air brakes. I loved that sound.

I decided I would do a backing turn and then face her the way I had come and the way out of the parking lot. I got it into reverse. And started moving.

The former owner came running up to the window by the driver's seat.

"No, no," he said. "Those brakes won't keep you out of a little gully back here. Use that emergency brake."

I grabbed the handle of a silver emergency brake that came out of the floor on the left. Nothing happened.

"It's that yellow thing there on the dash. Pull it up."

I'd wondered what that was. It was a yellow plastic knob about the size of the gearshift lever.

I pulled it, there was another *sssssssssss*, and the bus stopped.

"Always use that when there's any kind of incline," said the man.

I put the gearshift into neutral and left the motor running. It was time to move out toward West Virginia.

Again, I was ready.

The man took me on a tour around the outside of the bus. He showed me how to open the baggage compartment in the back, where the motor was, and explained that she had two forty-gallon gas tanks.

"What kind of gas does she use?" I asked. "Leaded or un-leaded?"

"Either one's all right," he said.

"Regular or high-test?"

"It doesn't matter."

Okay. I was ready.

▪   ▪   ▪

I said my final good-byes to the owner and his family. And with Annette following in the car behind me, gunned and clutched out of the parking lot toward Interstate 81.

I had three turns to make. One from the lot to a smaller road still on the hotel property. Then another onto the access road, and finally one onto the ramp. Two lefts and then a right. I misjudged all three, turning too late all three times, and three times ending up out on the shoulders before the way I wished to go.

Thank God for those shoulders.

I was so busy turning that I hadn't even tried to shift from first to second. Now I was on the interstate, headed north. I could see Annette in the follow car. It was time to shift into second.

I pushed in the clutch and shoved the gearshift forward as hard as I could. It got to neutral and would go no farther. I was losing speed rapidly.

Desperately, cleverly, I fished around until the gears went in and settled somewhere. I did not care where.

It happened. I was able to build up the speed. Was I in third? Fourth? I had no idea. After a few minutes I decided to try for what I hoped was fifth. I was successful, and suddenly I was really moving out.

It was then that I noticed the speedometer did not work. And I was hot. I turned on both of the fans on the dashboard. One of them faced me. I felt the air.

Cars were passing me. So were trucks. No problem. I was moving. I was happy.

Then, along the left side, I saw a police car coming up beside me. Its red light was flashing. The car pulled slightly ahead of me and I could see the officer. He motioned for me to pull over.

Speeding? No way. Cars were going by me like I was standing

still. Even if I was in fifth gear. Whatever, I hoped he would be nice to me.

Please be nice to me, Officer, sir. This is a big day for me, a big event in my life. You see, this is a 1946 Flxible Clipper. My dad started a small bus line in Kansas in 1946. It went broke, but it might not have if he could have bought a bus like this. Now I have it for him. So, as you can see, Officer, sir, what you have here is not a routine case of some crazy man driving around on an interstate in a rusty old bus. Would you like a ride?

I got the bus stopped rather efficiently and quickly and, most important, well before plowing into the rear of the police car, which had stopped ahead of me on the highway shoulder.

I decided to stay behind the wheel of my bus. Let him come to me. Let him come and see for himself what this bus was. Let him observe the fluted lights and the immaculate reclining seats, let him get a whiff of 1946.

The officer, the nicest of men, came from his car toward me with a smile. A smile. I opened the door. But he was looking at the temporary registration papers the former owner had taped down on the inside lower right corner of the windshield. He looked at them briefly, then came around to the door.

I jabbered: "I just picked this thing up. She's a 1946 Flxible Clipper. I'm driving her up to our place in West Virginia. She's in great shape here inside. . . ."

He said nothing. He just waved and walked back to his car.

Obviously, he was attracted by the fact that there were no license tags on my bus. Obviously, it was all right, though, once he saw the temporary papers.

Obviously, I was free to go.

Go I did. But again I could not find second gear. I ended up in what I was now sure was fourth, which was up in the farthest right-hand corner of the gearbox. I had skipped third as well as second.

Soon I slipped on down to fifth and again built up some speed.

For the first time, I noticed the noise and the ride. There

were loud squeaks and bangs and jarrings every time we crossed over the slightest bump on the pavement. I wondered whether the springs were broken. Could an axle break? What if a wheel broke off? Maybe the frame itself had rusted out underneath. The whole top of the bus could come flying off the chassis.

Or the steering column could snap. Or a tire could blow. A front tire that would probably send that bus and me down the side of one of these southwest Virginia hills I was now cruising up and down.

I decided not to think bad thoughts anymore. I concentrated on enjoying the looks on the faces of people in cars when they passed.

Hey, Daddy, did you see that old bus?

I did, son.

What's it doing?

Probably some old man with no house to live in. Now go back to reading your book, son.

Yes, Daddy. When we will be home?

Another six hours to Harrisburg, son.

I have to go to the bathroom, Mommy.

Hold it until we stop for gas.

Yes, Mommy.

■　■　■

Gas. My gauge showed that the left tank, the one I was using, was empty. I switched the tank and the gauge to the tank on the right. It was also empty.

I drove on awhile longer, until I could see a place off the highway that would be large enough to accommodate my bus and my turning problems, but that also had an easy off-and-on. A very easy off-and-on.

To the left I saw what looked like a large combination gas station and convenience store. So I exited, making sure in my mirror that Annette, poor Annette, was right behind me. She was.

I had seen and guessed right. It was perfect. The store was large, and so were the gasoline lanes. I had no problem swinging

the bus in and to a self-serve gasoline pump on my left. I stopped
the bus and turned off the engine. Annette came up and then
went inside for cold drinks, while I pumped the gas. Forty gal-
lons takes a lot of time, so I had several good swigs of Diet
Pepsi before finishing.

I went inside, paid, said some temporary good-byes to Annette and took my position again behind the wheel.

Casually, almost comfortably, I turned on the ignition and
pushed the starter. Nothing happened. Not a thing. Not a sound.
Not a whimper, not even a tiny little click. I turned off the
ignition and tried again. More silence.

I suddenly felt like a fool. What in the world had I done?
Here I was, in the middle of nowhere in a 1946 bus that I did
not even check out except by photograph before I bought it. I
knew nothing about the mechanics of buses. Nothing at all.
Why, oh why, would I relive the worst of Kansas Central? Like
Mom and Dad with Betsy, Susie and Lena more than forty years
before, here I sat with a bus that was broken. A bus that would
not run. A bus that was a bucket of bolts.

Oh, what a fool you are, Jimmy Charles Lehrer, said a voice.
It was my own this time.

I had no choice now, of course, but to see if I could find
somebody around who might fix this bus. Kansas Central, here
you are again. At least I had American Express and MasterCard,
and checks and even some cash. At least I would not have to
beg for credit.

I saw a small truck repair shop across the road. I headed for
it. There were terrific men inside the small office. I mean terrific. One was the boss, the other was a friend who had just
stopped by for some Saturday-afternoon talk. He was a retired
semi truck driver.

I told them about my bus at the store across the road. They
looked out the window and said: Don't worry. We'll be right
there. We'll get it going for you.

It was like having Dr. Wallace tell me that the bypass operation had worked.

They came over a few minutes later. And they both looked at her and admired her and fooled with wires and things, and finally concluded there was only one way to get her going. Pull her.

Like two heart surgeons, these two wonderful men did it. One got behind the wheel of the bus, the other chained a truck to her front bumper. With precision and confidence, they moved that bus less than ten yards before the motor caught. There was a *pop* and a *crack*, and the sound of the engine running like it was supposed to.

"How much do I owe you?" I asked the boss man.

"Oh, ten dollars will do it."

I gave him a ten, thanked him with more sincerity and enthusiasm than I had ever thanked anyone before in my life, waved again to Annette and drove off toward I-81.

This is my bus. It's a 1946 Flxible Clipper, just like one my dad could not afford to buy for his little bus line in Kansas. I'm taking it to our place in West Virginia. It was bought new by a hotel in the Poconos to take customers to and from the train station. Then a guy bought it and kept it in a garage for more than fifteen years. That's why she looks so good and new inside. Have you ever seen anything like it? And get a load of that smell of 1946.

I swung her too wide again coming out of the store's driveway. I could not make the turn onto the road. So I had to back up and turn and try again.

I managed. But I lived in fear that all of the scratching and screeching of the gears would cause the bus to die. And she would not start again. And I could not ask those two wonderful men to work their magic again.

I was hearing all kinds of voices saying all kinds of things by the time I finally did make it back to the interstate.

▪   ▪   ▪

Three hours later, I turned the bus, my bus, off West Virginia Highway 51 onto the mile-long gravel road leading to our house. Except for my continued fears about wheels and springs and my continued doubts about what I had done, there were no more excitements. I had exited I-81 at Inwood, West Virginia, managed three turns—two right, one left—onto 51 and headed east. Highway 51 was only a two-lane road, but it was paved and fine and I had absolutely no problems driving those last fifteen miles.

I clutched and shifted her down to first gear for the final few glorious yards down the gravel road. I had never found second gear and had about decided I probably never would. No matter how long I owned and drove this bus, I would always go directly from first to third.

But there was now some exhilaration, as I edged her over the railroad tracks and then a small bridge in front of our house. It was an exhilaration of being comfortable behind the wheel of that bus. Maybe, just maybe, I was right to answer the call of the Voice.

Think about what had just happened. I had never before in my life driven a bus. But there was something spectacularly natural about the way I had slipped in behind the wheel of this bus in that Roanoke parking lot and simply driven off. I had been around buses all of my early life, and still thought about and played with them now in my later life. But not as a driver, not until this Saturday in July 1989. There must have been something in me that made me sure I could, something that, by a process of osmosis, had seeped into my being and, pardon me, my motor skills.

I had imagined driving a bus so often and so intently as a boy in Kansas, and observed and admired others doing it as a young man in Texas that . . .

I think I may be overdoing it a bit. The point is simply that I knew I could drive a bus. And despite some turning and gearing problems, I had just done it.

Well done, Jimmy Charles.

Thank you, Voice.

I drove her to the end of the road beyond the house and to the barn, the place that would be her home from this day forward. This was a perfect place for her. I had had some gravel laid down to provide a proper flooring, in a space that I had measured ahead of time.

I eased her in to make sure she fit, and then eased her back out, careful not to turn off the motor or let it die.

With the motor still running (and the emergency brake on), I took a lot of photographs. Annette took some of me behind the wheel and standing at the door and in front. I was like the kid on Christmas morning posing with his new tricycle. Which was about the way I was feeling now.

The happiest moment came when I finally turned off the engine. I dreaded having to do it. I dreaded having to face the certainty that it would not start again. I dreaded having to look for a mechanic there around Charles Town to come and fix my bus so it would start. So I could do with it what I wanted to do with it, which was to play.

Click. I did it. The motor went silent. I sat for a count of four or five and then turned the ignition back on. And hit the starter. There was a whir, a pop, and then the magnificent sound of that engine telling me that all was well.

What had happened back down there at that convenience store in southwest Virginia had been a test of my bus character. Was I really bus man enough to stick with this? Did I have the bus guts to hang tough, the bus courage not to surrender at the first sign of a minor mechanical problem? Did I have the bus love it takes to persevere through trying times and other adversities?

I had passed the test. I measured up. I deserved to have this bus of my own.

She needed a name. I could not spend the rest of her and my life calling her simply My Bus or The Bus. What should I call her?

Betsy II. Of course. Betsy II. Hello, Betsy II. Welcome to the family.

The next week, I sent out small photographs of her with this xeroxed announcement, to friends far and wide:

Kate and Jim Lehrer

are pleased to announce
the acquisition on July 22, 1989, of

"BETSY II"

A 23-passenger, 1946 Flxible Clipper

She is in residence at Piedmont,
Charles Town, West Virginia.

NO GIFTS

16

Finally

As of March 1992:

Eight years later, I still live with the fear of feeling a little something tight across my chest and then dropping dead. Or of going to sleep and never waking up, like Grandfather Chapman. It will never go away and I know it. But it no longer affects anything I do or do not do. I no longer check the hospitals and the cardiologists when I travel. I go for days without even thinking about it. Sometimes when asked about my heart attack, I find myself replying as if I were reporting on a story rather than about myself.

I know the statistics. Seven years is the average staying power for a bypass. Something happens to require another, and that can be another heart attack. The death rate for people suffering a second heart attack is high—much higher than for those having Number One. But I do not spend much time thinking or worrying about it. I feel that I have done about all I can or want to do in the way of life-style changes to hold back the night. I am not interested in staying under the covers for the rest of my life.

In my most private thoughts, I honestly believe that heart attack in December 1983 may result in my living longer. It got my attention at a young enough age to change enough things to make a difference. I may be kidding myself, but it sure beats the alternative.

I have not had so much as a puff on a cigarette or any other form of tobacco since that December. I am at a point now that if they announced tomorrow that lab tests with white rats had proved conclusively that smoking was not bad for rats or people after all (anything is possible, à la Woody Allen), I would not start smoking again. For reasons of mess and smell, if for no other.

I still take a nap every workday, no matter what. I have missed maybe thirty times in all in the last eight years. That is remarkable, if I do say so myself. That brief daily respite from life is crucial to me.

So is the fact that I walk for one hour at least three times a week, sometimes more. It is a passion and a must in my life. I also play tennis and ride a bicycle regularly. I continue to watch what I eat. I stay away from red meat and sweets and high-fat foods of all kinds. Except on special occasions, or when my willpower completely fails me. My target perfect weight is 165, and I stay around there most of the time. I have had some problems, ballooning in late 1989, for instance, as high as 180. It was a stupid, disgusting thing to do, and I have put that kind of stupid, suicidal behavior behind me. (How did I take off the fifteen pounds? I ate less food and exercised more.) With the additional help of lovastatin, a cholesterol-reducing medicine, I now have my bad cholesterol way down and my good cholesterol way up.

My main advice for potential heart attack victims, though, has nothing to do with diet or cigarettes or anything like that. Go out and get yourself a terrific family before having a heart attack, is my advice. I cannot even imagine wanting to survive if I had not had Kate, Jamie, Lucy and Amanda around to care about me and to love me. I know for a fact that I would not have made it through in any way whole, if they and their love had not been there.

Jamie has even brought new ones onto the love-and-care team.

In June 1986 she married John O'Brien, a delightful young man she had met at Vassar. They have since turned Kate and me into grandparents, with the production of a girl and two boys— Kate Olivia, Luke and Ian. Being a grandfather was never something I thought about or lusted for, and frankly, in the abstract it was not even a particularly attractive prospect. But in the specific, it is a special and distinctive joy.

My second piece of advice is to get a job working with people who care about you. I cannot imagine getting through these past eight years without Robin, Les, Linda, Dan, Al, Charlayne, Judy, Roger, Annette, Peggy, Debra, Ros, Roma, Gregg, Lew and all of the other terrific people at *MacNeil/Lehrer*. Don't leave home with a heart attack without them—or people like them.

My plan is to continue to do the *NewsHour*, God and public television willing, for another five or six years. Minimum. That is with the assumption I continue to wake up every morning wondering where all of the fire trucks in the world are going. If I ever lose that curiosity, then forget it. Daily journalism is for the young in mind and spirit, regardless of age. (Some of the oldest people I know are twenty-three, some of the youngest sixty-three or older.) Its daily deadlines and other demands would be too much to bear under any other state of mind and spirit. I cannot imagine doing anything else on television besides the *NewsHour*. I hope economics and other factors never bring that to a test.

On January 31, 1992, our way of doing things received a good test. Robin and I moderated a debate on PBS among the five candidates for the Democratic presidential nomination. The candidates agreed to dispense with the usual opening and closing statements, time's-up bells and whistles, and other normal debate procedures. Instead, we divided the two hours into six sections, with Robin and me alternating the lead in questioning. But nothing was rigid, including the timing of the length of the answers. The candidates, as in real life, were also free to jump in and argue. Robin and I, also as in real life, even asked follow-up questions. We tried to run it in a way not calculated to demonstrate how much smarter and superior we were to these five men running for president of the United States. They deserved our respect and we gave it to them, as we do guests on the nightly program. (Showing contempt for politicians has become the new hallmark of some television interviewing. It is an outrageous pomposity, as well as a gross violation of our Skivvy Shirt Rule.) The public praise we received after the debate was terrific (show me somebody who doesn't like praise and I'll show you somebody who doesn't like anything), but the main value for us was as a reminder that our simple formula of serious talk plus serious fairness has value.

I wish J. D. Salinger felt that way. I am hanging in there to do the ultimate interview with him. Salinger's the only person out there I would do almost anything to sit down with.

Mr. Salinger, why have you lived as a recluse all of these years?

None of your business.

Well, sir, why have you not written anything in the last many, many years?

None of your business.

Are you ever going to write another thing?

None of your business.

I remain delighted about how my own writing is going. I don't mean the quality. That remains up to critics and readers. I mean the output and the delight I get in doing it.

Georges Simenon has joined Hemingway as a writing hero. The prolific Belgian wrote more than four hundred books, most of them set in and around Paris, where he had worked as a newspaperman. Many were about a brilliant but simple Paris detective named Maigret. I have most of the nearly fifty Maigrets that have been translated into English, and I seldom leave home on a trip without one. His so-called psychological novels are also great reads, particularly for anyone who writes and wishes to observe a master create place, time and atmosphere. His preferred way of writing was to outline a novel roughly on the back of an envelope, get a physical examination from a doctor, and then closet himself for eleven days and write the novel.

Simenon was also known for his extravagant appreciation of women. In an interview in his eighties, shortly before he died, he said that he had had sex with at least ten thousand different women. That certainly explained why he had to write so fast.

My words to live and write by are no longer solely from Hemingway. I am now an E. B. White man, too. He once wrote:

"I think the best writing is often done by persons who are snatching time from something else—from an occupation, from a profession or from a jail term—something that is burning them up, as religion, or love or politics, or that is boring them to tears, as prison, or a brokerage house, or an advertising firm. A great violinist must begin fairly early in life to play the violin; but I think a literary artist has a better chance of producing something great if he spends the first forty years of his life doing something else—grinding a lens, or surveying a wilderness."

In February 1992, Putnam published my fifth book in five years. It was *Short List,* the one about Mack getting on the Short List to be the Democratic nominee for vice-president. This book, the one you are now only minutes away from finishing, is number six. Number seven will be a non-Mack, post-*glasnost* spy novel called *Blue Hearts.* It's about two former CIA warrior agents who shared a special secret assignment after John F. Kennedy's assassination and now have a conflict about revealing their secret many years later. I also want to do a very different (for me) kind of novel about the fantasy love affair of an intercity bus driver with a passenger whose name he does not even know. My plans—serious plans—are to continue to write and have published at least one book a year until there are no more years.

I may even try to do a coffee-table nonbook, titled something like *Bus.* It would have pictures of old bus depots and buses, depot signs and cap badges, timetables and tickets. The intercity bus industry began in the 1920s, and now, barely seventy years later, it's almost disappeared. Only a skeleton Greyhound–Trailways company and a few solid smaller companies (Peter Pan and Bonanza in the Northeast, Jefferson in the Midwest, Kerrville in Texas) remain. The artifacts of those seventy years deserve to be preserved and presented in such a way that the general public can appreciate them. Not just the bus crazies like me. Make a book for them and the sales potential is a dozen or so. This one should be for everybody, for every coffee table.

Here's your Christmas present, Gladys.

Oh Harry, look at it. What is it, exactly?

A picture book about buses, Gladys.

Oh Harry, it's what I always wanted.

The Williamstown Theatre in Williamstown, Massachusetts, is producing a play of mine. It's called *The Will and Bart Show* now. It's the one that began as *The Great Man* and was first read and fooled with at the playwrights' workshop at the Sundance Institute in the summer of 1987. It's about two former Cabinet members—a secretary of state and a secretary of defense—who hold a deep, dark secret about the president they served. It has some thematic similarities to *Blue Hearts*, in that one of the main characters has a reason seventeen years later to reveal the secret, while the other very much does not. In the process, I get off some shots about keeping secrets and lying, my favorite Washington subject. I plan to write at least two more Washington-based plays—a kind of Capital Playhouse Trilogy. The second was going to be about a Senate confirmation hearing, but I may rethink that in light of the Anita Hill–Clarence Thomas affair. I am not sure I am capable of creating anything more dramatic than that. The third may be about a prominent Washington personality—maybe even a journalist—who is destroyed by an unfounded rumor.

I also want to do either a play or a novel—or both—about the short story writer William Sydney Porter, alias O. Henry. His life story, which includes time in Texas, Central America, New York City and an Ohio prison for embezzlement, has always fascinated me.

I have no problem "snatching" the time to write. That is thanks mostly to Kenny Kent and his encouraging me to eliminate as many energy-sapping happenings from my life as I could. It has left me with plenty of time to do what I want to do, which includes socializing, traveling and otherwise enjoying myself, as well as working and writing. The downside is that since my heart attack I have become passionate about what I want to do. That has led to my being impatient and unpleasant and, I guess, sometimes even resentful when something happens or is proposed that I see as a waste of my time and energy. I have none of either to waste.

The writing goes on no matter what else is going on. When I am into a Mack story or a play or something else I am writing, it is like having a low-grade fever. It is with me all of the time. I go away from it to do my work at the *NewsHour* or something else, but when I'm finished with that I can always come back to my story right where I left off. Without missing a beat. The daily nap also helps. It divides my day in two short hunks and makes it possible for me to write early in the morning before I go to the office and again in the evening after I get home. A little invention called the word processor also deserves some credit. It's given me speed and flexibility, and it has taken the drudgery out of rewriting and editing. I seldom leave home without my laptop.

There are many other personal things still to do.

I would like to go up to New Jersey and New York to do some research on the lives and times of Charles and Amelia Lehrer. What was the free-love socialist commune really all about? Where was it? What happened to it? What mark, if any, did Charlie Lehrer make on the political history of West Orange, New Jersey?

I would like to spend a week—maybe two—as an intercity bus driver. A real one. Put on a uniform and drive a regular run for some small company all by myself. I realize there are licensing and maybe other problems to overcome, but I am sure there must be a small bus company with small buses that operate a short turnaround route that would not mind having a substitute driver. I would work cheap, and I could even supply my own cap and ticket punch.

I'll be ready when the call comes. I take my lovely Betsy II out on weekends for regular rides on the roads around our place in West Virginia. I seldom get farther than a few miles from the house, and I carefully plot my routes to make sure I don't end up on narrow streets or at intersections that would make turning something beyond my skills. I have had to spend a little money keeping her mechanically functioning and viable. But nothing too much, because I do not drive her that much: only a few hundred miles a year so far, and that will most likely never change. One day I must get her painted in order to hold back the creeping rust problem. Maybe I'll do her up in the blue and yellow of Kansas Central. Why not? Make her a real Betsy.

I have thought, mostly privately, about acquiring another bus. Maybe an ACF-Brill, that thirty-seven-passenger mainstay of the Trailways companies in the forties and fifties. A man in Michigan has several on the market that are in near mint condition. I likewise would not mind having an Aerocoach, also a thirty-seven-passenger coach that had a brief life just before, during and after World War II, and then disappeared without much of a trace. The man in Michigan has a couple of those for sale as well. The prices for the ACFs and the Aerocoaches are reasonable—less than I paid for Betsy II. But those buses are bigger, and the storage and driving problems in West Virginia would be difficult. And yet . . .

Even if there were no Betsy II, the West Virginia house would be a joy and a pleasure in my life. A small stream flows through it, and on down the railroad track is a wetland, with all kinds of birds and small animals and rare and gorgeous wild flowers and other plants. Kate and I love to walk and ride bicycles on the C&O Canal, which is not far away. We also love to shop at the outlet stores—there are fifty of them—in Martinsburg, fifteen miles up the road from us. They have ruined us for paying full price on just about anything.

My bus collecting continues to perk along at full and satisfying speed. With the help of *Smithsonian* magazine, I finally added a real metal American Buslines sign to the collection last year. Don Moser, editor of *Smithsonian*, asked me to do a 250-word essay for a photo display featuring nine people who collected offbeat things. I wrote with passion about the value of the pack rats, the people who save the little and strange things of daily life. I said something about their being almost as important as the big shots who hold on to the Mona Lisas and the mansions. But the important parts of my passionate story were the opening and closing paragraphs.

The opening:

"For years I have been searching for an enameled metal bus depot sign for the defunct American Buslines. American was a delightfully unique company that provided free pillows and meals and a by-the-minute refund system for late arrivals on its main line between New York and Los Angeles. It disappeared into Trailways without much of a trace in the 1950s, but I am certain somebody somewhere has one of its old signs. I must have one and I will not rest until I do."

The closing:

"There are important people and organizations at work preserving the big things of life, like buildings and battlefields, but it is left to the rest of us to preserve items such as . . . well, bus depot signs.

"Which reminds me. If you should come across an American Buslines depot sign, call me. Collect."

That is almost exactly what happened. A woman called from California, although not collect. She said her husband had one of those American Buslines signs hanging in their garage. He would be delighted to let me have it.

I talked to her husband that evening. We made a deal. I now have that sign hanging in my office. Every workday I see it.

Another spectacular recent addition is too big to put anywhere in my office. It is a six-hundred-pound Trailways "Go Big Red" electric sign that I spotted over a deserted building in Sherman, Texas, a few years ago. Sherman is only thirty miles north of McKinney, Kate's hometown. We go there a lot to see her mother and other relatives. I had my eye on that sign for years, particularly after the bus station moved but the sign did not. I was unable to find anybody with whom to negotiate a deal. I also was not sure how I would get it down from that building and to Washington, anyhow.

But I happened to make the commencement address at Austin College in Sherman in May 1991. (The speech was to honor a loose—"Sure, sometime"—commitment I had made to an Austin College alumna, the actress Jayne Chamberlin. Jayne, who played the lead in *Chili Queen* in New York and Washington, died in a plane crash in South America.) I talked about taking risks, of course, but at the beginning I mentioned the soft spot I had in my heart for Sherman, and the lust in my heart for that old Trailways sign downtown.

Two months later, I went with Kate to our place in West Virginia for the weekend. And what, to my surprised and wondering eyes, did I see in the barn? That sign from Sherman! The president of Austin College, a man of wisdom and enlightenment named Harry Smith, had found the right people, gotten some college workmen to take it down and then had it shipped to me by truck.

It is a perfect pairing for another Trailways six-hundred-pounder of another vintage that the wise and enlightened people at the public television station in Cincinnati presented to me when I came out to make a speech. Both will someday hang from the rafters of my barn.

The major hole in my sign collection remains Dixie-Sunshine Trailways. I know one is out there somewhere. A retired driver in Denison, Texas, described what the signs looked like. Oval, DIXIE-SUNSHINE across the top, TRAILWAYS in the middle, BUS STATION around the bottom. I know I will eventually find and possess one. The only question is when.

If by chance you have such a sign that you wish me to have, please put it between two pieces of cardboard before sending it to me. I would not want a repeat of what happened with that Indiana Motor Bus Company sign after the first *Smithsonian* article.

Thanks.

ACKNOWLEDGMENTS

My friend E.J. Mudd was the first person outside the family with whom I discussed doing this book. She said, Do it. Neil Nyren, my friend and editor at Putnam, helped me find the way to do it. Others, some not mentioned elsewhere in the book, provided other words and acts of kindness and friendship during the past eight years. They are Howard Adams, Mollie and Jim Dickenson, Mary Ellen Greenfield, Robin and Hugh Jacobsen, Elizabeth Drew and David Webster, Lee Cullum, Molly and David Boren, Ginger and Douglas Keare, Colleen and Sam Nunn, Le and Ed Rowell, Mary Lynn and Nick Kotz, Peyton Lewis, Ginny and Roger Rosenblatt, Saskia Weinstein, Billie and Bob Kotlowitz, Wendy and Henry Raymont, Patsy and Ray Nasher, Helene and Bill Safire, Barbara and David Pryor, Susan Shreve and Timothy Seldes.

I am grateful to all of them.